Tik Tok Boom!

TRENDING FOR YOU
BOOK ONE

CHRISTINE D'ABO

ONE

Andie

I've never been much of a literary type, but I'm certain when Dante sat down to pen his infernal tale of woe he missed a circle—the Walmart photography center.

Don't get me wrong, most days I enjoy my job. I love the hell out of putting newborns into little bear costumes and sticking their tiny little bums into tiny little baskets to take their first pictures. Bliss. Their precious coos and squeaks fill my heart to the brim before I happily hand them back to their parents.

Or the elderly couples picking out photo packages so they can give physical pictures to family members who probably have a thousand digital ones on their phones already. The longer they've been together, the better, mostly because of the gentle teasing and soft looks shared between them as I buzz around arranging hair and straightening collars to ensure I get my shots as efficiently as possible.

Strangely, my hands-down favorite pictures to take are passport photos. Those are the conversations I leap into with far more enthusiasm than I ought to show. I genuinely get pumped to find out where people are traveling. The businesspeople who travel a lot for their jobs tend to be a bit jaded, the allure of the road long since gone—until you ask them about food. Oh my God, then I hear all about the best places, discovering where to find the best mole (Blue Iguana in Utah), best desserts (chocolate ganache torte at Pampas in Cupertino), or the best maritime donair (King of Donair in Halifax).

Then there are the first-time travelers and their unadulterated excitement as they tell me about their planned adventures—shit, there's nothing better. I immediately picture myself there with them, visiting countries I've only ever seen online, wondering if Iceland is as cold as I think it is, or if New Zealand's grassy hills have a different scent than what I've experienced here in Ontario.

Those are the good days. I *adore* those days. Need them to feed my soul so I can continue to function as an adult-shaped person.

But then there are days like today.

The previously undocumented circle of hell. There's certainly enough screaming to qualify.

"Okay, let's get some pictures done." I smile as I speak because sometimes if I fake happiness, it influences others. Holding my worn and dirty stuffed duck, I pump the squeaker in a mad attempt to grab everyone's attention. "Hey, look right here. Hello. Hi there!"

Not only is no one looking, but I seriously doubt anyone is aware of my existence.

The screaming four-year-old triplets, named—and I'm serious here—April, May, and June are in various states of climbing over the prop bench in the middle of the cramped studio. They're dressed in carbon copy outfits—purple and white polka dot dresses, black patent leather shoes, their curly brown hair pulled into tight ponytails that are strangled by white bows atop their heads. Their replicating likeness creates a bizarre morphing effect that somehow makes it appear as though there are a dozen toddlers instead of three.

Samantha—the mom—leaps into action, frantically trying to organize her chaotic children. "I'm so sorry about this."

"It's fine. I only need a minute to snap some pictures you'll love."

"Oh, that's good."

Then the toddler on the end turns and pukes into my garbage can.

Samantha has that weary droop to her shoulders that I often see in some of my college students. Her smile is present but so far removed from her eyes that it makes me believe real life Photoshop is a thing.

Let's take the eyes of a sleep deprived mom, the body of a super-model, and the smile of a psychopath. Perfect!

The smell of cooling McDonald's french fries, initially pleasant, begins to turn my stomach as the scent mixes with the tang of vomit. I feel more than a little guilty about standing there watching her, but I've learned from experience that a stranger jumping into the fray won't do much to help.

I want to go home. I want to disappear online and look at pictures of countries I can't afford to visit and excursions I'd be too chicken to attempt. Like ziplining through a jungle or kayaking in the Arctic.

"May, baby, I need you to calm down." Samantha wipes vomit from her toddler's mouth with a baby wipe, looking at me with obvious embarrassment. "I'm so sorry about this."

"Don't worry about it." I take a step closer to help, but the other two triplets glare me off before continuing to shout and tease their sick sibling.

It reminds me of my relationship with my sister, Cara.

The triplet on the opposite end of May—I think it's June—momentarily stops screaming as she stands on the bench and stares at something beyond me. I awkwardly twist, trying to spot what has caught her attention. My gaze snaps to the mocking yellow smiling smiley face on a sign declaring the rolled back price on a stack of *Blue's Clues* dolls.

Wait.

"Hey, do your girls like *Blue's Clues*?"

Samantha looks back at me wide-eyed. "They love it."

"Josh, Josh, Josh, Josh!" The triplets chant, first one, then the other two. Even May, who appears a delicate shade of green, is smiling and clapping her hands.

I want to slap myself directly in my silly face for not thinking of it sooner. My tablet is in my purse; it only takes me a few moments to retrieve it and search for *Blue's Clues and You* on Netflix. My smile this time is equal parts relief and joy as I turn my tablet to face them. "Hey, everyone! Heeeeerrreee's Josh!" I've never seen three children sit down that quickly before *in my life*.

Thank. God.

Samantha frantically buzzes around her girls, fixing ponytails and straightening skirts while I hold the tablet up for them to see, silently praying that they'll sit long enough to see this through. I tag-team handing the tablet to the mom so I can set up the camera ... and—

Snap.

"We just got an email!" Josh's cheery voice fills the photo studio.

Snap.

The triplets giggle at something Josh says.

Snap. Snap. Snap. I let out a soft sigh. "Okay, I think I got some good ones."

Samantha looks over the tablet at her children. "I was hoping for different poses."

Lady, noooooooooo!

"Sure, we can do that." I long ago perfected the art of smiling as I clench my teeth. "Let's try some of them standing."

I don't want to claim that I'm a miracle worker or anything, but I somehow manage to get pictures of them in *three* different poses. They even appear happy—mostly. Samantha's ecstatic.

"We have several photo packages you can choose from." I pull the pictures up on the computer and slip into the sales spiel by rote. I try not to go crazy with the upselling because honestly, this poor woman would agree to buy anything I put in front of her at this point. While my manager would love it, I couldn't have lived with myself. She settles on a mid-range package with the option of making a photobook online when she gets home.

Looking exhaustedly triumphant, Samantha pays for her purchase and begins to gather up her belongings, shoving them deep into a diaper bag that appears to have seen more than a few toddler battles. The triplets smile and wave once as she shoves them into the shopping cart, acting as though the last thirty minutes of insanity never occurred.

And this is why I'm happily child-free. I can barely care for myself, let alone muster the emotional strength to raise a child. No, nope, and no thank you.

I'm still cleaning up the props when Alex, my department manager, comes in. They freeze as soon as they get close to the garbage can, their face contorting into a grimace. "Shit, what's that smell?"

"Regurgitated McDonald's fries." I scoop up the bag and knot it off, hoping that will contain any further spread of the acrid scent. "How are you doing?"

"Transit was on time for once, so my day was made." They shrug before plopping down onto our small rolling stool. "Any other appointments or are you ready for your break?"

"I have two passport photos at four but nothing until then." It's a husband-and-wife booking, and as usual, I can't wait to hear every detail of where they're going.

Alex dramatically sighs, tips their head all the way back, and spins blindly on the stool. "Exciting." They stop nearly as quickly as they started, slapping their shoes against the floor. "You should go have your lunch break, then. If there's a puke-filled bag, that means you had a rough session. I'll get the rest of the cleanup for you."

What they're really saying is that I'm responsible for vomit disposal. "Thanks. I'll see you in an hour."

I grab my bag, shoving my tablet deep inside, careful not to scratch it against my personal camera's housing, and snatch up the offending garbage bag in the other hand. Giving Alex a small wave, I slip into the bathroom beside the photo studio to dispose of the vomit in the garbage can and bolt from the store.

The humid downtown Toronto air feels amazing.

I stand there basking in the warm weather until sweat beads and soaks the underside of my bra. There won't be too many more warm days like this now that we're creeping toward the middle of September, and I'm determined to enjoy every single one.

I might love the heat, but I swear after I turned forty-five three months ago, my body decided to revolt. Things that never used to bother me, now send my internal thermostat haywire. Have two glasses of wine instead of one? That's a hot flash, baby! Eat an entire large bag of chips? Let's be bloated and uncomfortable for three days!

Getting older sucks.

Surreptitiously rubbing my sweaty boob through my shirt, I slip the long strap of my bag over my head to rest across my chest and head toward the park. I don't get to relax outside very often because of my work schedule, so I do my best to take advantage of being outside whenever I can. Rent in Toronto is bloody expensive, and as much as I wish my part-time teaching job was enough to pay the bills, it isn't.

I teach night classes at St. Simon Community College, and at seven o'clock tonight I have a photography class with my newest group of students. I really should sit down with my laptop to prep, take the opportunity to get ahead of things. I rarely have extra time like this, and if I'm the least bit smart, I'd take advantage.

But because I'm an adult who can do what I want, I instead decide to take photos.

I almost immediately regret my decision as the heat from the sidewalk radiates up through my work slacks as though it were a broiler and my thighs are on their way to being well-done. I know things will be better once I reach the park; the grass and trees change the feel of the air. As long as I survive the short journey, everything will be fine.

I pull my camera from my bag, adjusting it so it bumps against my hip as I turn from the sidewalk onto the dirt and gravel path of the park. This is one of my favorites to visit in the city, not only because it's close to work, but because it has both a ballpark and walking trails. I'm always able to find someone or something interesting to photograph. Not that I normally do anything with my personal pictures. Well, not anymore. That's a dream long laid to rest, replaced with the need to eat and pay rent in a city that's far too expensive for my liking.

I love Toronto, despite sometimes feeling like the city doesn't love me back.

The park is busy today. There appears to be a group of students practicing cross country running around the community ballpark. The piercing sound of a gym teacher's whistle easily reaches me, making me cringe. I need to rest my brain and have some quiet, so I turn and make my way down one of the walking paths. The shouting fades the farther I go, replaced with bird song and the crunch of my footfalls against the dirt. The scent of dry grass and roses chases away the last of the vomit smell from my nose as I walk. I have my camera out, snapping the occasional picture of a bird, the flowers that dot the path, a heart cut into a tree that I've snapped before. With each picture I take, I feel the muscles in my neck and back start to relax.

This is nice. For a short time, I know I didn't have to worry about anything, that I can be me and ignore the stress of needing to pay my rent, of not knowing what to say to my sister who is coming for a visit in a few days. Hell, I can pretend that my life has gone exactly the way I intended. So what if I didn't get to do some of the things I've always wanted to.

Who gets to fulfill their secret dreams? Not the average person. Well, not the average person I know. I mean, sure, dreams can come true. People accomplish their goals all the time—going to school, getting the job they really want, finding love—but those are the normal goals.

I really wanted to move from my small hometown and come to Toronto to be a famous art photographer. So, I moved! I did that incredibly hard thing when I was nineteen, and I don't have a single regret.

But no, I'm not famous, but come on. How many people *actually* get to be rich and famous? I'm a forty-five-year-old GenXer. I long ago came to terms with the fact that I'm not going to take pictures for National Geographic or open my own art studio. I won't have pictures in Vogue or even be good enough to teach at a prestigious art school. I'd tried once and the reaction had been so far less than ideal that I didn't need a repeat performance.

I work in the Walmart photography studio and teach photography at a community college. There are worse lives to have.

I reach the end of the path and check the time on my phone. If I don't want to be late for my next appointment, I need to turn around and head back to the store. I don't want to go, but real life is once again knocking against my brain. Just as I turn, I see a man sitting on a bench off to the side near where I just walked, talking on his phone.

You know in the movies when you hear that silly record scratch noise when someone sees another person who's just so fucking gorgeous that their brain breaks? I'm certain I hear that sound in my head. For real. He's just ...

Dude.

I'm not normally a person who goes nuts over someone's physical attractiveness, but this guy hits every button I have in a way that I've never experienced before. He's around my age, maybe late forties or early fifties, and he has *that vibe*. Like he's been around and seen some shit, but he's cool with it. The kind of guy you sit down with at a party, and he casually tells you fantastical stories about his career but does it in such a way that you totally believe they're true.

From how he's sitting, I can tell that he has a small belly. The gentle swell that I know would be soft beneath my fingers if I were lucky enough to ever be able to touch the skin. I can picture him standing in a backyard, beer in one hand and his phone in the other, showing someone a funny YouTube video.

His hair is black but it's starting to go gray along his temples and sides. It's a little longer than most guys wear these days, but it suits his face. I can only see him in profile as he stares out at some distant spot in the park. He doesn't exactly look sad, but his expression is such that his call must be about something serious. My eyes keep drifting to the exposed forearm he has draped along the back of the bench, the flex of muscles visibly dancing that I can see even from this distance.

He is, hands down, the most attractive man I've ever laid eyes on.

Without thinking, I do the one thing I almost never do—I lift my camera and quickly snap a few pictures before he notices. Normally, I'd go talk to him and get his permission before taking any pictures, but there's something about that look on his face that screams *Leave me alone. I'm trying to sort out my shit.*

Still, I can't stop from moving closer, wanting to get a better shot of him, wanting to try and figure out exactly what he's thinking about that's causing the deep furrow of his brow and the downturned bow of his lips.

Snap.

I'm getting dangerously close to having him see what I'm doing. If he spots me, I'll have no choice but to approach him and ask for his permission to keep the pictures. A part of me hopes he will.

Snap.

Maybe I should pull up my big girl panties and go talk to him?

The worst that can happen is I bother him for a moment and he tells me to delete the pictures. My feet apparently agree with my brain because before I know what's going on, I'm halfway across the path toward him, my mind rehearsing possible scripts.

Hi there! I'm a local photographer and was wondering if I could have your permission to keep these photos I took of you.

Too boring and a bit creepy.

Hey, hi! I'm Andie. You're really fucking attractive, and I was hoping I could strip you naked and take some intimate—

Hahahaha. Yeah, no.

Hello. My name is Andie and I'm an amateur photographer.

Lies.

Hey, you're hot. Want to go on a date?

I can picture the look of rejection on his face without trying.

Mr. Handsome stands up and starts looking around the park, which stops me dead in my tracks. He's still on the phone but something has clearly changed with him. You know that sick, sinking feeling you had in school when the teacher was looking for someone to read the next passage from the novel you were study-ing, and you'd have done anything to shrink yourself into a ball so they wouldn't pick you? Well, that sensation erupts inside me when I realize he's looking for someone to speak to.

Now, I'm an extrovert. I normally can talk to anyone in any situation and get pumped. I'm the friend who gets invited to parties because I can bring anyone out of their shell. Where I *don't* excel is talking to attractive men. Inevitably, I say the dumbest shit ever and make a fool of myself. I've had a few boyfriends in the past; the brave few who stuck around got to see the real me. None of those relationships lasted, which is for the best.

Maybe this time it will be different? Maybe I'll look him in the eyes and the perfect thing will fall out of my mouth. It could happen!

I see him turn my way in my periphery, and it sends my heart racing. What little bravado I had, the fleeting confidence that had me believing I could go up to someone like him and strike up a conversation, *poofs* in a blink. Running will only draw his attention, so instead I turn toward a patch of clover on the grass and kneel to take some closeup shots, hoping he'll ignore me.

It's weird, but I know the moment he sees me. I feel his gaze on my face and body as though he's reaching out and running a finger down my spine. I snap several more clover pictures—blurry, too close, is that a chip bag?—despite my now shaking hands. The sound of his footsteps against the crushed gravel and dirt announces my worst fears. He's heading directly for me.

The realization and sudden rush of anxious energy has me standing so quickly, my head spins from the motion.

All thoughts of what I'm doing, what I hoped to say to him, flee my mind, leaving me with two realizations.

The first is that he's obviously coming to speak with me despite his ongoing call.

The second is that I now have to pee.

Whenever I get nervous about doing anything, my bladder decides to help get me out of the situation to the safety of the nearest bathroom stall. Most of the time, that's a helpful problem to have, but not when you're standing in the middle of a park and you're about to be approached by an absurdly attractive man. First, there's nowhere close to pee. More importantly, it's painfully obvious that I'm about to run away. I don't know why I panic but I do. The second I see that he's opening his mouth to speak, I blurt out, "I have to go to work." I turn and fast-walk my ass all the way back to Walmart.

Better to exist in the circle of hell you know than talk to an attractive man you don't.

TWO

Milo

Here's the truth—I like people just fine. I talk to people everyday via email and texts. I've been known to pick up a phone and call the occasional person who isn't my therapist. The problem I typically have with people is that they tend to exist out in the world, and I tend to exist in my condo. Not a lot of crossover there.

I have my daughter, Mia, and my home recording studio where I do voice-over work for cartoons, advertisements, and occasionally airport notifications. Our groceries get delivered, our entertainment is streamed, so there really isn't much reason to leave. It's strange to have a certain amount of name recognition and yet know full well no one has any idea who I am.

"Milo, when was the last time you left your condo?"

Dee is my therapist and is excellent at her job. I saw her in person before the pandemic, and she graciously continued to let me keep my sessions as phone calls long since her office opened again. I explained that it's more convenient for me and lets me be here for Mia when she gets home from school.

I glance out the door of my office and through the living room windows overlooking the city. "I went and got a coffee yesterday." That isn't even a lie.

"Did you go outside, or just into the PATH?"

The PATH is my underground refuge and how I convince myself I'm socializing, when in reality I keep my head down and avoid all eye contact as I make my way to the underground grocery store, coffee shop, or subway station.

"Milo."

I learned long ago not to lie to Dee. She's far too smart, and it doesn't help me deal with my issues. "Busted."

"Milo, we talked about this. Not only does Mia need to see you outside interacting with people, *you* need to do that as well. You're helping both of you."

"I know, I know."

I'll do anything to help Mia get over her rising anxiety. When her mother walked out of our lives four years ago, it nearly broke me. I tried so hard to make our marriage work, despite it being clear to anyone with a brain that we were completely wrong for one another. Rachel wanted to be out socializing, going to concerts, bars, parties with people and lots of noise. I'm more than content to stay home and watch Netflix, get takeout, or watch TED Talks from the comfort of my living room.

The longer we were together, the more explosive our relationship became. When Mia was born things settled for a while. Rachel and I compromised, learned how to function as parents, while we continued to rankle one another as a couple.

That's why when she left, I didn't see it coming.

Worse than hurting me, she hurt Mia. The bright smiles went away and the laughter evaporated. Mia became withdrawn as the two of us created a cocooned life in our condo. And when she started high school, things only got worse. It's why I returned to my semi-regular calls with Dee—to try and figure out how I could fix us both.

Plus, yeah, I have my own neurodivergent quirks I have to learn to manage. *Hello middle-aged anxiety. How are you today?*

Standing up carefully so I don't hit my mic stand, I step out into my living room and give my eyes a minute to adjust. "I've left my recording booth."

"Progress!" There's something in her tone that sets off my alarm bells. "Now, I want you to stay on the phone with me and go out."

"Out where?" I don't exactly have anything I need to do today. My groceries have already been delivered, and I've pre-ordered my UberEats for supper.

"It's a beautiful day. Surely there's something you can go out and do?"

"I'm in the middle of recording a commercial. I don't really have time to traverse Toronto."

I can practically hear her eye roll. "I'm not saying you need to go out for the day. Just thirty minutes. There must be something close."

"There's a park across the street."

"Perfect! I want you to stay on the phone and go to the park."

Even though I know there isn't one coming, I wait a heartbeat for the punchline. "You're serious?"

"You know full well I am. Take a coffee with you if you want, but get yourself outside into the fresh air."

There's no sense in arguing with her—I'm paying for this privilege after all. I put on my sneakers and do as I'm told. "I'm not going to be much of a conversationalist."

"You don't need to say a word until you get there. How's that?"

"Fine."

I hold the phone to my ear as I make my way to my target destination. People tend to ignore you when they think you're talking to someone else. Not that there's a ton of eye contact with Toronto residents; it's the tourists I have to look out for. I don't know if I simply have that kind of face, but whenever I go out, random people always seem to come up to me and start talking. Not only to ask directions—that's common, hence avoiding the tourists—but to *talk*. Mia says it's because I give off a major dad vibe, and who am I to argue?

The afternoon heat slams into me, and I take a moment to adjust after spending the better part of the last—I honestly don't remember how long—inside with air conditioning. The sun reflects off the glass windows that dot the side of my condo building, momentarily blinding me and stopping my progress. The sudden honking of horns has me jump while I let my eyes adjust to the light. I try and make out details of the park past the busy street. Yeah, all I can see is a dark blob stretching out of sight. I must make some sort of noise because Dee chuckles.

"At least I know you've left your building."

A bead of sweat is already making a path down my back. "You could have warned me it was hot out."

"It's Toronto in early September. What did you expect?"

I grimace. "Touché."

"The sooner you go to the park, the sooner you can get back inside."

"I hate it when you're right." With a huff, I stride as quickly as I can over the crosswalk. "What do you expect me to do when I get there?"

"I'll tell you once you're settled. I want you to find a bench to sit on."

There's an outdoor gym class happening, lots of kids running around with their teachers shouting encouragements not too far from me. Not exactly the atmosphere I prefer for this odd therapy session. It's been a long time since I was here last, but my memory of bringing Mia here to kick the ball around is as fresh as though it happened yesterday. "Ah, there's a path where there used to be benches. Give me a minute."

Thankfully, the farther away I get from the ballpark, the

thinner the groups of people, until I'm finally alone. It's curious not only being out here, but also knowing Dee is staying on the line waiting to continue our session. I normally have the sensation I'm under a microscope when we have our talks, and it takes me a while to feel better once we hang up. I usually lock myself in my recording booth and rehearse, pretending not to be the emotionally fucked up individual I am. Then I nap.

But being out here in the heat and sun with people at least nearby is taking more out of me than I assumed possible. My chest has tightened slightly, and when I sit on the bench, I have to take a moment to steady my breathing. Dee doesn't say anything while I run though some focus exercises, which are a blessing.

"Okay, I'm ... on a bench." I lean back and awkwardly drape my arm around the back of the seat, trying to look casual but feeling as though there's a neon sign above my head screaming "Hey, this guy has ISSUES!!"

A few heartbeats pass before Dee speaks. "What's it like there? Describe what you see."

What the hell does she want to know about? "It's a park. There's grass, rocks, and birds and stuff. There's a garbage can nearby and all I can smell is ... well, garbage."

"Very specific." A pause. "Why do you think I wanted you to come out here?"

"Because I haven't been out of my condo in a week."

"Just one?"

I try to remember the last time I went anywhere. "Three weeks. I had to pick Mia up from school when she had a panic attack in the bathroom."

"Milo—"

"I know, it's not good to stay inside like that."

It isn't even that I'm anti going outside. I'm not agoraphobic, and I really don't mind being around people. It's merely easier to be alone, to be present for my daughter, whose inner light seems to be fading with each passing day. Having a career that grants me the flexibility to work from my home at any hour of the day is a blessing. Because far too often I'll walk into Mia's room to find her huddled under her covers, eyes wide and shivering as the claws of a panic attack squeeze her little body. I need to be home, to be there for her. And if that means I don't get to go to a work gathering or get to see the latest blockbuster in the theater, fine. I can live with that.

Sometimes, though, I do miss sitting in the sunshine.

"Milo?"

Shit. How did I forget I'm on the phone? "Sorry. I was … thinking."

"That tends to happen when things get shaken up for us."

"Yeah."

"Do you think you might be able to do something for me?"

Whenever Dee asks that question, two things inevitably happen. First, I immediately say no to whatever she suggests. It's absolutely my self-preservation kicking in. Second, I always do whatever she suggests. Again, why pay two hundred dollars an hour for something if you aren't going to make an effort?

I let out a slightly dramatic sigh. "What?"

"Is there someone around you can talk to?"

"I picked this part of the park because it's typically quiet."

"There must be someone."

Glancing around, I see a woman squatting in front of— is that a chip bag? She's taking pictures with an expensive-looking camera, her short brown hair tucked behind her ear. "There's a woman taking some pictures."

"Okay, perfect. I'd like you to go up to her and ask her for directions to the nearest coffee shop."

"I know where Starbucks is."

"That's not the point. I want you to interact with her, short and simple. It will only take a minute, and then you can go back inside."

Dread curls in my stomach at the mere thought of engaging in frivolous interaction. "Why am I doing this?"

"I want you to look her in the eyes. Connect with someone who isn't Mia."

This is stupid. Dumb. Pointless.

I shift, turning toward her as my sudden burst of anxiety makes my brain itchy.

"And try not to come across as a creep."

That's encouraging. "Mia says I give off dad vibes."

"Of course, she'd say that. You're her dad."

Forcing myself to my feet, I start to walk toward the woman. Honestly, I don't think I could have told you anything about her, not until she stands straight up and turns to face me. Her eyes are wide, panicked. She's wearing a white shirt and black dress pants, and a large dark brown leather messenger bag is slung across her body. The strap is pressed directly between her breasts, and for a moment I wonder if she has a fedora somewhere because she's giving off Indiana Jones vibes. Time slows as I take in every detail I can; it's as though her very being seems to shine brighter than the world around her.

It's her light hazel eyes set in a round face, perfectly framed by her short brown hair, that catch my attention. They are the sort of eyes I could stare at for hours and never get bored. She's lovely. And freaking out.

I stop moving and open my mouth to ask her ... something? Right. Coffee.

Sucking in a breath to speak, I lose the opportunity to form the question because the next thing I realize, she's speaking— No, she's panic-shouting at me.

"I have to go to work." She turns on her heels and flees by me, down the path toward the opposite end of the park.

Great.

"I thought I told you not to be creepy."

"You heard that?"

"The International Space Station heard that."

I make my way back over to the bench. "I managed to look her in the eyes."

Dee chuckles. "At least we accomplished the spirit of the activity. It's fine that the end result wasn't what I'd anticipated."

With my eyes closed, I tilt my face up to the sky. "I get it."

"Get what?"

"That I need to put myself out there more."

I hear Dee make a little noise—the one I get when I don't understand what she's trying to tell me. "Why do you come to these sessions?"

"Because I'm trying to get better so I can be there to help Mia." It's the answer I always give whenever anyone asks.

Normally, Dee will provide a reaffirming response and then book my next session. When she doesn't say anything for a minute, I sit up straighter. "Dee, you still there?"

"I am." Another pause. "What are you trying to get better from? Specifically. What do you think is wrong with you?"

"Isn't that why I pay you? So you can tell me how I'm broken and figure out a way to put me back together?"

I laugh, but she doesn't.

"Milo."

Dee can say more with two syllables than most people can with a novel.

The sweat dripping down my back is starting to irritate me. "I need to get back inside. It's hot, and Mia will be home soon."

Dee clicks her tongue. "I'll have my assistant email you the invoice and a few options for our next meeting."

"Thanks, Dee. I'll talk to you soon."

I hang up before she can say anything else. Exhaustion slams into me almost as soon as I shove my phone back into my pocket. I need to get back to the condo and get cleaned up before Mia arrives. She's made it through a whole day of school and I've only had a few text messages from her. That means things went well and she'll be in a good mood. Maybe we can play *Mario Kart* before supper. Maybe tomorrow will also be good. Maybe my sweet child won't be plagued by her doubts and anxieties, and the universe will allow her to be happy.

I look down the path where the woman with the pretty eyes disappeared, then turn to head back inside.

THREE

Andie

I have this unbelievably awesome ability to take a snapshot of something with my mind and recall it later. It was helpful back in school when I had to memorize something for a test. I'd write everything down on a piece of paper, stare at it for a bit, and it would all sort of stick there. Not exactly a photographic memory, but something similar. It's why as a teacher I have an easier time remembering my students' names and faces than some of my colleagues do.

Unfortunately, it's also the reason I'm unable to stop seeing my mystery man sitting on the bench at the park. Sure, I have his picture on my camera. I can haul it up whenever I want, look, maybe drool a tiny bit, then put it away.

I can, but it's not necessary. His pensive expression has taken up residence inside my brain and won't go away. Who was he talking to on the phone that made him look equal parts annoyed, amused, and a little freaked out? His hair was sticking up slightly, as though he just finished running his fingers through it. I spent the better part of an hour trying to fall asleep the other two nights ago, wondering if the strands were as soft as they looked.

He really was incredibly handsome.

And a total distraction, considering where I am and who I'm with.

Get it together, girl.

The restaurant is busy; the white noise hum of chatter creates a little cone of silence around our table. It's been great having my sister, Cara, visit for the past few days. She doesn't come to Toronto very often, so when she does, I pull out all the stops and go full tourist guide on her. This trip I rented a car and we went to the Toronto Zoo one day and down to Niagara Falls another. I don't drive on the highways very often, so I did my best to appear relaxed and not white-knuckle it all the way there and back. Surprisingly, I did great.

We're winding her trip up with a visit to *Cielo Bar y Tapas*, my favorite tapas restaurant where my best friend, Holly, is the head chef. I always get a few extra treats sent out from the kitchen when she knows I'm here, which is amazing. My favorite? Her kaya tiramisu, a sweet Malaysian jam pastry. So freaking good! Not that I go out for this sort of food often—I don't have a ton of extra cash these days—so it's always extra special when I do. Doubly so because Cara is with me.

Currently, she's casting me little looks, her eyes occasionally narrowing on mine as though she's deciding whether to say something.

With the sweet remnants of coconut and shrimp clinging to my tongue, I lean in with my forearms braced against the edge of the table. "Are you okay? You seem off."

"I'm fine. This is tasty."

Look, it's important for me to say that I love my little sister. While we might not exactly be similar in personality, body type, or temperament, or have remotely similar life goals, interests, or world views, she's my sister and we have so much fun together.

Our childhood home had a big yard that backed onto an old logging trail. We'd run through the woods with flashlights, the sound of our feet thudding hollowly against the well-worn path, and pretend we were Jedi Knights on one of the Star Wars planets that we never could pronounce properly. When we got tired of that, we'd head down farther to the old, abandoned dump. It was decades away from use, with much of the garbage having long been disposed of. But there were still old machines, abandoned cars, a rusted-out drum that the other kids said used to be an incinerator. We'd play hide and seek in and around the rusted metal until it was dark.

Ah, the eighties.

But as we both got older and our interests began to diverge, I found myself spending less time with Cara. I wish I'd done more to keep our relationship closer over the years. It was hard though; my head was locked onto the future that wasn't in the Maritimes, and Cara wanted to marry Kyle, her high school boyfriend, and buy a house as close to Mom and Dad as she could.

Different paths in life and all that.

And yet, it doesn't seem to matter how long we're apart, or how little we chat together on the phone, the minute we're together in the same room it's like time rewinds and we're kids, running along the dirt trails behind our house. The buzz of crickets sounding in our ears, the glow of lightning bugs in the air, and the burrs that stuck to our socks from the bushes we ran through.

There aren't any burrs remotely close to the tapas restaurant we're sitting in. Cara is poking the side of a very tiny taco shell with the prongs of her fork. "Please tell me there's more."

I roll my eyes as dramatically as I can. "There's as much as we're willing to pay for."

"That's good. They won't feed me on the flight home, and if this is all I'm going to get before then, I'll make sure Kyle brings a pizza when he picks me up."

My brother-in-law would bring Cara the moon if she hinted that she wanted it.

"Look, if you're still hungry when we leave, I'll make sure we get you stocked up with snacks for the flight. Though, you're only going to be in the air for two hours. I'm sure you'll survive."

I shove a shrimp croqueta into my mouth, cocking my head when I realize that she keeps glancing down at her phone on her lap. "Is there a problem?"

Her face instantly flushes, which is the main reason she never got away with anything as a kid. "No."

"Kyle bugging you about your flight?" You'd never know it to see him, but all six foot three inches of her husband is nothing more than a soft teddy bear. A tattooed, long bearded, forest ranger of a teddy bear. "Give him a call if that will help."

"It's not Kyle." Cara groans as she pulls her phone up for me to see. "Mom says hi."

I also love my mom. I really, honestly, and truly do.

However ...

We haven't exactly seen eye to eye on many things over the years. She wasn't keen on me leaving home to come to Toronto for art school, though she always assumed that I'd move back to the East Coast once I got my big city dreams out of the way. When that didn't happen, she started with the passive-aggressive comments.

Wow, rent in Toronto is super expensive. Thank goodness the Maritimes aren't that bad yet.

I read about another gang shooting. It's so violent up there, I don't know how you feel safe leaving your apartment. At least we don't have to worry about it here.

My favorite is always when she clicks her tongue when I say something about traffic, or noise, or anything that can be construed as a potential negative. She inhales and whispers *Ah dear*, before exhaling a soft *nononono, no*.

Thankfully, I can hear none of that over text.

"Hi, Mom." I wave at the phone before popping another croqueta into my mouth. "Love you."

Cara dutifully types my message. "She says love you too."

"How many times did she demand that you ask me to come home?"

Cara's face scrunches up like a perturbed bunny. "Over the course of the trip, or just this meal?"

"The meal." I keep my voice steady, despite the disappointment I know is coming.

"Only four. She's restraining herself."

I smile on the outside, while I scream in my head.

Restraint is something my mother isn't exactly known for. I hate that she uses Cara as a conduit rather than talking to me directly. "At least you can tell her you tried."

"Thanks for that."

"I'm happy here. I know she finds that hard to believe, but I'd be bored stiff if I moved home."

There's no way I'll ever permanently go back. I love the Maritimes, but I'm far too settled here in Toronto to go back now. You'd think after twenty-six years Mom might realize she's on the wrong side of a losing battle. But no, no she does not.

I expect Cara to laugh this off the way we always do in these situations. There's nothing to bond siblings quite like coordinating a defense against a well-meaning parent. But when she doesn't say anything, I look up from the menu surprised to see her frowning at her plate.

"What's wrong?"

She glances up at me as she runs her finger along the bottom of her sweating water glass. "Are you?"

"Am I what?"

"Happy?"

"Of course, I am." If Cara ends up siding with Mom, I'm in for quite the battle. "Why wouldn't I be?"

She reaches across the table and takes my hand in hers, her skin cold and damp from where she's been touching her glass. "Hon, you look miserable. I know I've only been here for a few days, and I don't know everything that's going on in your life, but you just look ... tired."

The din of conversations from the other patrons around us pulses louder as the servers bring out a birthday cake for someone sitting three tables away, loudly singing their version of a birthday song. The disruption gives me a moment to collect my thoughts, not that I think it will do me much good. I'm not exactly a good liar myself.

Cara lifts an eyebrow as the waitstaff leave the table and the smattering of applause from the patrons dies off, meaning my short reprieve is over.

I straighten, smiling as genuinely as I can. "I'm fine. I just had a bit of a long week before you came. Did I mention the triplets?"

"Yes, you told me about the triplets."

"And then there was the whole issue with the backed-up toilets the week before. The smell—" I legit gag at the memory. "Nothing like raw sewage to ruin your week."

Cara holds my gaze but I pull away, needing to sit back and get some space between us. She doesn't move and her piercing gaze feels like the sun through a magnifying glass. The noise around us hollows out, collapsing inward leaving me painfully aware of my sister's concern.

"Have you done anything else with your art?" No hint of judgment in her voice, only curiosity.

"You know I haven't. I've been so busy with work and teaching that I ... I'm trying to go out on the weekend to take some pictures."

"Are you?" God, she's sounding like Mom now.

"I am! Look." I always have my camera with me—a habit I've maintained since graduating from art school. "I went out after work the other day and took some nice nature shots."

My data card is dangerously close to being full, though that's mostly because I'm lazy and haven't pulled my pictures onto my computer yet. When I turn the display screen on, the last photo I took is there—a random chip bag. Which means ...

I click the back button a few times and come face-to-screen with my mystery man.

When I got home that day I left my camera in my bag, still feeling the weight of the embarrassment from my hasty departure and not wanting to see his face again so soon. I assumed the picture was crap. It wasn't like I took any time to set up the shot, or accounted for the lighting. So I'm more than a little shocked to look down at his face shining up from the small display window and see that not only is it a damn good picture, but I also somehow framed him perfectly in a scene that took full advantage of the natural light.

Oh, shit. This is good. Like a once in a lifetime kind of picture.

And not something I can show anyone since I don't have his permission.

Because of course not.

I should delete him right now and forget that I ever laid eyes on him. My thumb shifts to the button; the little picture of the garbage can taunts me to press it. Instead, I use the scroll wheel to go back to the first few pictures I took of flowers, paths, trees.

Chip bags.

My nerves send a jolt of energy through my legs. "Here, look for yourself." I stick the camera out for Cara to take. "I need to pee."

The tables are far closer together than I'm used to—real life has mostly gone back to normal now that the worst of the pandemic is over. I skirt around various table corners and stride as quickly as I can to the washroom. Toilet stalls are my haven at work, a place I can hide for a few minutes when the pressures get to be too much, despite the amount of traffic.

I hate that I feel the need to hide from Cara, but I refuse to consider that while I might not want to move back home, maybe I'm not as happy as I let my family believe. Dating was more than a little difficult during the pandemic, to the point where I didn't go anywhere with anyone. I took as many pictures as I could inside my apartment, but that got old quickly. Then there was the dark period of my life where I dove into the bowels of Netflix, bingeing on some of the weirdest shows I could find.

Don't get me started on my Wordle situation and the need to find every knock-off I could.

I mean, we were stuck in a pandemic, and I was as far away from my loved ones as I could be. I ran home to visit everyone the moment I could, but the two weeks I stayed was all I could take. The old itch to move, to get out on the road and go see anything, hit me hard.

And sure, I didn't go anywhere, didn't book that vacation I wanted to take, go on that cruise I constantly looked at online, but that was for practical reasons. The ships weren't safe yet. The vaccine boosters were still being tweaked. The airlines were imploding and losing luggage.

I was a scared child stuck in a forty-five-year-old body.

The usual.

Okay, I need to get my shit together and get back out there to face my sister. I'm happy. No, I don't want to move home, but I'm due for another visit. Yes, I'm out there dating again and I'm sure I'll meet someone, even if it doesn't turn out to be a long-term thing.

I'm *fine*.

Wait, I do need to pee.

Ten minutes later, I'm sitting back down at the table. "Sorry about that. Anyway, yes, I'm taking pictures and I'm happy. You can reassure Mom that if there was a problem, I'd be the first to tell her."

Cara is still staring down at my camera, her eyes wide and her lips parted. "Hon, this is really freaking good."

"It's just flowers and trees."

She holds up the camera, and I'm once again face-to-screen with my mystery man. "Who's he?"

Now, just because I can't get him out of my head doesn't mean I want to have a full-on conversation with Cara about him. The next thing I know, she'll be trying to find a way to locate him and set us up on a date or something.

"Some guy I saw in the park." I shrug, wishing I'd been smart enough to delete the picture before handing it over. "I need to delete that."

"No!" Cara clutches the camera to her chest, looking equal parts horrified and offended. "Don't you dare. This is … no. He's sexy as all get out."

When I'm face-to-face with someone who genuinely likes one of my photos, family or not, my immediate reaction is to tell them they're wrong and here are all the reasons why. It doesn't matter if I'm craving that sort of approval only seconds before I get it, I can't help but grind that approval to dust in my head.

And yet …

Leaning forward so my chest is dangerously close to my plate, I can't pull my gaze from him. Yup, the photo really does live up to the image that's planted firmly in my head. "God, he really is."

"You need to do something with this. *Anything*. Post it online."

"I can't. I left the park before I was able to talk to him and get his permission." It breaks my heart, but I do have ethics and I don't know this man's life. He could be on the run from someone, or merely wouldn't want his face plastered all over the place.

Cara turns the camera back around to look at him some more. Holly chooses that moment to step out of the kitchen. The moment her eyes find us, she grins and makes her way expertly between the tables.

"Andie! I thought I saw you out here when we sang to table eight." We do that awkward hug thing where I'm sit-standing half out of my chair, and she's half bent to give me a side hug. "I have crap on my apron."

"Holly, you remember my sister, Cara."

"I do! Welcome, and I hope my food hasn't disappointed."

Cara laughs in a completely adorable way that I've always wished I could replicate. "It's amazing. I'm just not used to such small portions."

"You can try all sorts of dishes that way." Holly's smile is wide and makes her eyes sparkle.

"Expensive little dishes." Cara shakes her head. "Sorry. That was rude."

"Not at all. How about I send out a little something extra to tide you over." Holly winks. "Chef's treat."

"You're amazing." I point at the mostly empty shrimp croqueta plate. "More please?"

"Coming up," Holly says with a nod and a smirk.

"Wait, before you go. Did you see Andie's photo?" Cara sticks my camera out for Holly to see. "Isn't this a good one?"

Holly *ooohs*. "Andie, honey, this is amazing. I like how it tells a part of a story. Makes me want to know what happens next."

"See, that's two people who think it's amazing." She smiles at Holly, who grins back. "You have to keep it."

"Sure, I can keep it. But I can't do anything with it."

Crossing her arms, Holly gives me one of her exasperated eye rolls. "You need to find one of those photography contests and enter it. I've been telling her this for ages now, but she won't listen."

"Andie's stubborn. She makes up her mind about something, and that's it."

Holly glances at the kitchen door. "I have to get back. Andie, hon, we need to do drinks again soon."

"Call me and we'll make it happen."

Cara waits for Holly to leave before leaning in. "You're making a mistake with that photo."

"Did you not hear what I just—"

"There's a way. There must be." She looks down at him with a sigh and hands my camera back. "This is the sort of photo that makes the cover of magazines. And if you were a finalist, or hell, even won, Mom wouldn't be able to say that you're not living your life and should come home every two minutes."

Shoving my camera back into my bag, I laugh. "Mom would still find a way to encourage my relocation. She's never approved of me being here."

"It's not that." Cara sighs as her gaze slides away.

"What is it, then?"

My sister has always been the peacemaker in our family. She long ago perfected the art of walking the line between knowing when to spill the truth and when to hold her tongue. And I long ago perfected the art of knowing when she's holding onto something that she wants to share.

Right now, there's something she's keeping from me.

"Cara?" I say it in a sing-song way, so she knows that I know.

She sighs again. "It's not mine to tell."

"I can't help if I don't know what's going on."

"I know." She picks up her water glass and takes a long drink. "I promise I'll say something if I think you need to know."

"Okay." There really isn't anything else I can do or say at this point. I glance down at my bag by my feet. "He really is sexy as fuck."

"Right!" Cara's grin chases away the sudden cloud over us both. She leans closer as she glances around dramatically as though looking for someone trying to listen in. "Seriously, you need to find this guy so you can use the picture. Or date him. But at least be able to use the picture. It deserves to be in a contest so people can see your talent."

I find myself leaning in as well. "Someone like that is probably already married with a dozen children."

"You shouldn't judge." She wags her finger at me. "He could be gay."

"With a dozen children." I roll my eyes. "Either way, I wouldn't know where to start."

"You'll figure it out. Just don't give up on yourself or your dreams."

"Those dreams are long gone. Not many forty-five-year-olds are starting out with a new artistic career. I'm an average photographer who takes family portraits and passport photos, and I'm okay with that."

"Bullshit. You're good at this stuff. You've just never given yourself permission to try and make a go of it. You've convinced yourself that you're going to fail before you've started."

"I did try. And I did fail."

Cara's face turns red.

She was on a high school trip the week of my art exhibition, leaving only Mom to attend. Literally the only person. That night I mentally went through every possibility of how to get out of the show once I realized no one was coming. I got up to faking an alien invasion when Mom walked over, kissed my cheek and asked if I wanted her to buy my ticket home.

That, yeah, that hurt.

Cara waves away her embarrassment. "That was then. You need to find this guy, get whatever permissions you need, and enter it into ... I dunno, something. Prove yourself wrong."

"Maybe. Hey, what time's your flight?"

"Nice topic change. I have plenty of time."

Thankfully, she takes the hint and we talk about her trip and what we'll do the next time she comes up. The whole time in the back of my head, I wonder if there's a way I can find him and get his permission to use the photo. Because that's the only way I can justify getting in touch with him. It's not like I can explain the stalkerish behavior that would be necessary to find him otherwise.

Yeah, hi. I know I randomly took your picture in the park and ran away, but I scoured the city trying to find you and wanna have a coffee? How about getting naked?

Horrible idea.

Even if I manage to locate him to get his permission to enter a contest, isn't that still weird? Is there a contest that would make the effort worth it? It's been so long since I've thought about putting my stuff out there beyond my social media accounts, I'm not sure where to start.

I'll probably fail again, and that's the last thing I want to deal with.

And ... shit, I'm totally doing it again. Cara is right. I do talk myself out of doing things before I give myself a chance. I don't know what scares me more—the thought that I might do it and fail again, or that I'll succeed.

Because then, I'll have *expectations*.

Shoving that emotional baggage back into Pandora's box, I lock my attention back on Cara and our conversation before she's gone, and I'm once again on my own.

FOUR

Andie

It doesn't take me very long to realize I have not one, but three problems.

First, my mystery man is hot.

Second, he is my exact catnip kind of hot. The sexy dad who's probably super capable of doing things like killing spiders, basic home repair, and dishes. Why my brain has latched on to competency as my kink of choice, I can't tell you. But it has. I guess I could have worse problems.

My third and final problem is my realization that Cara's right. Her suggestion to use the photo for a contest is a good one; her voice echoes long after I drop her off at Pearson to catch her flight home. I have to at least see if it's something I can feasibly manage, even if I don't see it through.

I start by dumping the file onto my computer to see what I can do to it in Photoshop. There's no reason to go chasing after this guy if I can't get it to look the way I want. I adjust the exposure and tweak the color balance, then lay a filter over top of him to see if I can make it any better.

Then I remove all of that and start again.

And again.

A part of me is content to stare at the man knowing that shortly after I took this he stood up, walked my way, and our eyes met for one glorious moment before insecurity had me running. He'd been engaged in some sort of serious conversation, but when he stood and I felt his attention shift to me, it was as though someone had driven an electrical current deep beneath my skin. I became immediately aware of the precision of his gait, and that I was the sudden object of his attention. The memory of seeing his blue eyes locked on me, the ripple of his forearm as he clutched his cell phone, kicks my libido up to a gazillion.

In retrospect, he probably saw that I'd taken his picture and was coming to talk to me about it. Which makes finding him slightly more problematic. If I were in his position and someone hunted me down to get consent after the fact, I would demand that they delete the photo and *never pick up a camera again.*

I sigh and go back and tweak the color balance some more.

What I'm not going to do is pack up early and walk through the park in a vain attempt to find my guy again before I have to head to the college. And I certainly won't sit on the same bench he was on and take my laptop out, pretending to work when what I'm really doing is trying to look busy and not like a crazy park stalker waiting to see if he'll happen to come by.

I mean, I do. For nearly an hour.

No luck.

I have to leave because a swarm of wasps buzzing around the nearby garbage can are coming far too close for my liking. The last thing I want is to get stung and then try to act upbeat while teaching the importance of aperture sizes when setting up various photo shoots. I take the longest route possible to the bus stop, peeking into windows of businesses, coffee shops, and any ground-level stores I can. The chances that he's not from around here are slim. Most people stay in their little section of Toronto unless there's something specific they need to do. If he was at that park eating lunch and taking phone calls, he has to be from somewhere close.

Unless he was visiting from out of town, in which case I'm screwed.

How the hell am I supposed to find this guy? I could show his picture around, but that kind of defeats the purpose of wanting to get his permission before using it in the first place. There has to be some other way. I just need to figure out what that is.

My photography class this semester is in the basement of St. Simon—the floor that goes from freezing in the summer, to fucking melting in the winter. Nothing like ancient HVAC systems to keep things interesting. The old school has those wooden handrails and decorative panels with the shellac that gives off that oddly metallic scent. I refuse to use them, mostly because I hate how the smell sticks to my skin, and the pink soap they put in the giant metal dispensers never seem to work well enough to scrub it off.

My classes are usually full of a mix of people. Some are first-year students who need an art credit before they move on to the specialized courses of their programs. Some of them are taking a one-year certificate and my course is mandatory. I have a few people who are one-offs, taking my course for their own interest. Having all these different people at different stages makes for an exciting class. It also requires me to be a bit creative with my assignments, ensuring that I can not only meet all their needs, but also not make assumptions regarding life experiences.

They mostly like me. I'm not a hard-ass when it comes to being on time (shit happens), and I always give extensions if people have a reasonable request. Even if they don't have a reasonable request, I'll usually give an extension. Night classes are hard at the best of times, and enough of my students have trauma from their high school days; I'm not about to pile more shit on them. We get through the program requirements, they learn what they need to move on, and I receive the joy of seeing their photography skills improve.

It's all very much win-win.

Tonight, I'm late—see? It can happen to the best of us—and they're in various states of sitting and standing when I come in. The room isn't anything special, big enough to comfortably seat twenty-five students, but small enough that I don't have to shout while teaching. The bank of computers lined along the back wall are barely sufficient to run the programs we use in the program. The one time I asked for some upgraded machines I was told in no uncertain terms that I was lucky to have what I did.

Apparently, Photography 101 isn't a priority.

Who knew.

"Hey, folks. Sorry about that."

"You're late!" Lucy Xaio sits cross-legged on her chair in the front row of the classroom, grinning at me as she chews her gum. She's my youngest student, and she tends to keep me on my toes.

Fatima taps Lucy's desk and clicks her tongue. "Ms. Matheson, we don't mind."

Lucy grins at us both, clearly teasing. "At least it means less time for Photoshop."

"I thought you liked Photoshop." I slide my laptop onto the small desk that's designated for instructors, type in my password to log in, and carefully set my camera bag beside it.

"Love it. Where *were* you?" Lucy pushes her Raptors ball cap off her forehead.

"Yah, where were you?" That's Ronald Johnston piping up. Ronald is by far my most gifted student. He understands concepts nearly as quickly as I explain them. His challenge is lack of attention, most likely due to a case of undiagnosed ADHD. "You're never late."

"Except for that one time she came in hungover last semester." Oh, Mrs. Babineau. This is her third time taking my class and I'm convinced she's been failing on purpose. Her husband passed away two years ago and if I had to guess, I think she's lonely.

The rest of the students sit down, but they're all very obviously waiting for me to answer. No, I'm not about to confess that I was hanging out at the park looking for my mystery man. "I was working on a photo and lost track of time."

I don't talk about my Walmart job, or my experiences as a photographer to my students. Other than Mrs. Babineau, I'm not sure anyone else would care about what I do outside of the class. So when Lucy, Ronald, and Fatima all share a look, I know the next fifteen minutes are about to be a write-off.

"What photo?"

"I thought you were just a teacher?"

"Do you have an art studio?"

There's additional muttering from around the room as I sit on the edge of my desk. Looking at each of them in turn, I know it's best to answer quickly so I can move on to my lesson. "First, there's no such thing as being *just* a teacher. I'm only part time here at the college. My day job is a photographer at Walmart. No, I don't have an art studio. And I was considering entering a contest with a photo I'd taken, but I don't have informed consent to use it, so I'm just playing around for now."

Pandemonium explodes. Lucy and Fatima are up and coming to my desk, clearly making a beeline for the laptop, while Ms. Babineau slowly makes her way past the other students toward me. "My dear, you've opened a can of worms you'll need to deal with now. Better show us the picture."

"Ah, no. This really isn't on the curriculum, and like I said, I don't have his permission to show the photo or anything like—"

"You really shouldn't leave your Mac unattended." Lucy is already walking away with my laptop, a group now formed around her.

Shit. "Give that back! Immediately."

"Ooooh she has a bunch of great pics." Lucy keeps walking,

and the rest of the students block my way, preventing me from getting my laptop back. "Anyone else want to see?"

"Me!"

"Yes."

"Send them."

"Absolutely not!" With my hands pressed to my cheeks, I fight off my surging panic. "Besides, we need to start our lesson on aperture settings. We can't afford to fall behind."

Lucy grins. "And airdropping the class in three, two, boom."

Shit. This is bad. Like, seriously awful. "Lucy, stop whatever it is you're doing. That's my private property."

I feel the energy of the class shift. I'm on the losing end of the situation. They're all talking, laughing, pointing at the images on their phones—I think they're enjoying my art. I also know the second they find the photo of my mystery man.

Ronald twists around to look at everyone. "There's some of a person, and that would be the only reason she'd need permission. The last few files."

"Oh my God, this dude's sexy AF." Lucy stands up on her chair, her mouth agape.

I pinch the bridge of my nose unable to keep from sighing. "Lucy, get down. You're going to fall."

Thankfully, she listens, her sneakers slapping hard against the floor tile.

"Which photo?" Fatima asks, staring at her phone as she scrolls through the list. "Oh. Yes."

There's no way I can stand here and watch as the entire class fixates on the photo. Turning my back to them, I mentally drown out their voices and comments, hating how my face flushes at the unexpected attention.

"Dude, this is really good," Lucy says, sounding impressed.

"I had no idea you were so talented." Mrs. Babineau chuckles. "He's very attractive."

"Sexy AF." Lucy laughs. "That's what you need to say, Mrs. B."

"Yes. He's sexy AF."

Someone please murder me with a spoon. It would be less painful.

There's nothing weirder than hearing a woman in her late seventies say AF, clearly not knowing what the acronym means. I mentally correct myself on that point when I turn around and see the mischievous look on her face.

"He's a stranger and you're all objectifying him."

Fatima's eyes grow wide. "You have to find him. The world needs to see this."

Another blush heats my face. "He left the park before I had a chance to ask him." *Liar.* "I've gone back a few times hoping to run into him, but no luck. Unfortunately, as good a photo as it is, it will have to stay in my private collection."

"I bet we could find him." Ronald poked Lucy's shoulder. "It wouldn't take much to get something out on social media."

Fatima turns in her seat. "I bet Toronto TikTok could find him."

"Yes. Absolutely it could." Lucy holds up her phone. "We need to do this."

"No!" While it's wonderful that they're so invested in helping me find him, this is getting out of control. "Again, I don't have permission to use his—"

"I can make a video and post it to my account."

My mouth falls open when I realize it's *Mrs. Babineau* talking. "Please, tell me you don't have a TikTok page."

She beams. "The kids ask me questions and I offer them relationship advice. Plus, I like the sea shanties."

What kind of bizarro world have I fallen into?

"I'm putting out an SOS to all my T-dot peeps. We need to help Ms. Matheson find her mystery man. This woman needs to know who you are!" Lucy is up, phone in hand with Ronald and Fatima behind her.

"Don't you dare!" I chase them to the back of the room, but somehow Lucy has already paused her recording and is typing something. "Look at this sexy dude! We need to find him because Ms. M has a *question* for him."

I'm trying to juke my way through the group, but everyone is once again on their feet. "Lucy, you really can't use that."

Lucy races to the front of the class and leans against the old blackboard that never gets used. She holds out her phone again and grins at it. "People. Ms. M is dope and we need to help her. Look at that photo and tell me if you know who he is. Better yet, sexy AF guy, get in touch." She then starts typing something again. "I'm using #helpMsMatheson #sexyaf."

"Got it!"

"Me too!"

Before I know what's happening, the entire class is talking and making their own videos on TikTok. The chiming of videos playing and being shared fills the room. It just as quickly dies off.

There's a soft beep, and I turn my attention to Mrs. Babineau, the only person still in her seat. Her phone is pointed at me. She turns it around and smiles at her screen. "Okay, my dears, can we help Ms. M find her sexy AF friend?" She presses a button, then slips her phone back into her purse.

My mouth has fallen open again. "What. Did. You. *Do?*"

"Life is too short not to take chances," she says, crossing her hands in her lap.

Looking into her eyes, it's clear to see the pain there, to see the regrets. She's been with me long enough that I know those words come with experience that I have yet to ... um understand. Something tightens in my chest and for unexpected reasons, I feel as though I'm going to cry.

"Ms. Matheson, it's fine." Fatima beams at me. "Everyone's on social media. He looks great! He won't care, and it's the best way to track him down. I have more followers on Insta, so I'll hit there."

"No!" I shout louder than I intended. It instantly quiets the class. "Take it all back. All of you. Unpost it."

Lucy shrugs. "It's out there now. I've already had ... three hundred views."

Stunned, I shake my head. "But it just went live."

"Up to a thousand," she says, shrugging again. "I have active followers."

Clearing my throat, I look around the room at the sea of suddenly expectant faces. "I ... don't have permission. You don't understand."

Shouts fill the air as two of my quieter students, Sandra and Phillip, stare at their laptops, heads together. Philip looks around Ronald. "There's the Toronto Icon photo contest coming up in a month. You could enter that."

"There's a whole search page full of contests that accept international submissions." Sandra's small smile lights her eyes. "I'll send you links to the best ones."

I clap my hands together, feeling true anger. "Okay, *enough*. You all crossed line, and I'm putting an end to it. This is Introduction to Photography, not Social Media 101. Sit down and get to work on your own assignments. *Now!*"

Everyone filters back to their seats looking cowed, and I return my now-closed laptop to my desk and pull out my notes for the night. How did things go so far so quickly? This is exactly the opposite of what I wanted to happen. All I can do now is pray that nothing will come of it. Most social media posts have limited range, and I hope this will die a quick and quiet death.

Because really, how many followers can they possibly have?

FIVE

Andie

My phone starts blowing up at five in the morning. Not that I'm in any state to be fully aware of what's going on —because five in the morning. I blindly mute it, roll over, and go back to sleep. When I come to around seven-forty and pick up my phone, I have ... oh so many messages.

I'm not normally a person who has more than one or two text chats happening at any one time. And yes, while I have Instagram notifications coming through on the rare occasion when someone comments on one of my posted photos, that's maybe once a week.

Not multiple notifications a minute.

Ding.

Ding.

Ding.

Bloop.

Ding.

Dear God. What. Is. *Happening??*

My naïve thought that nothing would come from the TikTok and other social media posts evaporates when I see that people have not only picked up the hashtag, they've located my Instagram and Threads accounts and added my @ to their threads.

I stare at my phone for a few more minutes, stunned at the speed at which the notification numbers are going up, and up, and up. I've gone viral? Me? Which makes absolutely no sense to me given that I haven't done anything. Well, not directly.

There once was a time that I would have loved for this to happen. For everyone in the world to suddenly become fixated on my photos, sharing them with their friends. I used to long to become so popular that I'd have publishers reaching out to me, each wanting to be the one to take my coffee table book to market. That I'd somehow, against all odds, become famous.

But now?

Ding.

Ding.

Ding. Ding. Ding. Ding. Ding. Dingdingdingding.

It's a nightmare my brain can't deal with. I flip to my contacts and fire off a quick text to Alex.

> Hey, I'm not feeling good. Think you can find someone to cover my shift?

There's a pause before the indicator pops up announcing that Alex is typing a response.

> OMG U VIRAL!!! THE FCK!!!

A sob pops from my mouth before I'm aware it's en route. Nope, I'm not going to cry over something this stupid. I was a child of the eighties; a latch-key kid who survived full-sugar Kool-Aid, jumping off sheds, and biking without a helmet. This is social media, not the real world. I will act like an adult and deal with this the best way I know how.

I'll ignore it.

Taking a second to wipe my eyes, I let out a little huff and respond.

Are you able to find someone to cover my
shift?

Yes. NP. U good?

"Of course, I'm not fucking good, Alex."

I'm fine. Thanks and I owe you lunch.

Cool.

I'm about to put my phone down when it rings. The number that flashes on the screen is Holly's, one of only a few people I want to talk to. "Hey."

"One of my prep cooks showed me the TikTok with you and your picture. My God, that's insane. Hon, are you okay?"

"Not really. I ... my students took my laptop during class. Everything happened so fast."

"What are you going to do?"

That's the million-dollar question. "I think I'm going to go for a walk."

"Shouldn't you, I don't know, do something about this?"

"What the hell can I do?" I always assumed going viral would be a rush of excitement, not a chest-compressing grip of anxiety equivalent to watching a train barreling toward you.

"Nothing, I guess." Holly hesitates. "If you find yourself near the restaurant, come in and see me."

"I will." The phone continues to buzz against my head. "I have to go."

"Talk soon."

Tossing my phone on my counter, I run into my bedroom and get dressed. I leave my phone where it is, slip on my sneakers, shove my wallet into my camera bag, and bolt.

Toronto offers a multitude of opportunities to take interesting building and cityscape shots, to see the city differently from the normal heads-down I've-got-to-haul-ass-and-get-to-where-I'm-going way. I jump on the bus and head down to the waterfront.

I need to clear my head.

It's quiet as I walk, taking pictures of landscapes and animals. No people. No faces. Nothing that will get me into trouble. I try to wrap my brain around what is happening and what, if anything, I can do about it. Every time I start to work my way down a path mentally, all I can see are his blue eyes, his mouth slightly open as he stood there staring at me in the park.

Any goodwill I might have had with him before now is no doubt gone. Somehow, I've become the villain of this story, and I don't like it in the least.

To distract myself, I take more photos. I find some graffiti that looks cool and snap a few different angles of that. It's a sunny day, and Lake Ontario is clear and blue. I wander around for hours, going close to the CN Tower and the aquarium, but there are far too many people hanging out for my liking. Because I'll see someone doing something cool and want to take their picture. It's inevitable—like when someone tells you not to do something and you weren't even thinking about it *until* they mentioned it. From that point it's all you can think about. So, I leave.

Instead, I pick up some takeout—forgive me, Holly—before I hop back on the bus to my apartment. It's still light out, despite being well after suppertime. The air in my apartment is cool and holds a hint of mustiness from the air conditioner in my widow. My phone is on the floor a good half foot from the counter where I know for a fact I left it. For half a second, I think there might be someone in the apartment who knocked it over. Then the phone buzzes several times in a row, chittering and vibrating in place.

Great.

As much as I would love to avoid this, there's no way it's going away unless I take some action. I might have to delete my Instagram account to make things stop. Go nuclear on what little social media I have.

Or I can just turn off notifications. Idiot.

The vibrating stops instantly, and with that gone I feel as though I can breathe a bit easier.

The first thing I look at is the list of text messages. A good number of them are from my students. I always share my cell number with my class in case any of them need to get in touch regarding an assignment, or if they need to let me know they can't make it to class.

Grabbing my takeout and a bottle of white wine—a lovely Portuguese that was only nine dollars—from the fridge, I plop myself onto my couch and prepare to discover what going viral means. I don't bother with a glass, instead unscrewing the cap and drinking it straight from the bottle. Lucy has by far sent me the largest number of texts.

> OMG Ms. M sorry!
>
> U good??
>
> getting tons of pings
>
> we need a plan
>
> Ms.M??
>
> people are obsessed with u!
>
> obsessed!!!

There once was a time when I would have assumed she was exaggerating about the whole obsessed thing, but given how many mentions I've received, it's a safe bet she's right. As much as I need to address Lucy's role in my current predicament, I don't have the mental energy to deal with her. That will be a tomorrow problem.

Okay, next thing I need to do is look at missed calls, of which there are five. Two from Cara and one from Mom—those can also wait until tomorrow. It's the two from the college that jolt my heart and instantly turn my stomach into an acid pit. Holding the button to activate my voice mail, I wait to hear who is on the other end.

It's probably nothing.

"Ms. Matheson, this is Carly Rowe from the dean's office. He would like to see you in his office tomorrow morning at nine a.m. I was told to inform you that this isn't an optional appointment."

I want to throw up.

The phone prompts me to press seven to erase the message; I hit that number so hard I swear I nearly crack the screen. I'm not given much of a reprieve as the lilting tone of the messaging system continues. "Next message."

"Matheson? This is Jean Robichaud." I've only heard the lightly French-accented voice of the college dean a few times in my tenure as a part-time instructor, but there's no mistaking him. "My assistant should have already set up the appointment, but I wanted to make damn sure you knew this meeting wasn't optional. My office. Tomorrow." If it were possible to slam down a cell phone to disconnect a call, Robichaud would have done so.

Fired. I was going to get fired.

SIX

Milo

"Dad? I think you've gone viral."

I just finished recording an ad for a local radio station and came to the kitchen in search of a snack. While I use the building's exercise room daily, I try to limit my snack intake to a reasonable amount. Being fifty, my stupid metabolism has slowed, making it no longer possible to eat whatever the hell I want, whenever I want.

So I can only have *one* mega Jos. Louis treat a day instead of my normal three.

I shove half of the chocolate cake into my mouth and chew around my words. "That's cool." Having a sixteen-year-old in high school has in many ways kept me keyed into the current young-person's cultural phenomena.

With my job, there are legitimately a few ways that I can go viral. The most likely being one of my voice clips getting memed. I'm more than a little surprised that it hasn't happened before now. I've voiced some weird characters over the years; it was only a matter of time.

What I'm trying to say is, I'm not particularly worried by Mia's statement.

"Which clip is it? Wait, wait, let me guess." What weird thing have I done recently? "Was it from *Bo Bo's Unnatural Adventures*?"

"No, it looks like it's—"

"Oh wait, it's older isn't it? Ah, probably McGuffin from *The Academy for Ghouls and Villains*." I drop my chin to my chest to shift my throat into the right position to do McGuffin's voice as I shuffle-bounce my way over to where she's sitting on the couch. "You're late, Ms. Mia. Off to detention with you!"

"No, Dad, it's not that." She holds up her cell phone for me to see something. "It's a TikTok showing a picture of you."

Wait, what? "The only picture of me that's out with my name is my head shot on my agent's site."

Mia rolls her eyes. "It looks like you're outside at a park or something. Look."

There's a young woman wearing a Raptor's hat with a giant picture of— Yes, that's absolutely me directly behind her. "I'm putting out an SOS to all my T-dot peeps. We need to help Ms. Matheson find her mystery man. This woman needs to know who you are!"

A bunch of hashtags pop up, but it's the picture I can't look away from. That's me sitting there, talking on my phone to Dee at the park. Taking Mia's phone, I watch the video loop so I can stare at the photo again.

It's quite good, and the woman who took it clearly has talent. I just wish it wasn't me who has become the subject of her viral search. "I don't recognize this woman."

"Oh, I don't think Lucy took the photo. She's just trying to find you."

I peer down at Mia, who's blushing. "Lucy?"

"I've been following her account since the Raptors won their second championship." Mia shrugs the way she does when she's trying to pretend she's not excited about something. "She's funny."

Panic tinted with a touch of rage jolts through me. I force my hands to relax and let my jaw unclench before I respond. "And the person who you think is funny just put out a video with my photo that some random person took of me when I wasn't looking?"

"It's not Lucy's fault. Ms. Matheson took the picture. Lucy's just trying to find you." Mia is on her feet, hands on her hips, and those big brown eyes are fully wide. "It's a good picture of you."

It's one thing for a voice clip to go viral for one of my commercials or a bit from an animation I'm a part of, but this is something completely different. Being known as a voice actor, even a famous one, comes with the added benefit of being able to walk down the street without anyone recognizing you. I never give face-to-face interviews, which maintains my privacy and keeps me out of the spotlight.

It's one of the things Rachel and I fought over before the divorce.

Who the hell would have seen me when I wasn't paying –

In a blink, the woman from the park flashes back into my head. How can I possibly have forgotten her and the camera she was holding? Well, that's not true. I haven't forgotten *her*. I haven't been able to get her look of surprise out of my head. The way her lips parted to reveal a soft pink tongue. Those stunning light hazel eyes that were such an unusual color, I could get lost looking into them.

But the fact she was holding a camera? Yeah, that slipped my mind.

I was so focused on the mission Dee sent me on, I didn't consider what she might be doing there.

With a camera.

Near me.

Shit.

"Well, poor Ms. Matheson is out of luck." I hand Mia's phone back to her and promptly shove the rest of the Jos. Louis into my mouth. "Bye."

"Dad, wait!"

On a good day, Mia's not exactly enthusiastic. She smiles and will occasionally laugh at some video or other on her phone—mostly of kids falling or perfectly cut screams—but rarely do I see her beaming with excitement. It catches me off guard in the best possible way as she dives in front of me, her hands braced on my arms to prevent me from moving. God, I love my kid. I'd do anything for her.

"Hear me out."

I can tell already that nothing good is going to come from this. "What?"

"Why don't we reach out to her?"

"I'm sure you could talk to this Lucy person and she'd respond. Some influencers are good like that."

"No, no, not Lucy." Mia blushes. "I mean, yeah, but no. I think you should talk to Ms. Matheson."

"That's a terrible idea." I would kill and die for Mia, but every fiber of my being knows following up with this woman is a terrible idea.

Mia shrugs. "She seems cool."

"I thought you didn't know who she was?"

Rather than back down, Mia takes her phone out and scrolls through something. "Okay, I saw this earlier and wasn't going to tell you, but the picture and the TikTok videos are everywhere now. Like, I think even on Facebook where old people go. So, you should see it. So, you know what people are saying."

She hands me the phone and there on the screen is the woman from the park. She's standing in what looks like a classroom, appearing every bit as panicked as she did when I approached her at the park, yelling at her students to not post the photo. This is clearly someone who was caught up in the middle of something outside of her control and didn't know what to do.

I've seen that look in the mirror enough to recognize it.

"You should reach out to her. Say hi."

"Terrible idea." I give Mia her phone and disappear into my recording room.

When Mia doesn't immediately appear in my door, I figure I've managed to get past her obvious fixation on the photo and viral videos. Still, I wait a solid ten minutes before I open my email to see if my latest contract has any updates they want me to make on the commercial I recorded—

Mia jumps into the doorway, her phone casting light across her face, giving her a maniacal appearance. "Her name is Andie!"

"Shit, Mia!" I swear my child is going to give me an honest to God heart attack one day. "Please don't do that."

"Sorry." She doesn't look the least bit contrite. "She's on Insta, and I don't know why but on Threads too."

Gravity takes hold as my head tilts back to rest awkwardly against my chair. "You need to let this go."

"Daaaaaddd." Mia does this full-body standing flop thing with her arms that relays her absolute annoyance at me. "You're no fun."

"I'm fun. I just have zero interest in talking to this woman."

"Why not?"

A perfectly valid question, though one I don't want to get into with her, probably ever. "Don't you have homework?"

Her small cringe tells me everything. "Just a project."

"When's it due?"

"Tomorrow."

"And how much have you done?"

"Some."

I perfected my dad look of *stop trying to bullshit me* long ago and don't need to say anything else. Mia holds my gaze for a moment before she groans dramatically and marches off to her room, hopefully to do homework. The temptation to ride her about staying on top of her work always hovers in the back of my mind, despite knowing she'll get it done. Mia is a lot like me that way, leaving things to the last minute before mostly sticking the landing right on the deadline. It's a stressful way to live at times, even if it's the only way I know how.

Speaking of which, I have work of my own.

I open an email and stare at the words for a solid minute before I realize I'm mindlessly reading a Bed Bath and Beyond twenty percent off coupon. "Shit." I delete it and move on to the next email, this time from my agent, Bruno—someone I give a shit about. I read the first sentence, then read it again, forcing myself to focus on the words. When I reach the bottom and realize that I haven't processed a single phrase of what he said, I lean back in my chair and press the heels of my hands directly against my eyes.

I can't the get woman's—Andie's—panicked expression out of my head. That look of sheer *holy shit, what the hell is happening and how can I stop it* is so relatable to me, I feel as though had I been there with her in that moment, I might have been able to help. Instead, we're both in a situation that clearly neither of us asked for. Things will settle down for her. There really isn't any reason at all for me to reach out to her and see what exactly she wants. In fact, I have no doubt the internet hive-mind will move on from their need to locate me and on to something else. Things will go back to normal within a day, two at the most.

Sitting back up, I read the email once again.

Interesting. Yup. Sure.

I'm on my feet and at Mia's bedroom door before I consciously know what I'm doing. I knock, wait approximately half a second, then open it, leaning my body weight against it for support. Or to hold myself back. I'm not sure which.

"Why does she need to find me?" Yes, I could just as easily search online, but I haven't seen Mia this excited in a while. We were a team, after all, and if I'm going down this road, I'd rather have her by my side.

She's sitting cross-legged in the middle of her bed, a textbook open in front of her and her Chromebook off to the side. When her gaze snaps to mine, I'm shocked at how quickly her expression morphs from dejected to absolute glee.

"I don't know, exactly. But I'll check Lucy's feed to see what she says." She has her phone in her hands, but just as quickly seems to hesitate and pull in on herself. "Unless you don't want me to. I mean you're the one in the picture."

If it was just myself, I don't think I would have proceeded with this discovery process. But Mia, is so excited by Andie and this whole going-viral thing that I know in my heart I won't be able to say no to her. Maybe this is the exact sort of thing I need to do with her to help her move beyond her anxiety.

If only it were that easy.

"See what you can find out. But don't *actually* reach out and tell them that you know me or anything like that. This Andie person might want nothing more than for this to blow over, and we'd only be making things worse."

"There's no way she'd not want to talk to you."

"Mia …"

She lets out a groan. "Fine. I promise."

"Thank you, baby." I wag my finger around the general direction of her homework. "Do that first."

"I will!"

She totally won't.

Instead of going any further with that, I close her door and retreat to my recording booth to catch my breath and mentally bask in the glow that is my daughter's enthusiasm. Sitting in my chair, I take a moment to organize the pens and various sticky note pads strewn around my desk, rearranging the sticky notes I've pressed onto the frame of my secondary monitor.

This situation is wild. Why would this go viral in the first place? Don't people have anything better to do than want to shove two strangers together?

The picture hardly looks like me.

My Discord notification dings as a little icon next to Mia's avatar appears. I open it up to see she's simply dropped a Threads handle: @photosbyandie.

Great. She's a photographer and probably needs me to sign a waiver or something. This isn't going to be the grand romance that Mia no doubt has in mind, which is for the best. So what if Andie *is* one of the most attractive women I've seen in a while.

None of that matters.

I now have her contact information and can follow up with her. In theory. If my brain will give me permission to follow through with something like this. Sooner or later, I'll have to either do something or find a way to put a firm end to the craziness. Thankfully, my cell phone rings, saving me from having to decide for the time being.

Even if I did hit follow on her account.

Later. I'll look later.

SEVEN

Andie

I make the effort to dress up nicer than my typical jeans and comfy T-shirt that I usually wear to the college. Unfortunately, the synthetic fabric from the shirt sticks to my sweaty back, making my already uncomfortable situation doubly so. I was never one to get in trouble. Not as a kid growing up, nor at work, nor really in any facet of my life. I'm so damn boring—probably the reason I've never really risen above the middle of the pack a day in my life.

Boring people rarely stand out.

The waiting room walls are covered with school sun-faded recruitment posters. The one across from me has an assortment of students hanging off one another in a large group, large white letters asking to *join our school today*. I catch myself jiggling my leg as I sit on the uncomfortable wooden chair and force the bouncing to stop. While I'm nervous, there's no reason to announce it to the entire world.

"Mr. Robichaud will be out in a minute." Carly, the administrative assistant for the dean's office, breezes into the room with an easy smile on her face. She disappeared to do something almost as soon as I arrived, leaving me to panic alone.

When she presses a glass of water into my hand, I can't help but stare dumbly at it. "Thank you?"

"You look like you're about to faint. I thought this might help."

"I look that bad?" I drain the glass quickly and thankfully don't choke. The last thing I need is to start coughing because that will be the exact moment he comes out.

"You're white as a sheet." She gracefully sits down behind her desk, her red curls bouncing around her shoulders as she does. "Jean's not that harsh. He just needs to clarify a few things and you'll be fine."

The door to Mr. Robichaud's office swings open and his steely gaze snaps directly to me. In that moment, I know exactly what it feels like to be a bug under a magnifying glass. He pushes his black-rimmed glasses up his nose as he tilts his chin down and narrows his gaze.

"You're Matheson." It isn't a question.

I have to force myself to take a breath before I get to my feet. "Yes, sir. I'm Andie."

He lets out a noise that I think is a growl, but it could easily be a groan. "Come in." He doesn't wait for me; he disappears back inside.

Carly glares at his retreating back and holds up her hand for me to wait. "He's not normally a bear. Just be honest with him. He appreciates bluntness."

"Now, Ms. Matheson!"

My feet are moving the rest of me into his office without a second thought.

"Shut the door."

Mr. Robichaud is already sitting behind his desk. It's one of those old school wooden ones that's far too big for the size of modern offices; it takes up an excessive portion of the space. There's a large blotter calendar covering the center, a cup full of pens, and a pile of the requisite school swag that always seems to accompany anyone who works for St. Simon. There's only one chair for me to take, directly opposite him. He points at it when I don't immediately move, which only serves to send a jolt of embarrassed heat through me.

"Sorry." Unlike the graceful Carly, I practically stumble into the chair. "Mr. Robichaud, I just wanted to—"

He raises a single eyebrow and I immediately shut up.

"Ms. Matheson, how long have you worked for us?"

"Ah, about eight years now. I'm just a part-time instructor, but I've always hoped that one day I'd be able to—"

His hand rises again, instantly stopping my mouth from moving. I would pay money to wield that kind of power with a simple gesture.

"I see on your file that you've completed the mandatory annual HR employee program regarding our school's ethics. You even aced the training quiz on your first attempt." He sits back in his seat and grips the arm rests. "That tells me you know exactly how you're supposed to act here as an employee."

"Sir, I didn't—"

"Which is why I was shocked when it was brought to my attention that one of my staff not only ignored our policies on privacy and our code of ethics, but that the offense had occurred in one of our classrooms."

I don't know why I get to my feet, but having the physical height advantage in that moment helps calm me. "I know I didn't have permission to post the photo, which is why I didn't do it. My students took my laptop and airdropped it without my consent. And while that's ultimately my fault as well, I didn't actively do anything that went against the rules of the school. Sir."

Based on the shocked expression on Mr. Robichaud's face, he hadn't expected my reaction. Look, I might not be someone who handles conflict particularly well, but I'm also not a doormat.

"If one of your students stole your property, then we need to address that. If I can have their name and—"

"No."

It's his turn to get to his feet. "Excuse me?"

"The student in question made a mistake, but the situation came about because I lost control of the class. If anyone is going to receive a reprimand for what's happened, it will be me." I cross my arms for good measure, hoping it will make me look strong.

In truth, I'm hugging myself.

Mr. Robichaud's hands are on his slim hips, his body canted slightly toward me. He holds my gaze, and for a moment I think we're going to descend into a staring competition. When he finally sits back down, I realize that I've somehow successfully defended myself.

Go me?

"This might be the case of a situation that got out of hand, but that doesn't change the result. A photo of a man you don't know has gone viral. We can't put the genie back in the bottle, so you need to find him and get his retroactive permission to use it."

"I've tried. I was looking for him before all this had happened in case I wanted to use it for a contest or art show. I ... He was just some random man at the park. I don't know how to find him, hence the TikTok."

Why did I panic when he was coming to talk to me? All of this could have been handled with a simple conversation and an email, and I wouldn't have found my life on this strange path.

"That's a shame." Mr. Robichaud taps his finger on the last Friday of September. "If you can't produce a release form, I'll have no choice but to put you on unpaid administrative leave."

"*What?*"

"I can't make an exception to the school policy, no matter how unfortunate the situation is. We can't afford to have the precedent of leniency set, or someone will take advantage of it." Some of the tension in his shoulders seems to disappear. "I can give you time, though. You have two weeks to track him down and get the release."

It takes every bit of my control to keep from crying. "Two weeks. Okay, I can do that."

Holy crap, that really isn't a lot of time.

"Bring it to Carly as soon as you have it." He turns, and begins to type on his computer.

Well then, that is apparently that.

I don't exactly remember leaving his office, or the building for that matter. It isn't until I step outside into the warm summer air that I come back to myself. I stand there, giving myself a moment to collect my thoughts, to sort through exactly what the hell this means for me.

Two weeks to find a man who to this point has been elusive. If the call out on TikTok didn't work, then what luck will I have looking on my own? Maybe rather than fight it, I should lean in, ask Lucy for more help, and put out a personal plea? I'm sure she'll be all over me going on her feed with a video.

Or maybe I'll give up and start looking for another job.

Because the reality of my situation is if I lose my teaching position, I won't be able to afford my rent. I don't live in luxury, but I'm comfortable. I've been in the same second-story apartment for the past ten years. My landlord is a good guy, reasonable with his rent increases over the years, and always there for me when I need a repair. If I have to leave, the chances of finding a new place I can afford on my own is a tall order.

No, I have to find this man and get his signature so I can get past this and go back to my normal, boring life.

And that's all there is to it.

BY THE TIME I climb into bed, I'm physically exhausted. Despite that, there's absolutely no way I'm going to sleep because my mind won't shut off. I affectionately refer to it as my loud brain moments. My internal monologue, the constant chatter that my brain engages in throughout the day, is noisier than normal. It's almost to the point where I'm completely distracted by the city noises echoing to me from the street below.

There's only one solution.

I press speed dial and lean back against my pillow. "Holly, hon. You done work?"

"I just got out of my car and am heading into the house." She sounds exhausted, the usual sparkle gone from her voice.

"You okay?" I hate asking because I know she rarely tells the truth. Holly hates to *impose*.

"Yes. No. Just a super long day with an extra side of bullshit."

"Do you want to talk or would you rather I let you go?"

"No, no. It will be good to talk to someone who doesn't hate me."

"How could anyone hate you? You're fucking adorable."

Holly was one of the first people I met when I moved to Toronto. We took the same English elective and hit it off immediately. And while I might not have a ton of friends, the ones I do have are like family to me.

Holly chuckles, sounding more sad than tired. "That's a long story and you called me for a reason. So, spill."

"Oh, I don't want to bother—"

"Spill. It."

It doesn't take me long to fill her in on the meeting I had with Mr. Robichaud. When I finally finish, I let out a huff. "Now I have to find him. For real." When she doesn't say anything, I clear my throat. "Holly?"

"Still here. Just ... I thought I was having a bad week. I knew when I saw the video you looked panicked. I just hadn't realized how bad things would get for you."

"It blows."

"Sucks and blows. What have you done to try and find your Mr. Perfect?"

My face flushes and I squirm in bed. "I never said he was

perfect."

"I've known you long enough, so you can cut the bullshit. That man's so painfully your type, I don't think we could have hired someone better suited for you." I hear her flop down onto her couch. "And you haven't answered my question."

"I went back to the park and looked for him."

"Okay. That's a start. What else?"

"I, ah, well. I think I'll see if Lucy will make another video?"

"Didn't she put out your contact information? Have you checked your social media? Email?"

"I haven't yet."

"Why not?"

Because I'm a giant coward who is apparently terrified of being somehow rejected by a total stranger. "I've been busy."

Holly groans. "I'm going to hang up on you now and you're going to check your socials."

"I can do it—"

"I won't condone your procrastination. Goodbye!"

"No, Holly don't hang up!" But she's already gone.

Great. Now I have to *actually* do the thing.

I bought a super long charging cable for my phone for nights like this. I can lay in bed doom scrolling and not have to worry about my battery dying on me. I open the Threads app on my phone, ignoring the number of notifications I have sitting there, and instead mindlessly scroll through my feed.

When I bailed on Twitter and jumped over to Threads, I lost my enthusiasm for social media. Still, I've been careful to curate who I follow over the years, not wanting to get swamped with too many trolls or bots. It's a hodgepodge of topics: K-pop, Marvel movies, Bridgerton fans, and of course other photographers. Those are the accounts I tend to follow a bit closer than the rest, especially if they're people I went to school with. Some of my classmates have done well for themselves, and it's gratifying to be able to live a bit vicariously through their experiences.

What I'm not anticipating is the sheer number of them who tagged me in a retweet of Lucy's TikTok.

You know when you realize you can't put off the inevitable any longer and you get that baseball-sized pit of dread firmly in your stomach? And how you can't help but squirm from the sheer embarrassment of the situation, though you're all alone and no one is there to see you?

Just me?

That's how I feel when I realize I have no choice but to meet this situation head on and see who or what tagged me. If I'm lucky, maybe someone really does know who my mystery man is, and I'll be able to get my release form signed.

There's a ton of speculation, threads upon threads of people guessing who my Mystery Man might be. Some internet sleuths are wondering if this is some elaborate ruse on my part to try and get my name out there. There's also a ton of threads that have added my handle to discussion threads that are less than flattering.

Why people are so hateful online is beyond my comprehension.

There isn't an easy way to filter through everyone who's reached out to me. To make matters worse, my DMs are open to everyone. That means a massive number of people texting me with suggestions, comments, and more than a few propositions for sex.

Why the hell do so many people want pictures of my feet?

"I don't understand."

I'm about to toss my phone beside me when a DM comes in through Instagram and catches my attention. Sitting straight up in bed, I read it, then read it again.

It's from account @VoiceBoxMan and he only sent me one line.

Hey, I hope you made it to work on time.

"Oh my God. It's him!"

EIGHT

Milo

The can of beer I've been holding is still mostly full; the condensation covering the outside dampens my fingers. Why I opened it, I'm still not certain. No, that isn't true.

Mia was getting ready for bed when she locked herself in the bathroom. I might have missed her sobs, but I've trained myself to be hyper aware of her shifting moods. She was off after she finished her assignment, but she refused to tell me what's going on.

When I heard the muffled sobs coming from the bathroom, I immediately knew whatever was wrong had shifted beyond normal teen angst. Thankfully, it only took me about an hour of talking through the door to calm her down enough to get her to unlock it. I knew better than to press her on what triggered her; she either tells me or she doesn't. Instead, I sit on the floor with her and pull her into the firmest hug I thought she could handle. She took her clonazepam to help with the anxiety, which makes her drowsy, and I tucked her into bed before retreating to the kitchen to dig a beer from the bottom drawer.

Tomorrow morning will likely be hard. If I have to guess, there's more than a fifty percent chance I'll go in to wake her and she'll be shivering under her blankets, taking school off the table.

I've finished the ad recording today, so that gives me some flexibility to take tomorrow off.

Thank God for small favors.

Still holding my beer, I sit down in my chair to look out over the city. I'm terrified of heights, and despite living on the fourteenth floor of my building, I can't get too close to the window without feeling nauseous. It's easier when it's dark out, and as long as I don't get too close, my vertigo stays muted. This chair is perfectly positioned so I can fully appreciate the beauty of Toronto at night. The lights and sounds of the busy city are a balm in an odd way.

When Mia is like this, I feel so alone in the world. I'm drained, not knowing how to help her, not knowing what tools she needs to be able to function as a person in an indifferent world. Still, sitting here looking out over the city lights somehow helps. Knowing there are millions of others in the city takes some of that loneliness away.

A little bit.

I pull my phone out and without thinking, find myself opening Instagram and searching for Andie's profile again. I stop and stare at the image of the woman who's somehow become lodged in my brain. I followed her account earlier but haven't taken much time to look through her posts. Photos from around the city are labeled with names that are familiar, but the images are strangely foreign. It's not that I don't believe they were taken in Toronto, but the way they're framed helps me see them from a totally different perspective.

Exactly the way her picture of me looked.

Impulsively, I open a DM to her, my thumb hovering over the letters as I try to figure out what to say. I can imagine she's getting slammed with messages, so the likelihood that she'll either not see one from me or will outright ignore it is strong. How the hell can I convince her that I'm the man in the photo without coming across as weird or creepy?

The memory of her large eyes, that panicked expression before she yelled and fled, bubbles back to the front of my mind. There were only the two of us there, so I'm the only one who knows what she said before running. I smile as I thumb the message into the app and tap the send button.

> Hey, I hope you made it to work on time.

There, that's fine. Right? Not creepy? Though it's too late now to do anything about it, except wait and see—

The magical bouncing three dots appear almost immediately, telling me that someone is typing a response. I sit a bit straighter, swallowing a generous mouthful of beer before setting the damp can on the floor. Depending on her response, both my thumbs might be required. I'm not about to half-ass this one.

When her words pop up on my screen, I laugh.

> So, yeah. Hi! Sorry I freaked out there. You just...looked intense. I don't do intense.

I'm certain that's the first time I've ever been referred to that way.

> I guess it's my turn to apologize. My daughter says I give off major dad vibes so I assume everyone sees me as harmless. I didn't think about how it looked. Strange guy approaching a woman alone in the park.

There's a slightly longer than expected pause before her next response comes.

> I think it's difficult for children to see their parents as anything other than parents. Know what I mean?

I totally do. There are some days I wonder if Mia knows that

I'm a person in my own right, with my own desires and needs. It's been so long since I did something for myself, I don't remember what it was.

Dee would have *thoughts* about that.

The three dots pop up again, followed by another longer text.

> I'm glad you reached out. I'm really very sorry about the photo of you getting out there without your consent. It wasn't my intention for that to happen.

I can somehow hear the earnestness in her text.

> It wasn't malicious. No apologies necessary but accepted.

Another pause before the dots appear.

> Thank you. I was a bit panicked to be honest. Ah, this is going to be weird but I'm hoping we can meet up so I can get a signed release form from you. I hope? My students didn't realize at the time that putting it out there broke my school's code of ethics, and my job is legitimately on the line. I won't use the photo for anything at this point, but it would help me out.

If Mia were sitting here with me, she'd probably tell me that this is fate or something pushing me and Andie together. But I've been on the receiving end of the pressures of working for a corporation and how little wiggle room there is when it comes to violations.

> Of course! When and where?

> Tomorrow? At the bench in the park. You can tell your wife (or husband!) that I won't keep you long.

Ah.

Of course, she thinks I'm married because I mentioned Mia. Not the first time I've run into that assumption.

> I'm single, but I'll let my daughter know. What time?

> Oh. Wow, sorry. I'm not normally this much of an asshole. Ah, how about 3 pm? I'll be done my shift then.

> Sounds good.

I hope Mia will be okay by then so I don't have to cancel. Maybe if she knows I'm going to see Andie, that will be enough to help pull her out of her depressive state for a while. It's worth a shot.

I hold my phone, not quite ready to let the conversation go, but I don't have a clue what to say next. When Andie goes quiet, I wonder if she's gone offline or if she also doesn't know what else to say. I wait another moment before thumbing one final message.

> I really loved the photo you took of me. Thank you.

When she doesn't respond, I tuck my phone back into my pocket, pick up my beer, and watch the city lights move below me.

Tomorrow will be interesting.

NINE

Andie

W hen I walk out of Walmart and it's raining, I throw out a silent prayer that this isn't a sign of bad things to come. I reach into my bag to dig out my extendable umbrella and the back of my hand brushes against the folded paper inside. I printed off three copies of the blank release form and shoved them into my bag before bolting from my house this morning, genuinely nervous that something unexpected would happen to prevent me from getting his signature.

And why the hell didn't I ask for his name?

I was mortified when he said he isn't married because that's exactly the sort of assumption I try so hard in life to avoid. Once we agreed upon a meeting time, I tossed my phone and buried myself deep beneath my covers. I didn't see his compliment about the photo until this morning, far too late to respond.

Despite my nervousness this morning, I took the time to put makeup on and made sure to wear my kind-of formal black T-shirt with my dress pants. It's all about professionalism and has nothing at all to do with the fact that he's an attractive and apparently single dad who approaches strangers with a singular focus and intensity so strong he sent me running.

It will be *fine*.

Water from the sidewalk splashes across my shoes, dampening the cuff of my dress pants. It slowly bleeds upward as I pick up the pace. I had a last-minute walk-in about twenty minutes before my shift was scheduled to end, which means I'm going to be late if I don't hurry. If, after everything I've been through to get him to agree to come, I miss him because I'm late? I'll scream.

Then I'll probably cry.

The park is mostly empty except for a group of women jogging. Their loud talking sounds equal parts muted and grounded, as though they're having a conversation in another room rather than halfway across the lawn. The green of the grass and trees is vivid, a stark contrast to the gray sky, both of which highlight the women's red and blue running outfits, so they stand out from the background. My hand moves to the top of my camera in my bag before I realize what I'm doing.

No. Nope. No fricking way am I going down that road before I've managed to resolve my current crisis. My luck? One of those women is a movie star or a social media influencer and I'll end up creating another internet storm. I can only handle one crisis at a time.

My feet slow as I approach the bench where I first saw my mystery man—*why the hell didn't I get his name?*—and it's empty. I'm only five minutes late. He can't have come and gone already. Right? He knows I need his signature on this release form or else I'm going to lose my job.

Right??

It's fine, he's just late like I am. No big deal. I'll hover until he shows up, then we can get this over with. I resist the temptation to check my phone for the time for a solid thirty seconds. I half pull it from my pocket, glance at the digital display, and shove it back inside. After another five minutes, I check again as dread creeps up and adrenaline pumps through me.

Water is beading in large pools on the bench, leaving me

nowhere to sit. I'm used to being on my feet all day, so it's fine. Despite really needing to sit down from the weight of my nerves.

Screw this.

I pull out my phone again and this time open Instagram.

> Hey! Just wanted to check to see if we're still on?

Not too desperate-sounding, but firm.

Not that he responds. Which, shit, why does this entire situation have to be so complicated?

"He's not coming." I speak the words to my phone; hearing the dejection in my voice makes me feel even worse.

He isn't coming, and I'm going to get fired.

Rather than prolong my misery, I turn and start to walk back down the path. I get about halfway when I hear a shout behind me.

"Andie!"

I spin around, my umbrella shedding water in an outward spiral my mystery man comes bolting toward me. He's wearing a black dress shirt that's soaked and pressed to his chest like another layer of skin. His brown hair is short enough that the rain makes it look good, wet and slicked to his face.

He comes up to me before doubling over, his hands braced on his knees. "I was in a meeting." He holds up his hand as he catches his breath. "They wouldn't shut up."

God, he's attractive. "That's okay. I was late too and, ah, I thought I'd missed you."

When he stands up, I realize that while he's taller than me, there isn't as much of a disparity as I remembered. His blue eyes are ... wow, and he didn't shave this morning, giving him the appearance of that casual scruff that's hot on some guys.

He's *definitely* one of those guys.

My brain takes a moment to catch up to the fact it's still

raining quite hard out and he doesn't have an umbrella. I step forward and lift mine up to cover his head. "It will help a little."

"Thanks." He somehow smiles with only his eyes.

My mouth dries, and I have to force myself to swallow. "Ah, hi. I'm Andie."

"I know." He stares a second before shaking his head. "I'm Milo. Nice to properly meet you."

Milo. The name suits him. Protected from the direct rain, his hair is starting to curl. I want to reach out and brush the water away so I can see more of those curls form and—

What the hell am I doing here?

"Release form!" I speak far too loud considering how close he is. "Right. Yes. Here." I reach into my bag and find the folded and now damp paper. "Ah, I wasn't expecting rain."

With his head cocked to the side, he smiles at me. "That's fine. I think today has us both a little thrown off."

It's such a simple thing to say, but it helps ease my panic. "Yeah, this has been so weird."

"That's an understatement." Milo looks around before pointing back down the path. "Let's head to the bench. We can talk for a minute, and I'll look at your form."

"Okay."

Turning together, we start walking as the trio of jogging women head toward us. I ignore them as best I can when they stop their conversation and openly stare at the two of us while they pass. We don't say anything as we walk, which kicks my nerves up a notch. My internal monologue is running through dozens of opening sentences, topics, something that won't make me sound like a weirdo. I've nearly decided on the right thing when we get to the bench, and I look down.

"Oh, it's wet."

Of course, it's wet, you idiot. It's raining out!

"That's fine. I'm already soaked." Milo sits and turns to brush the water away from the spot beside him.

It doesn't really help dry anything, but the gesture is appreciated. I sit down and hold the umbrella out so it kind of covers us both.

And here we are.

Milo half-smiles at me as he unfolds the paper and begins to read. "It really is a release form."

"Yes. I mentioned that in the DMs."

"I know. I was half expecting this to be some joke or something." He shakes his head and pats down his wet pants. "Do you have a pen?"

"Right. Yes." I hand him the umbrella as I search for a pen in my bag. "I normally have one in here in case I have to take notes or something. Really, I mostly do online consent forms, so I'm not used to this. I could always email you one if I can't find one ... Never mind. Here."

Yanking it free from beneath my camera, I hold it out and grin. My eyes meet Milo's and my stomach does a weird little spin when I see that he, too, is smiling.

Oh.

Oh, dear.

I feel my face flush and I can't stop from squirming on the bench. Maybe it's a good thing that it's raining out. Nothing like a dousing of cold water to keep one's mind out of the gutter.

He plucks the pen from my hand, and I'm only a little disappointed when I don't have the forethought to accidently brush my fingers against his. He quickly turns his attention to the sheet and signs.

"Don't you want to read that?"

"After everything we've been through? If this is a scam or something, then you deserve to be able to pull it off."

"It's not a scam."

He glances up at me, his grin widening. "You don't strike me as the scammy type." He hands me back the papers and my pen. "There you go. All consented."

I've never been with another person in my life that I equal parts want to get to know and want to flee from. There isn't anything creepy or off-putting about Milo; if anything, he's instantly likable. But there's a part of me deep down that knows the longer I spend in his company, the more his presence will complicate my life, and I don't like complicated.

"Now that you have that form, have you thought any more about your plans for the photo?"

"I honestly don't know." I hadn't considered what might happen once I got to the other side of this TikTok nightmare. "It doesn't even feel like it belongs to me any longer."

"It's an excellent picture. It would be a shame for you to never do anything with it. You should sell prints, or whatever photographers do."

"I doubt anyone would buy it." I stand up and shift out from under the umbrella, ignoring his little huff. "Thank you for signing this. I can send you a copy of the photo if you'd like. Seeing as you're the subject, it wouldn't be right for you to not have it for yourself."

Milo stands as well and holds out the umbrella for me to reclaim. "I didn't mean to upset you."

"You didn't." I groan. "This situation's been a lot. Everyone has an opinion about me, you, and this photo. I guess I hadn't realized how stressed I've been." What I should do is go back to my apartment and crawl inside a hot bath with a glass of wine.

What I *want* to do is share a glass of wine and have Milo crawl into *me*.

Milo nods and peeks out from under the umbrella to look up to the sky. "Sometimes it's easier to hide and let everything pass by before you need to face the world again."

Something in his tone tugs at my heart. "Exactly."

There's no reason at all for us to continue to stand here in the rain, staring at each other. I have what I came for and he no doubt has a life to get back to. And yet, neither of us move to leave. He licks his lips, and I can't tear my eyes away from the pink tip of his tongue. I press my hand to the side of my throat, drawing his attention. The rain is letting up a bit, but we both need to get changed out of our wet clothing. Naked, with damp skin and his curly hair, our clothing piled on the floor ...

Not together. No, no, nonono. Bad thoughts, Andie. Bad, naughty, dirty—

"I should give you my phone number!" I cringe at my enthusiasm. "I mean, in case you have questions about the release form."

He straightens. "Yes, that's a good idea. I mean, legally. Or in case your boss has questions."

"Yeah, he might want to check with you ... ah personally."

"I'd hate for you to still be in trouble because we didn't exchange phone numbers."

I'm very much aware that we can contact each other via social media, but this is practical. Adults do this sort of thing all the time, and I'm an adult. Mostly.

Milo pulls his phone out and hands it to me. I fumble my way through adding my name and number to his contacts and hand it back.

"Wait." He holds up the phone and snaps a picture of me. "To add to the contacts so I remember who you are."

"Right, yeah. That's cool." I look over my shoulder, half expecting someone to be there watching. "I should probably go."

"Me too. Mia will be home from school soon."

"Mia's your daughter?"

"Yeah."

"Good, cool. Okay. Umm, have a good day." I turn and walk away only to look back over my shoulder and see him still standing there watching. He gives me a little wave before walking in the opposite direction.

I don't realize I've been smiling the whole way back until I get onto the bus and my cheeks hurt. I have the form signed, I've given him my number, and I only mildly embarrassed myself. It's just a matter of time before the uproar over the photo dies down, and then I'll be able to go back to my normal routine. It's not like anything else can possibly go wrong.

TEN

Milo

Mia's phone becomes a curious weight in my hand as I stare at the shaky video on the screen. I honestly don't remember seeing anyone else at the park when I spoke to Andie. I mean, sure; in retrospect the three women were obviously there, but even if I'd seen what they were doing, they were far enough away I wouldn't have paid much attention. They, however, clearly recognized us.

"Oh my gosh, they're so freaking cute! Just adorable."

"Did you see the way she smiled at him? That girl's painfully in love."

"I'm impressed she tracked him down. The power of TikTok!"

A blast of text accompanies the video, as well as a song I'm not familiar with. Some sort of swelling pop number that makes my teeth ache. The video ends with a flurry of giggles, only for it to loop around again. Then again.

Watching myself talk to Andie from afar feels otherworldly. In the moment, I didn't notice how nervous she was, but the advantage of seeing everything from afar makes it obvious. The way she tucked her hair behind her ear, fiddled with the umbrella handle, how she fidgeted on the bench. It's clear seeing it on the phone that we were equally overwhelmed.

And yet watching the video, I'm still drawn to the way her hip jutted out to the side as she shifted her weight. I don't need to see her eyes to remember the way they sparkled when I agreed to sign her form. Andie is this enchanting mix of nervous and outgoing energy that pulled me in far faster than any other woman I've ever spent time with.

And that, well, terrifies me.

I glance over at Mia, who's hovering close by. Today has been better than yesterday. Mia got up, took her meds, and ate without prompting. It's as much of a relief as it is disconcerting to see her calm and smiling after one of her dips. I'm not so naive to think she's better; she's simply been able to grab hold of her emotions once again and keep them in check. Mia is one of the strongest, bravest people I know.

She catches me looking and smiles. "She's pretty."

My daughter is many things, but subtle isn't one of them. "Yes. She is."

"Are you going to go on a date with her?"

"No."

"Why not? You said you think she's pretty."

"Mia—"

"Dad, she clearly likes you!"

I hold out the phone, not wanting to watch the scene play on a loop again. "She needed me to sign a paper so she wouldn't be in trouble with her job anymore. That's all there was to it."

No lies are spoken on this day.

And yet ...

The memory of the way her face flushed when she suggested putting her number into my contacts, and the way her nails clacked softly against the screen, flashes of chipped purple nail polish against the glowing surface comes rushing back to the forefront of my sex-deprived brain. I haven't been this fascinated by someone since Rachel and I first met back in college. Not that on the surface Andie and my ex have anything in common. Rachel was all bluntness and focus on the future. Everyone knows where they stand with her, whether they want to or not. It's the thing that both attracted me to her and, in the end, drove a wedge between us.

I foolishly thought I'd be able to soften her edges.

She foolishly assumed I'd follow her into the spotlight.

If Andie hadn't found herself in an impossible situation and needed me to sign the paper, I might have run the other way, like I should have done with Rachel. Unlike my ex, Andie doesn't appear to have the same sorts of edges. I wanted to sit on that bench in the rain and talk with her, to watch her emotions dance across her face. For the first time in a long while, I wanted to stay out in the light.

Stay in Andie's light.

"So, you're never going to see her again?" Mia has this ability to ask a question in such a way that it sounds as though she's pleading and annoyed with me in equal parts. These are the rare moments when she sounds very much like her mother.

That's a thought my deep-seated guilt pushes aside as quickly as it arrives in my brain.

"Sweetheart, this whole situation is just wild. She didn't intend for us to meet, let alone for her photo to go viral. The last thing I'm sure she wants is to see me again."

Mia crosses her arms; her phone sticks out like an odd appendage. "You're a dork. She gave you *her number*. If she hadn't wanted to talk to you again, she wouldn't have done that."

I want nothing more than to argue with her, but it's difficult to find a flaw in her logic. "She might have felt obligated."

"Dad." She groans and lets her head fall back for a moment. "I'm leaving you to your sins to go do homework." She spins on her heel and marches to her room.

"Wait. What sins?" Dear God, I hope she doesn't mean porn.

"Stupidity." She shuts the door on me.

Which is good because I need a moment to figure out what the hell just happened. Being fifty and having a sixteen-year-old means I'm constantly playing catch-up with the lingo of the day. YouTubers, TikTok stars, Instagram reels—Mia is always showing me people and things that keep me young and at the same time make me realize just how old I am. Middle age is a state of mind, and I've done my best to toe the line between acting my age, understanding the media that my daughter consumes, and enjoying the descent into social media madness. Being a voice actor means I get to hear myself in video games that are played by people and then shared on YouTube. But it's the memes that blow my mind—everywhere one minute and gone forever in the next.

Not that I'll have to worry about memes when it comes to this video with Andie. Well, maybe the photo of me will get riffed on a bit. Yeah, not sure how I feel about that. My carefully constructed anonymity bubble is starting to develop cracks, and while Dee will no doubt think this is a good thing, I'm more than a little terrified of what might happen.

It takes all my strength to not go online, and instead turn my attention to my email. I've recently been contracted to do some voices for a video game expansion, and the script hit my inbox this morning. I'm reading through the notes when my phone rings.

Shit, I have an appointment with Dee. And I'm late.

"I'm so sorry." My default is to apologize, even if I really haven't done anything wrong. I cringe, knowing what's coming.

"Why are you apologizing?" Dee is always great at calling me on my bullshit. "I called you."

"But I'd forgotten about our appointment."

"Yes, you've been busy."

For a second I think she means the script I've been reading. Then it hits me. "Oh, you saw the video."

"Both of them." While Dee would never openly laugh at me,

there's no mistaking the humor in her voice. "So, how are you feeling?"

My head falls backward. "I'm fine. Well, it was a bit stressful when I realized that Andie's job was in danger and I was the only one who could help her. But that's over now, and everything should go back to normal."

There's a pause that stretches on for what feels like an eternity. I hate silence, mostly because in my experience bad things follow long stretches of nothing in conversations. Statements like *Why would you think something like that?* or *God, you're an idiot* were the norm when I was married. With Mia, long silences usually mean she's spiraling, and I never know how to handle that. The panicked despair brought on by my parental incompetence, of never knowing quite the right thing to say or do for her, is sadly a common sensation.

I hate it.

I feel the muscles in my jaw relax when Dee finally lets out a little sigh and says, "I have a question for you."

"Give'r."

"Do you want things to go back to normal?"

"Yesss?" Why does it feel like I'm walking into a trap? "I don't exactly want to be the center of a viral video any longer than necessary."

"Milo, why do we have these calls once a week? You're spending a lot of money to talk to me, to work on your mental health and improve your life. But when an opportunity presents itself to put all these strategies we've worked on into action, you run away."

It's my turn to be silent.

"My job is to help you. I would never force you into doing something that would harm you."

"I know that, Dee. I trust you more than anyone." After Rachel left me, I went to a dark place. Between knowing I needed to be strong for Mia, and Dee's help when it came to working through my emotions, I somehow came out the other side ... not so much stronger, but at least slightly more resilient.

"Might I make a suggestion?" There's something different in her tone, as though for the moment she isn't speaking to me like my therapist.

"Of course."

"I think you should take advantage of this newfound fame. You've come quite a distance since your divorce, but the one thing you seem to be resisting is putting yourself back out into the world where you can be seen."

"I'm not ready to date. And I don't think Mia is ready for me to date either."

I've been asked by some of my online friends why I've never joined Tinder or one of the other dating apps over the years. Mostly, I don't want to introduce a bunch of women to Mia only to have things fizzle out. She doesn't deserve to be subjected to my dating failures.

"I'm not saying you need to date Andie. But it might be a good opportunity to make a new friend. To go to the movies at a theater or something. The two of you have been through an experience that not everyone can fully understand. Going viral. Wouldn't it be nice to have someone to talk to about it? To commiserate? To show Mia that crazy things can happen to you and there's a way you can overcome and move past them?"

"I—"

"Just think about it."

What else can I do? "I will."

And I do, long after our call is done and I should've returned to reading my script. Dee is right that going viral is such a bizarre situation, it's hard to explain to someone else. Will I need to worry about being approached whenever I step outside my condo from now on? Will I miss the attention when it inevitably stops? Will Rachel see these videos and come try to take Mia from me?

No. That's sadly something I'll never have to worry about.

My internal monologue is still chatting up a storm when Mia emerges from her room. "What's for dinner?"

Shit. Food.

"What are you in the mood for? Pizza? Subs? Sushi?"

Mia slides onto the stool beneath the kitchen counter, only to drape her body across the surface. "But father. I am hungry now. I shall perish if we wait."

"So dramatic."

"How about we order pizza and to distract me while we wait, and we talk about how you and Andie should *totally* start your own TikTok." She says the last part so fast it might have been one word.

Ignoring her, I pull my phone out of my back pocket and hit speed dial for the pizza place at the bottom of our building. "Hey, it's Milo. Yes, the usual. Thanks, eh?"

"Daaaaad. You're not paying attention to me." She turns her head so her hair flops across the counter. "Why won't the two of you start a TikTok account?"

My heart does this happy little skip at the thought of spending more time with Andie. My mind has put on loop the way she touched the side of her throat at the park. The way the rain rolled down her face, tracing a path across her skin that I wanted to follow with the tip of my tongue.

Shit. Nope. Really don't want to pop a boner with my daughter right here.

Clearing my throat, I shift to hide any potential evidence of my appreciation of the idea. "One, I didn't say I would or wouldn't. And two, you can't assume Andie would want to do something like that. The poor woman has been through a lot because of me."

"No, she went through a lot because of the video that was posted with your picture. You didn't directly do anything."

I cock my head to the side and really look at her. "When did you start sounding so much like an adult?"

She rolls her eyes. "I'm sixteen. It was bound to happen sooner or later."

God, my baby is sixteen.

"I had a session with Dee today." I don't normally talk about my therapy. Mia has her counselor and I have mine, and I never dump my problems on her in any way that could impact her own healing process. "She suggested I take advantage of what happened here and put myself out there a bit more."

Mia sits up straighter.

"She didn't say I should go on social media or anything crazy like that. But she did suggest that maybe I should try and become friends with Andie."

"Yes! And you could both start an account! Dad, it would do so well. Everyone is totally in love with the two of you online. You'd have so many views and follows it would be insane." Mia's face is flushed, and her eyes have grown so wide I'm scared she's about to have a panic attack.

"I don't think anyone really cares about us. We're just the story of the moment."

She stares at me, her sudden excitement dropping away. "Yeah."

There's something terrifying about her mood swings, about how close to the surface her feelings are. "Yeah what?"

"It's probably better if you didn't. You're great at starting things, but you suck at seeing them through." She pushes herself to her feet. "Let me know when pizza comes."

My stomach sours and my chest aches as I watch Mia return to her room. There's no way she can know that those are the exact words Rachel said to me the day she told me she was leaving. That despite Dee confirming I didn't do anything wrong—that my ex had been trying to find a way to justify wanting to leave Mia and me—the accusation is still lodged deep in my psyche.

I clutch the edge of the counter and hold on for dear life.

Maybe I should reach out to Andie and see if she'd be interested in doing something like what Mia suggested. Not only would I prove to Mia that we can both grow and change, but it would be a chance to form a new friendship with Andie. I could kill two birds with one stone.

The more I think about it, the more it feels like the right thing to do.

Maybe.

ELEVEN

Andie

T he air conditioning in Dean Robichaud's office has been cranked up to the arctic setting, which means barring an obvious arm-cross-for-cover, I have to hope my rock-hard nipples aren't showing through my shirt. Dear God, I've had the odd hot flash over the past year and even I wouldn't turn the temperature this low. If someone told me they could see my breath, I would totally believe them. I'm sure he likes the cold and not that he's deliberately choosing to make visitors uncomfortable.

At least I hope that's the case.

As he requested, I arrived with the signed release form in hand hoping I could just drop it on Carly's desk and run away. It's the end of office hours, and I timed things so I'd have the excuse that I needed to be in the classroom. In and out, easy-peasy.

But *of course*, the dean is in his office and wants to see the paper for himself.

Today, Mr. Robichaud has on a light blue tie and a dark blue shirt—a combination I wouldn't choose myself, but he somehow pulls it off. He's equal parts attractive and intimidating, which I know is a major turn-on for some people.

Not for me.

I. Am. Terrified.

He's sitting at his desk, not directly looking at me as he reads. I get the impression I'm being evaluated as much as the form is, so I do my best to keep still. Mr. Robichaud is the type of person who makes me instantly self-conscious. If we met casually, I'd be too worried about saying the wrong thing around him to ever relax enough to enjoy his company. Like right now, I can't tear my gaze away from the movement of his eyes as he scans the page. Each second it takes him feels like a lifetime of dread building.

This is the opposite of how I feel about Milo.

The release form is a standard one, and it shouldn't take him long to confirm that everything is in order, and yet I've been standing in the middle of the arctic for a solid five minutes now. It could be five years for how long it's taking him to finish.

He makes a clicking noise in the back of his mouth as he sets the form down in the middle of his desk blotter like some strange reverent prize. "I'm surprised you were able to get this signed so quickly."

"Honestly, I am too. He saw the video and reached out to me through social media. I don't think I would have been able to find him on my own." When he doesn't say anything in response, I take a tiny step forward. "I do have his contact information if you'd like talk to him yourself. He mentioned he was okay answering any questions or concerns you might have."

"That's fine." He picks up the paper and holds it out for me. "Have Carly make a copy for our records."

The dread that's been clawing at my chest eases slightly at his words. "I will. Thank you, sir."

"Don't thank me. You're still on thin ice. If I hear any complaints at all about your conduct, your teaching, anything, school policy dictates I must put you on unpaid leave. Is that clear?"

"Yes, Mr. Robichaud. Crystal. You really don't need to worry.

That photo was a one in a million shot. I'll never take another that good again."

"Fine." He glances up at me across the top of his glasses.

Trying not to wrinkle my hard-fought release form, I bolt from his office and am relieved to find Carly still behind her desk. "I'm sorry you had to stay late for me."

Carly either heard what Mr. Robichaud asked, or she's been his assistant long enough to anticipate what he wants. Either way, she takes the release form from my grasp and saunters over to the photocopier. "It's fine. If I leave before six on most nights, I take it as a win." She glances over at the office. "He's a bit of a workaholic."

"He shouldn't make you stay just because he wants to burn the candle at both ends."

Carly smiles as she slides the paper free of the photocopier. "He doesn't. Here you go."

"Thanks." With his warning still ringing in my ears, I point toward the exit. "I have to get ready for class."

Carly smiles and shoos me away.

Leaving the office feels as though I've escaped a dragon's den with a single gold coin, but more importantly, with my life. I managed the impossible—got the release form signed and walked away with my job intact. Now I can return to my normal routine of working at Walmart and teaching here at the school. I never have to worry about that photo or needing to figure out what to do with it, ever.

I may never see Milo again.

I stop walking halfway down the stairs when that thought comes front and center. It's not as though we had any sort of reason to meet up again, not really. We shared this bizarre viral moment and now our lives are going to return to normal. Which is a good thing, right?

Except, I've been unable to get the look on Milo's face out of my head. I replay our conversation on the bench over and over in my head, only my imagination has him leaning forward to kiss me hard, push his fingers through my hair and squeeze, to cup the side of my face with his other hand as my groin pressed hard against him.

I reach for the handrail as I look to the ceiling and give my head a shake.

I do not have time for a sexual fantasy in the school corridor, not with my class starting up shortly. "Get it together, Andie."

The room is full, everyone already sitting at their desks chatting in super hushed tones. It's weird and more than a little unnerving after having just come from the dean's office. "Hi everyone."

The muttering instantly stops, and I realize Ronald is blushing and Fatima is looking anywhere but at me. Mrs. Babineau isn't in class, which is a shame because she would have filled me in immediately as to what's going on.

Lucy just looks smug.

"What are you all up to?" I cross my arms and lean against the edge of my desk. "And don't tell me nothing."

"We were just looking at some fan fiction," Ronald blurts out, the pink of his cheeks deepening in color.

Oh no.

I know better than to ask the question I'm about to, and yet there's no way I'm *not* going to ask. I'm far too nosy for my own good and may or may not have an account on Archive of Our Own that I'm occasionally on, hunting for new content.

I take a breath and lean forward slightly. "What fan fiction?"

Lucy groans and I think she mutters something before giving a little shrug. "About you and Milo."

Now, there are probably several ways I could have handled this revelation; with poise, grace, and plenty of tact. I could have laughed it off and immediately turned to today's lesson. I could have given them a small lecture on in the inappropriateness of fantasies between real life people, and how it can be harmful.

Instead, I gasp, "People have written porn about me?"

Several people in the class snicker.

Lucy cringes. "It's not porn! God, Ms. Matheson. It's just some stories that people have made up about you and Milo and your future babies."

"One fic already has twenty-three parts." Fatima's confession sounds painful to speak.

"Wait. None of you are writing this, are you?"

The shouts of panicked denial are at least reassuring.

Ronald looks as though he wants to die. "You're our teacher. That's just ..."

"A whole kink that I really never want to be a part of." I look each and every person in the eyes. "Ever. Do we understand?"

I'm greeted with a chorus of dutiful nods.

Fan fiction. Oh my God, people are making shit up about my personal life.

I want to die.

"Let's get to work. I've marked your assignments and your last quiz. Everything should be updated in your student portal. Now, let's open your textbooks to chapter five and talk about exposure compensation."

There's something to be said for ignoring your problems.

I HAVE THE EARLY SHIFT, opening the Walmart photo studio. Normally this is fine, but today I'm more than a little tired. On my way, I grab a grande, no-room Americano with an extra shot from Starbucks so I can make it through until three when I can go home. Maybe I'll have a nap or something. Rest long enough for my brain to reboot and get out of this crazy mental loop of doom I find myself caught in.

Last night I had a hard time falling asleep; my brain refused to let go of the idea that people out there are writing fan fics about us.

I should have given in and looked them up to see how bad the damage is, but I just couldn't. My own imagination is doing quite enough work in the Milo fantasy department; the last thing I need is a twenty-three-part story to obsess over.

I yawn into the plastic cover on my cup and take a sip, shuffling into the darkened studio. I turn on the computer and am walking around to hit the lights when Alex appears in the door.

"Hey, you." I wave before turning my attention to the prop box. "I didn't think you were in this morning."

"I wasn't supposed to be." There's something off in their voice. "I have to talk to you for a minute."

I don't have much of a sixth sense about things, but I'm good enough with people to know when something bad is about to come my way. Alex is a delightful person—they're fun and caring and hate conflict, despite being a department manager. So, when they won't meet my gaze, I know deep in my gut what's about to happen.

"You're going to fire me."

Alex sighs, their gaze locked onto my shoes. "It wasn't my call."

"Is it about the TikTok video? I wasn't the one who posted it."

"I know, and I tried to convince management of your innocence. The problem is that," Alex says, pointing to a group of young girls I hadn't noticed. They're hovering by the *Blue's Clues* display, their phones up and pointed at me. "People have been coming in basically waiting to stalk you. We had a group of high school students kick up a fuss yesterday when we wouldn't tell them when your next shift was. The district manager happened to be in and suggested we fire you to prevent further disruptions."

"But ... I haven't done anything wrong." Panic threatens to short-circuit my brain—the last thing I need right now. "Can you actually fire me for this? Is this even legal?"

Alex cringes. "Yeah. There's store policy that you signed when you started. Being a disruption to the store, potential safety issues. The district manager gave me a list."

"Oh."

"I'm so sorry, Andie."

I think I'm going to vomit. "It's not your fault."

"It's not exactly yours either," Alex says, shuffling from side to side. "You're a good employee. A good person. Maybe once this all blows over we can hire you back."

"Yeah. Thanks." Not that it matters. I take another look around the studio, not knowing what to do. There isn't anything I *can* do. I pick up my coffee, retrieve my bag, and hand my keys and cards to Alex. "You take care of yourself."

"Are you going to be okay? For rent and stuff?"

That's the million-dollar question. "I'm sure everything will work out. You have my number, so keep in touch. Okay?"

"I will." They give me a hug before awkwardly pointing toward the door. "I, ah, have to escort you out. Maybe call an Uber now? I have a feeling your fanbase might want to talk with you if you're lingering outside."

Damn. "Sure. Yeah."

I call an Uber on the app, and when the car is only a minute away, Alex walks me to the door. Without another word or glance behind, I duck into the car. The door slams shut behind me.

"Hey." My driver pulls away from the store. "How's your day going?"

I worked so hard to get Milo's consent for the photo to save one job, I didn't consider my other one was in jeopardy.

"Miss?"

"Sorry." I smile at him, swallowing past the lump in my throat. "I've had better."

I gently bang the side of my head against the window, and breath through my panic until I get home.

TWELVE

Andie

After getting fired, I approached my day the only way I know how. I made a list. Technically, I made many lists, but they were all sub-sets of the main list. Yes, I enjoy the order of writing things down and making little dots that I can later check off. The title of my current endeavor is boldly stretched across the top of the page. I drew a slightly wiggly line beneath the words as though to keep everything in place.

Things To Do Now That I'm Mostly Unemployed
  - Sulk
  - Cry
  - Sulk some more
  - Open a bottle of wine
  - Doom scroll
  - Figure my shit out

That last point is where I know I'll have to actually start doing something. With my wine poured—it's lunchtime, close enough to five o'clock—and my nose blown, I straighten in my seat and get to work.

I start with a quick rundown of all my upcoming bills, and how much money I have in the bank to cover them. I'll be able to lean on my thin savings, which will buy me some time while I look for another job. That thought shifts me to making a list of potential places I can apply to work. There are some photo stores that might have an opening, not to mention a few box stores. My concern there is being discovered by some more "fans" and being fired from those jobs as well.

I then make another sub-list of All The Ways My Life Now Sucks Because I'm Internet Famous. I leave a few open bullet points on that one. At least I don't have to worry about outside stalkers at the college. St. Simon's might be an old building, but they've installed high tech security with badges that keep non-staff and students out of the buildings.

When my stomach growls, I go in search of my lunch bag. There's no sense in letting a perfectly good egg salad sandwich go to waste. I sit at my tiny kitchen table and stare out the window. I have a list, but I sure as hell don't have a plan. Holly will be sleeping still, so I can't talk to her yet. I'd call Cara, but that would make her worry about me when there really isn't anything she can do.

My phone is in my hand, so I mindlessly thumb through to the recent calls screen. Mom's number is at the very bottom of the list sending a pang of guilt through me. You can't exactly have a relationship with someone if you don't put in a bit of effort. I hold my breath and hit dial. It rings four times, and I'm about to hang up when the sound stops, replaced by a small intake of air.

"Andie?"

"Hey, Mom."

"You okay?"

Of course she jumps right to the chase. "Yeah. Why would you say that?"

"It's lunchtime. You never call this early, let alone on a weekday. So again, are you okay?"

Mom is one of those people who does not appreciate small talk or beating around the bush. I learned that at an unfortunately young age. The comfort I foolishly thought I might receive for my plight I know I won't get. I love her, but once again I realize that sometimes I don't exactly *like* her.

Quashing my disappointment, I smile as I speak, knowing she'll hear it in my tone. "I had today off and thought I'd call." Not exactly a lie. "What are you doing?"

The humming sound she makes tells me she doesn't believe me. "I was heading out to church. We're hosting the homeless for a meal tonight, and I volunteered for kitchen prep."

"That's good of you."

"The work needs to be done. Help the people who can't help themselves." An awkward pause stretches on for several seconds. "Andie, are you … baby, are you okay?"

I'm not. Of all the people I know, I could use Mom's no-nonsense practical nature to help figure out what I should do next. And if I ignore her inevitable *Well just come home* comment, I might even receive some good advice.

"Andie?"

"I'm sorry, I should have realized you were busy. How about I give you a call on Sunday like normal?"

The pause is heavier than before. "Sure." Mom's Maritime accent stretches the single word out to *shore*. "I'll be here."

"Okay. Have fun at church. Love you."

"Love you too."

I hang up before she says anything else. Or before I break down and start crying. Why I can't have an easy relationship with her the way Cara does, I don't know. She's never been cruel, and mostly has supported me when I needed it. She just never wanted me to move away from home, and I think always thought that I abandoned her to pursue something I couldn't achieve.

Maybe a part of her is right.

No, with everything else going on, there's no way I'll let myself fall down that rabbit hole of mental angst. I might be underemployed for the moment, but unlike the people Mom is off to spend the afternoon preparing for, I *can* help myself.

I open the Instagram. There's been little slowdown on the number of people contacting me, both via DMs and by adding me to their conversations. Instead of ignoring what's there, I take the time to sift through the newer messages. Lots of lewd remarks, a bunch of fans commenting a lot of *Yass queen!* and the like. What is interesting are some of the offers.

Companies wanting me to try and promote their makeup, drinks, apps, and games; photo companies wanting me to endorse their cases, tripods, and any sort of accessory you can imagine. There are so many offers, I can't tell which are legitimate and which are scams. To be honest, I assume they're all scams.

I fall down a deep, dark rabbit hole of searches for so long that when I look up, the sun has started to dip below the horizon, my neck is sore from being hunched over, and my battery is low. I sit back and let out a sigh, wishing someone were here to hear it.

What's wrong? Do you want to talk about it?

My inner voice sounds strangely like Milo's. He seems the sort of guy who would give a shit about a friend when they're having a bad day. Introvert or not, there's an accessible kindness to him that was readily apparent from our brief encounters. He was the subject of my photo and the TikTok search, but he didn't really express much in the way of anger, annoyance, or any other negative feelings.

He clearly hasn't heard about the fan fiction.

The urge to call him, to check in and see how he's doing, whether his boss discovered what's going on and if it's negatively impacted him, is strong. Should I tell him about the fics? Would that make things even more awkward than they already are? I pick up my phone again to text him, until that lovely intrusive thought machine starts to kick in.

What if his boss found out and he's now in trouble the way I am?

What if he's been fired or something and now hates me because this is all my fault?

What if his daughter has been negatively impacted by all this and Milo is now super upset with me and everything?

What if he *has* found out about the fan fiction and is now, like, super embarrassed about how he and the size of his cock is being portrayed, and he's now writing his own fic to make that very important correction?

What if—and hear me out on this one—he's been on the run from the Mafia and is now in mortal danger because I took a random picture of him in the park?

That last one is truly ridiculous, but at the moment my intrusive thought machine is pumping full speed ahead. It also keeps circling around to the whole fan fiction idea. Because I no longer have a job to keep myself distracted from everything that's happening, it's difficult to keep from mentally floating into the sea of chaos that is going viral.

Instead of letting my brain continue to do its thing, I stand up, dump my now hours old sandwich into the composter and get back to the very adult task of budgeting.

Crawling into bed later, I'm only slightly less panicked about my situation. I have enough savings that I'll be okay for a month, maybe two if I'm super careful and don't buy anything beyond the bare-bones basics. I'm not fully unemployed, having dodged the bullet with my teaching position, but that won't be enough to keep my bank account from dropping quickly.

I'll need to do one of two things: get another retail job to keep myself afloat or take one of these maybe scam-ish promo opportunities. The retail job will most likely lead me back into the same situation I was in at Walmart. The other? I don't know the first thing about sponsorships or where I'd promote something like that.

My brain is way too tired to think any more serious thoughts. I'm not going to come up with a solution immediately. Really, I should have called Holly, or Cara, or hell, even Mom again at this point, just to have someone to talk things over with. And yet, every time I pick up my phone to do that, I come up with another excuse to not press dial.

Embarrassed. I'm embarrassed.

Instead, I turn to the other thing I haven't been able to get out of my mind since learning of its existence.

I knew there was no way I *wasn't* going to check out some of the fan fiction on AO3, so I came prepared with a glass of wine. The only thing better than ignoring your problems is facing them slightly tipsy. Now, it's important to step into the fan fiction pool prepared for the weird and wonderful, and actively embrace the expansive imaginations of the writers. If as a reader you're prepared to do that, you'll find some amazing stories.

I've never read one that features me, though. I've always had to insert myself into the typically generic character who is pulled into whatever fanbase story I picked to read. So, it's weird to see that there's an actual category for myself and Milo under the Real People tag. Not a ton of stories—we're not talking Supernatural or Star Trek here—but enough that I have to scroll down.

Twice.

I click one randomly and can only read through the first few sentences before I start skimming. It's a *Fifty Shades* retelling only with myself and Milo and—

Oh my God, that's ... wow.

I'm no prude, but it's a bit bonkers reading something that's supposed to be about you. The assumptions people have made based on a small snippet of video and a photo are wild. *I* am apparently wild.

And flexible.

I wonder again if Milo knows about this. Or if he might be into some of this stuff.

That's a conversation I don't necessarily want to have.

But my brain is more than happy to provide a mental slide show of everything that's being described. It's not hard to insert myself into the scene—Milo standing there shirtless, his gaze hungrily roaming across my body. I'm the intruding photographer, there to snap a picture of him but accidently get caught.

"How dare you come into my home and take a picture of me." He grabs the back of my head, pulling it to an awkward angle. "You need to be punished."

"I'm so sorry." I lick my lips as the top two buttons of my shirt pop open to reveal my ample cleavage. "I promise I'll do whatever you want."

Whoa boy.

Bookmarking the fic, I close the page and take a few calming breaths.

I find myself pulling Milo's number up on my phone and thumbing a quick message.

> Hey! Have you ever read any fan fiction?

My thumb hovers over send as my inner critic lambasts me for wanting to reach out to him. We've moved on! Hell, he might not want to talk to me at all.

Still, there's no reason whatsoever to talk to him about *this*. Knowing that someone out there has speculated on the size of his cock might not be the flattering compliment one might assume it is.

Fuck it.

I hit send as I gulp down some more wine. I'm getting dangerously close to hot flash consumption levels, but I'm beyond caring tonight. Look at me. Instead of freaking out about finances, I'm reading sex stories about myself and texting a man who was probably happy to see the ass-end of me back at the park. I wouldn't be surprised if Milo has blocked my number and won't ever see my—

The sound of a bike bell—my text notification—startles me into nearly spilling my wine. I sit up straight as a smile stretches across my face.

> Please don't tell me we have fics. My daughter
> will murder me.

I don't realize how badly I wanted him to answer until his words appear. A warmth spreads through me as I relax and try not to fat finger my response.

> I will lie to you then. No fics at all. Nope. None.

There's a pause as the bouncing dots dance on my screen; it's vaguely hypnotic. Finally, his reply pops up and I burst out laughing.

> Did they make my cock a respectable length, or
> am I crushing your cervix?

I shake my head.

> Let's say I'll never walk straight again.

My Instagram notification icon pops up, and I impulsively click on it. I forgot to make DMs private again, which means anyone is able to talk to me and send me a message if I don't know who they are. There are a few more messages from brand accounts, but most seem to be either bots or guys who are looking to hook up. I open one randomly, only to see a grainy dick pic.

Another text from Milo pulls me out of that.

> What are you doing?

> Made the mistake of opening a DM. Face 2
> face with a dick.

Shit. Sorry.

> Is it your dick? If so, we need to talk about how
> to take better selfies.

Milo doesn't respond, which is only mildly disconcerting. I flip back to the messages and go down the list blocking and reporting anyone who sent me an inappropriate picture or made a threatening comment.

I get through about ten when Milo finally texts again.

Are you okay?

> Yeah. Why wouldn't I be?

I'm tagged in some of these too. The @ comments are horrid.

> Welcome to being a woman on the internet.

Another pause and dancing dots from Milo.

This is absurd. I never thought I'd find myself out there like this. It makes me worry about my daughter.

There's one of two ways I can handle this. I can continue to text him and keep this safe distance between us. Or ...

I take a breath and hit dial on his number.

THIRTEEN

Milo

I'm not so much of a macho man to admit I might have let out a tiny, surprised squeak when Andie's number comes up as a call. I rarely use the actual phone anymore, relying on texts, emails, and online shopping for most things. If it had been any other person, with the notable exception of Mia or Dee, I probably would have declined the call and continued with texts.

Strangely, I really want to hear her voice again.

"Hey." I have to swallow to get some saliva going.

"Not sure how you feel about calls, but I figured this was faster than typing." Her voice was deeper than I remembered, huskier.

"Calls are fine." *Liar.*

"I can totally hang up and we can keep texting."

"It's fine. This way I can close my eyes and chill." Totally a lie. I couldn't stop my gaze from bouncing around my room.

"Okay. Cool." A soft sigh trickles through the line to me. "Where are you?"

"In bed." I cringe at how inappropriate I made that sound. "I was trying to sleep and failing miserably. It's a pretty boring room if I'm being honest."

"Oh? Why's that?"

"I live in a condo quite high up. I keep the blinds closed because," I don't want to get into my whole fear of heights, so I give her the line I tell anyone who ever asks, "the lights from outside are a bit much. I do have a couple of nice floor lamps that cast long shadows across the wall and ceiling."

"Really?"

"They look like possessed spiders."

I hesitate but it only seems fair to reciprocate the question. "And where are you?"

"Also in bed. I wasn't trying to sleep though." She chuckles softly as I hear her take a sip of something. "Thanks for accepting my call. I have wine and it was getting challenging to text and drink."

"I can imagine." I'd need wine by now too if I'd read some of the comments she's been dealing with all this time. I bend my leg so it tents the sheets away from my body. "*Are* you okay?"

Andie doesn't respond immediately. "I think so? It's been a weird day."

"It's been a weird couple of days. Weeks." The thought of everything that's happened is a weight on my chest.

"I had dreams of being famous when I was a kid, but the reality has turned out to suck." She sounds so alone, lost, I impulsively want to find her and pull her into a hug.

Instead, I try to make her laugh. "Well, being internet famous is different from celebrity status. And it could be worse."

"How so?"

"We could be a meme."

Andie groans. "Can you imagine having one image haunt you for the rest of your days?"

"At least your picture of me at the park is a good one."

"So was the Sad Keanu meme, and he was only on a lunch break."

We both chuckle, and I sink deeper into my mattress. It's been a long time since I chatted with someone with zero expectations. It's nice.

"You said you were worried about your daughter?"

Normally, any conversation about Mia and her challenges sets me on edge. It's not that I'm embarrassed to talk about it. Not at all. It's simply that over the years I've grown exhausted by suggestions on how to help Mia from people who don't understand what we're going through.

She just needs to get out of her room.

Have you tried signing her up for an exercise program?

My depression improved the minute I started running.

Water. She's probably dehydrated and just needs to have more water.

It's gotten to the point where I'm unable to bear hearing another suggestion, even if it was valid. The only people I'll listen to are Dee, Mia's therapist on the rare occasion when I'm asked to attend a session, and Mia herself. Anything else drains my batteries faster than I could ever express.

"Oh, I'm sorry. I didn't mean to pry."

The sound of Andie's sincerity jolts me. "No, not at all. It's just ... I don't normally talk about her with people."

"I get it. Between people judging you and offering unsolicited advice, I bet it's exhausting."

Wow. "You're the first person who understood that without me having to explain."

"I've had my own challenges over the years. Not mental health concerns, but explaining things to my parents that ... Well, they just don't understand. I'm the lone extrovert in my immediate family, and yeah. They didn't always get it. Get me."

Her voice is soothing, warm, and any trepidation I might have felt bleeds away. I turn my head and look at the back of my closed bedroom door. "Mia has severe anxiety and depression. Her moods shift from day to day. It's a bit like riding a roller coaster, I imagine. I can watch her start to go up this track of happiness. It builds and builds and then she'll crash hard and fast into a hole of utter despair. It started the week before her first day of high school and it hasn't stopped."

It also coincided with Rachel leaving, but I'm not ready to have that conversation with Andie. No sense in scaring her off immediately.

"Mia has been thrilled at what's happened to us though. Genuine joy and not a manic thing. So that's been great."

"Aww, I'm glad something positive has come out of this insanity." Andie chuckles, and the sound does inappropriate things to my groin.

Because while I like to think I'm a nice guy, I'm still a nice guy with a dick.

"You would have laughed at her. She thinks we should start our own TikTok account and take advantage of all the hype."

I didn't expect the soft *"Huh,"* that comes through. It doesn't exactly put my radar on high alert, but I do open my eyes again and push myself up to a half sitting position.

"Dude, have you gotten any offers to endorse things? Or job offers? Even my Twitter feed is full of that stuff and I never go there anymore."

"Twitter?" I laugh when she groans loudly.

"I refuse to call it X. So stupid." The sound of fabric moving through the phone reminds me she's in bed.

We're in bed separately together.

I press down on my cock and hope that will stop.

Focus you asshole. "I haven't, but that's probably because people don't have all my socials yet. Give it time and I'll be swamped."

There's a pause and the image of Andie running her hand through her hair flashes through my head. I get out of bed and start pacing around the room. Much better than the alternative of touching myself while we're on the phone.

Andie's hum through the phone tickles my ear. "It's an interesting thought."

"What is?"

"Starting a TikTok account. I mean ... apparently, we're recognizable? If those women in the park are any indication. It might be fun. Ah, I mean, if you'd want to spend time with me." Her nervous laugh makes me want to pull her into a hug.

"I'd love a chance to spend some time with you." My breath catches in my chest, and I have to stop and clear my throat to get things moving again. "It's also a good way for us to control the information that's getting out there. We only show people what we want them to see and that's it."

"I can't imagine we'll have that many people want to follow us anyway. I mean, it's one thing for a photo and video to go viral, but when there's a constant stream of content from a couple of GenX-ers, I imagine the kids will get bored and move on."

"Totally agree." The more the idea stays in my head, the more I like it. "It might be a great way for me to help Mia too. Something she could be a part of without the pressure of needing to be in charge."

"Yes! Mia should totally do it with us! I don't know the first thing about that platform, and I bet she would know the hot trends as they were emerging."

I turn and look out my bedroom window across the bright lights of the Toronto skyline. "Are we really going to do this?"

"I ... yeah. I think so?"

I don't know what it is in this moment, why I suddenly feel calm and settled. It isn't as though Andie and I are going on a date or entering into some sort of romantic partnership. No, it's that I've found myself stumbling into this strange friendship with a woman who has zero expectations of me. I can be myself, not worry about having to impress her. And if things don't work out or we get bored with being internet famous, we'll both be able to walk away from this with our hearts and egos intact.

It really is the best of possible scenarios.

"We should get together and come up with a plan on how to move forward with this."

Andie yawns, though it's clear she's trying to cover it up. "Absolutely."

There's no way I'm going to keep her up anymore. "I'm going to try and sleep again, but maybe we can meet up and chat?"

"A chat is a great idea."

"Tomorrow? I know a nice little café close to where I live." While I don't think I have anything to worry about, I'm not at the stage where I'm ready to give her my address. This has the added bonus of me getting out of my condo—something I can totally brag to Dee about during my next session. "I'm a bit of an introvert, but this is my go-to spot. They make a mean cappuccino and have excellent lemon loaf."

"That sounds amazing. Ah, I'm ... Well, not really available until around three, is that okay?"

She probably has a shift at work or something. "You're in my calendar. I'll see you then."

"Okay. Thanks. Night."

"Goodnight."

There's a slightly longer pause than I would normally expect before I finally hear the call disconnect. Why I wasn't the one to hit end, I'm not sure. It's a pleasant oddity not wanting to stop the conversation. In the few interactions I've had with Andie, I've been charmed and wanted to draw those interactions out as long as I could.

That isn't how I normally do things. Even with my family— with the exception of Mia—I quickly hit an interaction wall and need to peace-out of the conversation. And here I am, standing half-naked in my bedroom with a hard-on and warm fuzzy feelings about a woman I hardly know.

Life is so odd at times.

"Right. Sleep."

I take a step toward it and stop again when my cock pops up behind the elastic waistband of my boxers. Normally in this situation, I jerk off before going to sleep. If not for the fact I'm going to see Andie tomorrow, I might have done that. But I know myself well enough that if I jerk off tonight, there's no way in hell I'll be able to look her in the eyes tomorrow.

Just no.

"Cold shower it is."

I hope it will be enough to keep me focused on what we need to talk about tomorrow. The last thing I need is to film a video in which the entire world can see what Andie does to me.

Or worse.

For Mia to see.

FOURTEEN

Andie

Milo texted me the address last night, but I was a wee bit drunk by that point. I check what he sent when I crawl out of bed and stand, bleary-eyed, glaring down at my phone. Right, we're meeting this afternoon. At a café. I'm going to sit across from him at a nice dry table and stare into his intelligent blue eyes and somehow avoid coming across as a totally overenthusiastic dork. A hopefully not hungover overenthusiastic dork.

What time is it?

Shit, I slept through to lunch.

Painfully more awake than I was a few moments previous, I scramble and put the address into Google maps to see where the hell I have to go. The café isn't far from the park where we met—not at all surprising for a man who's a self-proclaimed extreme introvert—which means I can take transit and get close enough to our meeting spot without needing to walk far. He must live in one of the condo buildings nearby, and this is the closest place that makes excellent lemon loaf.

I'm going on a not-date with Milo to talk to him about everything that happened, and to see what he thinks about me taking one of these sponsorships. Oh, and to confirm that we are in fact going to start a TikTok account. It seems a bit insane.

It *is* a bit insane, and yet I know I'm going to totally do it.

As I stare down at the screen, a message from Holly pops up.

Hey you. Coffee?

I swear there are some days when I'm convinced my best friend possesses the other half of my head. I need to talk this out with someone before I plunge head-first into a bad idea.

Dude, yes.

I'm at the Starbucks across the street. Come over when you're ready.

I don't bother responding and instead make a beeline into the shower hoping my brain will finally kick in. As the cold water blasts my face and rushes down my body, my guilt sinks in. Convincing Milo to make a TikTok account with me without telling him that I'm mostly unemployed was a shitty thing to do. I have to confess my true situation and get that sorted as soon as I see him.

I towel dry my hair, get dressed, and head out to Starbucks.

Holly is already at a table, two coffees in front of her, reading something on her phone. I plop myself into the seat across from her as she slides a cup to me. I take a sip and moan. "You're a goddess."

"I'm not really feeling that today."

My slightly hungover brain clears instantly as I look her over. "What's the matter?"

Holly is one of the most amazing people I've ever met. She's an intuitive chef who could craft a gourmet meal out of peanut butter and croutons. She's also extremely capable in all aspects of her life, which is why I'm mildly panicked when I see her blink back tears.

"Holly, hon, what's wrong?"

"Just work stuff."

"Okay." Nothing is ever just *work stuff*. "Talk to me."

She takes a super long sip of her coffee, followed by a sigh. "The owners have hired a new chef. Which I knew they needed to do to replace Camille for the day shift. But. He's their nephew and he has ideas on how things should be run." Though her hands don't move, I can hear the air quotes in her voice around the word *ideas*.

"I thought they were letting you run the kitchen. That's your ... But they love you."

"They love their nephew more." She chuckles. "I still have a job; they made that clear. I just don't know how well we'll get along."

"Oh, hon. I'm sorry. That sucks." Holly and I are similar in that we've both had clear dreams of who and what we wanted to do with our lives since we were kids. The only difference is that she's seen hers through to success.

"Enough of that. What's going on with you? You're hungover on a Thursday morning and not at work."

It's my turn to sigh. I draw a breath and let everything spill out. My students taking my laptop, the video, meeting Milo, saving my job, getting fired, and finally my upcoming not-a-date. By the time I finish, her mouth has fallen open and her eyes are practically bugged out.

"Holy crap. And here I thought I was having a bad week."

"I didn't mean to one-up your bad week or detract from it." My coffee has grown cold enough that I'm able to drain half the cup far faster than is reasonable. "This was a mess of my own making. Now I have to tell him that I really need to do this TikTok thing so I can maybe get a sponsorship to pay rent. Which means I need to keep my mental movie of the sexy, sexy fan fic of us out of my head. 'Cause that will be fucking awkward."

"Fan fic?"

I wave my hand. "Don't ask." Leaning forward, I take her hand in mine and squeeze. "What do I do?"

"Be yourself. Be honest. Milo sounds like a good guy and will understand."

I give her hand another squeeze before letting it go. "Thank you. I hope so."

"Speaking of which, what time are you meeting him?"

"At three," I say, looking down at my phone. "Shit, I missed the bus. I'll have to Uber it."

"I can drive you."

"Really?"

Holly smiles and everything feels better than it did a few minutes ago. "Of course! I have extra time before I need to head home and get ready for work tonight."

"You're amazing. Let me go get some things, and I'll come back here."

She's already on her feet, her purse slung over her shoulder. "I'll come. No sense in me haunting here any longer than necessary. Besides, I can check out your fridge and see what you've been eating."

"Oh, come on. I eat."

"Not properly, you don't."

"You're never allowed to meet my mother."

At least I'll have another set of eyes to make sure I don't look as hungover as I feel.

MY HEART POUNDS as I race through the crowd of people on my way to the café. Traffic was heavier than either Holly or I anticipated, and she ended up dropping me off a block away from The Pear Tree. I walk-run past people who don't understand that *I have places I need to be, dear God, move!*

When I finally see the café's awning, I slow down and catch my breath. Sweat covers my back, and I know my face is probably moist in the most unflattering of ways. I hope Milo is also late and I'll be able to get cleaned up before he arrives. That thought is dashed the moment I step into the café and see him sitting in a booth on the far side.

Great.

A waitress comes over and smiles at me. "Hey. Welcome to The Pear Tree."

"Hi!"

"You look hot in the uncomfortable way." She reaches over the counter and hands me a glass of water. "Take out or dine in?"

Milo is looking over and I can't stop myself from waving. "Hey! Sorry I'm late."

He cringes as he smiles and waves back.

"Shit, I embarrassed him."

The waitress glances over at him and grins. "Good luck with that one. He's been coming in here for years, and he barely looks at anyone. I mean, he has good reason, but that's not for me to share."

"Ah, okay." I feel Milo's eyes on me and a shiver rolls through my body. "At this point we're just friends."

She leans in a bit closer. "You let me know if there's anything I can do to help. Most of the staff here are emotionally invested in seeing him happy." She winks and steps back. "What are you having?"

It's a lot for me to take in, so for the time being I push what she said and all it implies to the side. "Could I have an iced coffee and a piece of lemon loaf?"

"I'll have it on the table shortly."

"Thanks so much."

I need to let out a sharp breath before I march over to the booth. While I'm not exactly nervous—total lie, I'm freaking out—the last thing I want to do is make Milo uncomfortable. *Rein yourself in, lady. You can be a lot.*

"Hey!" I plop down opposite him, jeans squeaking as I slide across the pleather bench. "Sorry I'm late."

"Hey yourself." He looks over at the waitress behind the counter. "You two looked like you were having an intense conversation."

"Who?"

"You and the waitress."

"Oh. Yeah. I think she was checking me out so she could update the others on the gossip."

Milo frowns as he runs a hand through his hair. "What gossip?"

"Well, maybe not gossip. But you're clearly a regular who they've formed a parasocial bond with."

"I ..."—he taps his finger on the table—"don't think that's what that term means."

Waving away his correction, I allow myself to look into his attractive blue eyes. Like, I know I'll still be able to see them long after we've parted. They don't sparkle exactly, more like a shimmer that bespeaks his obvious intelligence and wit. "So. How ya doing?" I smile at the sing-song way I said it. Apparently, he brings out my silly side.

Milo leans forward, and I find myself mirroring his position, leaving our faces dangerously close to kissing range. "I found the fan fics."

And there comes my super blush. "Did you see the one 'A Rainy Day Proposition'?"

"All I could think of reading that one was don't leave the soaked clothing on the dining room table. You'll ruin the finish."

"And who uses produce as a sex toy?"

Milo shakes his head. "Frozen peas in a condom?"

"It sounds painful." I shiver at the thought.

Milo meets my gaze evenly, his eyes sparkling with amusement. There's something enthralling about the way he looks at me, as though he just thought of the punchline and can't wait to share it with me. And while I might be a bit awkward from time to time, I'm someone who likes to be in on the conversation, who would share that joke with Milo in a heartbeat.

Enough of that. I sit back but leave my hands laced together on the table. "Were you waiting long? My friend dropped me off and we hadn't realized that they'd started construction on the corner."

"It's all good. I answered emails and was reading about some new recording software I want to buy." I watch the tension in his shoulders bleed away. His gaze roams across my face, but it always comes back to my eyes. That intensity, despite being tinged with humor, threatens to do things to my body that I'm not prepared to deal with.

"So, TikTok," I say far louder than I intended. "Are we really going to do this?"

"Yeah. I mean, I'd like to if you're still game."

So many things I'd be game to do with you. "I am. But I need to be upfront about something before we go any further." I take a deep breath and barrel forward. "I got fired."

"What!" He bangs his knees on the edge of the table as he tries to stand up, before falling back into the seat. Between his near-shout and the rattle of dishes, every eye snaps to us. Milo looks as though he wants to melt into the floor. I turn and wave at every-one, which sends their gazes scurrying to find something else to stare at. "Sorry. Its just, I thought the consent form I signed fixed that."

Oh right. "No, no. Sorry. That was my teaching job. That one is fine. But I also work at ... err, worked at Walmart in the photog-raphy studio. I needed both jobs to afford to pay rent and eat occa-sionally."

The thought of never being able to take my beloved passport photos again suddenly makes my throat tighten.

"Andie, I'm so sorry."

When his hand covers mine and gives it a squeeze, another elec-trified shiver rolls through me. Milo pulls his hand away quickly as the waitress chooses that moment to bring over my food and drink. "Here you go. Everything okay?"

"Yes, thank you." Milo smiles but doesn't make eye contact with her.

"I told him I just got fired from my job and he's now worried that it's his fault." I don't know how, but one look at Milo's pained expression and I know it's true. "Which it wasn't."

"Ah, I'm sorry to hear that." The waitress smiles as she steps back. "I hope things work out for you."

"I'm sure they will." I wait for her to get out of earshot before continuing. "I have more than enough savings to get me through for a while, but I'll need another job. Toronto is expensive."

"And you think TikTok will give us money?"

"Well, not TikTok directly. But maybe this?" I slide my phone across the table for him to see. "I don't know the first thing about sponsorships and stuff, or if this is legit. But I thought you might."

Milo pulls a pair of reading glasses from a case on the bench beside him. Whoa baby, he slides them down his nose just the right amount to look sexy. He then licks his lips and I nearly ignite on the spot.

Maybe frozen peas in a condom isn't a half-bad idea after all.

"I can have my agent look at this if you're serious. I normally have him review any contracts that get sent my way." He sets my phone down and pulls his glasses off. "Honestly, this looks like a bit of a scam."

"Oh." I become a live-action rendition of a deflating airbag.

"We can still do this, and maybe we can find some actual sponsorships. But are you sure? It might be easier for you to find another job."

I could tell him I think our "fans" will probably hunt me down and there will be another situation that might cause me to lose that job too. That this idea makes the most sense and has the bonus of spending more time with him. Instead, I find myself telling him the truth.

"Since I was a kid, I wanted to be a famous photographer. I came from the Maritimes to Toronto to go to school, to put myself out there and make my dreams happen." Shit, there's that stupid lump in my throat again. I take a drink of water before pressing on. "I don't know why, but it feels like getting fired was a good thing. I have a chance to try this and get my art recognized by the masses. I might crash and burn, but at least for once I can honestly be able to say that I've made the attempt."

My gaze falls to the back of his left hand, to the rise and swell of his knuckles. I force myself to look him in the eyes and instead of pity or judgment reflected there, I see only understanding. "Then I'll help you."

"Wait, I don't want you to feel guilted into this."

"I'm not. I have my own reasons, and I'm happy they line up with yours."

Is he? I can only take him at his word.

"Do you think your daughter will participate with us?"

"I haven't asked her, but I know she'll jump at the chance. Mia lives on that app. If I was a better parent, I'd probably do something about that."

I catch my hand moving to touch the side of my neck and instead, reach for the iced coffee. For a guy who is apparently clueless when it comes to flirting, he's good at dragging those tendencies out of a woman. "It would be good. Having another person with us."

He cocks his head to the side and grins. "Why's that?"

"Ahh, I mean. It would just be good to have another person in case one of us is sick or we can't be there to record one day."

The last thing I want to say to him is that I hope his daughter will act as a bit of a buffer between us. I know I'm less likely to act on my attraction to Milo with his daughter constantly present. We'll just be friends hanging out, having a good time. It will be awesome!

He leans forward again and makes sure he has my attention. "I'm thinking bottle smashing."

I open my mouth to say something, but nothing comes out.

"I know you want some sponsorships and stuff, but we need to build our presence. Think about it. We can do all sorts of crazy things around Toronto. Fun things! You know, like going to one of those places where you get all dressed up in protective gear and smash the shit out of bottles and stuff."

Why does this feel so natural and somehow conspiratorial at the same time? "Do you have anger issues I need to be worried about?"

He laughs. "Surprisingly, no. There are lots of things around the city that I've always wanted to try, but for one reason or another, never bothered."

"Didn't bother with? Or couldn't do?"

A shadow passes over his face, and for the briefest of moments I think he might get up and leave. But as quickly as it came, the darkness leaves him. Milo sits back, taking a piece of my lemon loaf with him. "My job is flexible. Having a set schedule with you, though, will ensure I make the time to get out there and do some of these things."

"Okay, that sounds like a plan." I haven't given much thought to what running a TikTok account with someone will entail. "Do you think your daughter will participate with us? How many of these videos should we plan? How do we film them?"

Panic. I'm officially panicking.

He taps the table next to his coffee cup. "I haven't asked her, but I know she'll jump at the chance. Why don't you come over to our place and the three of us can do a test run? We can figure all the details out then."

There's something in the way he presents the offer, the softness of his smile and the slower cadence of his speech, that feels like it's a huge deal or something. Given what little I do know about him and Mia, it probably is. "Are you sure? We can always meet some-where else. The park or library?"

He shakes his head. "Unless you'd rather not come to my place. I get that also might not be comfortable. We're still getting to know each other."

It's strange. I'm not exactly the type of person who goes to a guy's house to hook up; no one-night stands for this boring middle-aged woman. Being adventurous—while something I've always longed to do—isn't my default in life. And while no one out there would say going to Milo's place to meet his daughter and make a TikTok account is even remotely on that scale, for me it kind of is.

Ignoring my trepidation, I look him straight in the eyes and smile. "I'm okay with going to your place. If I think things look sketchy, I'll bolt."

Milo laughs loud enough that the people at the table beside us look. "Fair enough."

"It wasn't that funny."

"It's just odd. Mia has accused me of being the most boring person in the world on more than one occasion. But both you and I know boring doesn't always equal safe."

The response I had planned flies out of my head. It always catches me off guard when a man acknowledges the unfortunate realities of dating as a woman. "Yeah. Thanks."

Milo nods. "So, only if you're comfortable, I'd love for you to come and meet Mia at my place. I do need to warn you that she'll probably hint that I'm lonely and you should totally date me. I'll ask for your forgiveness now and please let her down easy."

Well. That's interesting. "You're really *not* into dating."

"I haven't been for a long while." The change of his tone and the look on his face tells me that's far as he wants to go on the topic.

"Are you sure *you* want me to come over? All of this will even-tually blow over and our lives will return to what they were. If you'd rather things go back to normal, it might make more sense for me to keep my distance."

Milo turns to look out the window. He doesn't say anything immediately, and all I can do is sit there and wait. Eventually, he turns back and smiles again. It's different from before, softer. I can't be certain, but it feels as though his protective mask has slipped ever so slightly, and I'm catching a glimpse of the part of Milo he doesn't share with others.

"Dee—that's my therapist—she's been telling me for a while now that putting myself into situations that are uncomfortable for me might help me push past some of my challenges." He gives a little shrug. "I haven't had someone in my home in ... Wow, a long time."

For the first time since we found ourselves thrust together in this strange series of events, I look at Milo and feel that, despite not spending much time together, we're similar in many ways. Maybe this is one of those weird universal turns that happens for a reason. Maybe, perhaps, *possibly* we really are meant to smash bottles together in a safe room.

I clear my throat. "Why don't you talk to Mia and if she's okay with everything, text me your address. I teach Tuesday and Thursday nights, but I'm free all weekend."

"Yeah, okay. Sounds good." He smiled as he reached out and stole another bite of my lemon loaf. "What are you up to for the rest of the day?"

"Groceries and then a long bath before I have to teach tonight. I'm still sadly recovering from my wine." I did *not* want an order of hot flashes with my alcohol. Being perimenopausal sucks.

"Groceries. That's something I need to do too." He pulled out his phone. "Instacart for the win."

"I have an independent grocery in the bottom of my building. Tamara would murder me if I had someone deliver stuff that wasn't takeout."

Milo chuckled. "The joys of city living."

We chatted for a few minutes before the conversation came to a comfortable silence. I stand almost at the same time as him and walk over to the counter to pay my bill.

Milo smiles at our waitress. "I've got both."

My face flushed. "You don't need to do that." The last thing I want was for him to think I couldn't afford anything.

He holds up his hand. "Consider me paying it forward. You're going to have to put up with me a bit longer."

The waitress looks between the two of us and grins. I can only imagine what she's thinking.

Stepping outside into the early fall heat shakes away the embarrassed confusion that has fallen over me. "I'll have to come back and get more loaf." Lacing my hands behind my back, I try not to rock on my feet, not wanting to appear more nervous than I am.

Milo looks as awkward as I feel. "Loaf is good." His gaze darts around. "I never know how to walk away from social situations."

"How about this?" I stick out a hand and wait for him to take it. "Thank you so much for meeting me. I'll wait for your text after you talk to Mia. Have a great day."

Milo takes my hand to shake it. "Talk to you soon."

The warmth of his hand around mine sends a tingle down my back. It ends as a shiver that races through my body. As he pulls away, his fingertips brush the inside of my wrist, sending a second, far stronger pulse of arousal through me.

I spin on my heel and stumble a step before finding my footing. There's no way I'm going to look back at him, despite feeling him watching me. Because clueless or not, Milo will have picked up on what that simple touch did to me.

Whoa boy.

FIFTEEN

Milo

W et lips, wide pupils, and the tiniest of gasps. I haven't been able to get Andie's reaction to my not-so-accidental touch of her wrist out of my head. I narrated an audiobook once where the hero did that to his love interest, and her resulting desires were something I've never forgotten. What the book didn't specify was the reaction that simple, soft caress had on the hero who performed it.

My cock has been hard off and on since I watched her walk away from me.

I've become obsessed with Andie in a way I don't think is healthy, or even possible given my lack of interest in dating. And yet, despite all the flirting we did in the café, the gentle teasing that sparked something to life that I'd thought long dead, it was that tiny caress that ignited the fire inside me.

I want to know what she looks like naked.

What she sounds like if I nuzzle the soft spot behind her ear.

What the hollow of her throat tastes like.

"Did you empty the dishwasher?"

I lean against the counter to hide my erection. My gaze finds Mia's; she's standing in her doorway frowning at me. "Pardon?"

"Is it empty?"

Sadly, the boys are both very full. "Just about."

I take out the last glass and turn to put it away. "Now it's empty."

Mia emerges from her room with an armful of dishes. "Good."

Dear Lord, please save me from a teen daughter's dish collection. "Mia."

"I was studying!"

"Three plates, four bowls, a mug, and a cup?"

She shrugs and deposits them on the counter. "I didn't say I studied all at once."

"Where are the spoons?"

She cringes. "I think I brought them out already."

"At least tell me your room is clean now."

"It is." She walks away, pausing after a few steps. The frown on her face is sudden, the lines cutting deep. "She's not going to come *into* my room, right?"

"No, baby." Mia's bedroom is her safe space. The last thing I want is for her to feel intruded upon. "Not unless you want her to."

"I don't." She heads back to her room and turns around to face me as she enters. "It's clean, though. In case."

"Fair enough."

Mia is visibly nervous, and despite her squeal of excitement at the suggestion of Andie visiting, I worry I'm making a terrible mistake.

"Have you figured out what we should do for our first video?"

That brings a smile to her face. Thank God.

"Not yet. I'm torn between two trends."

"Title of your autobiography?"

"Dad, that joke is so old." Her eye roll pairs perfectly with a sigh. "I'll be in my room. Plotting your demise." She shuts the door loudly, leaving me to deal with her dishes.

While I saw Andie only a few days ago and we've chatted

multiple times via text since then, I'm also nervous about her visit. It's a big deal to have anyone in the condo, let alone a woman who's meeting my daughter. Not that I think Andie will do anything to make Mia feel uncomfortable. Not intentionally. But Mia's mind has a way of latching onto something I assume is innocuous and spins it around until her anxiety turns it into a massive *thing* we have to defuse. I never fault Mia when it happens, but that doesn't lessen the stress at the time.

It's a hard line to walk on a good day, let alone when we have something unusual planned. Normally, if I say too much about Mia's challenges to people, they get awkward and panic about saying the wrong thing. That, in turn, makes everything horrible. Yet, if I say nothing, people inevitably push her too far and I end up spending the next several hours trying to comfort her and reassure her that she isn't broken or weird.

I don't want that to happen with Andie.

I *like* Andie as a person and a friend. And if my raging libido is anything to go by, I'd like the opportunity for something more with her. I don't want to invite her here and to make her uncomfortable. Or worse, have her upset Mia and then feel guilty about it.

I spent a little time on Reddit reading threads about how to introduce someone new into your teen's life without building up expectations. While everyone has different stories and situations, the common thread seems to be not to force things. On either party.

Maybe it really would be easier to keep my relationship with Andie as friends and nothing more. It would save headaches if Mia decides she doesn't like her.

When do you get to have something for yourself?

I quickly push that selfish thought aside, ignoring the way my inner voice now sounds like my therapist's.

Instead of dwelling on the negatives, I clean. I shove the cache of found dishes into the dishwasher and give my open concept condo a quick once-over. The joys of having everything open: it's easy to spot a mess. Conversely, it's also the worst thing about living here. What I would give to have a space of my own that I could leave chaotic. To be able to ignore the need to organize and tidy, and leave piles of crap wherever I want. Treasures to discover later. My recording booth is the only spot that Mia doesn't come into, but it's little more than a closet, and I can't exactly have a bunch of things in there.

Some day, maybe we'll buy a house outside of Toronto and spread out.

Probably not, but it's a nice thought.

A quick glance at the clock tells me Andie will be here soon. She texted me when she got on her last transfer, so I was able to give Mia a heads-up before for her arrival. I like to give Mia time to mentally compose herself before guests arrive.

Who am I kidding? *I'm* the one who needs to prepare.

That moment Andie sat down in the booth, I became hyper aware of her. The way she tried to fight the urge to touch her hair, how her gaze dropped to the table every time she started to smile. I could see her pulse throbbing in her throat, and it brought all sorts of crazy images to mind.

Me licking that spot. Me pressing my lips to it while I teased her breasts with my hands, just to see if I could feel the rhythm change.

Right on time ... there's that boner again.

My phone chooses that moment to chirp at me, sending me jumping around to face it. Shit, that's my building intercom. Andie! Lunging for my phone, I scoop it up and answer it.

"Hey! It's Andie. I'm in the lobby waiting to be buzzed up."

Another wave of doubt washes through me, but I quash it. Mia and I need to step outside of our comfort zone to start learning how to handle our challenges. Having Andie over is a good way to begin that process.

It has to be.

"Hey yourself. Buzzing you in now. We're on 14, unit 1412. Elevator is on the right when you come in the door."

"Awesome. See you in a few."

I hold the button to open the door for her a bit longer than normal before I take a breath and give my place another quick once-over.

"Mia, Andie's on her way up."

"Okay!"

When she doesn't immediately appear, I know she's probably dealing with her own nerves. Best to let her emerge under her own terms. The knock on my front door comes far faster than I anticipated, and wow, my heart is pounding. Who knew a speed cleaning was such a major cardio workout? Opening the door, I grin, my cheeks feeling as though they're stretching beyond normal.

"Andie!"

"Hey!" Her face flushes as her teeth graze her bottom lip. "This is quite the place."

I step back, letting her into the condo. "It's not overly extravagant. But I like the location, and the restaurant on street level is to die for."

"I live above a convenience store. This is heavenly."

We stand there awkwardly for a moment; my brain is slow to catch up to the fact that I'm the host. "Make yourself at home."

Andie toes off her sneakers and takes a few tentative steps forward. "So, this is where we're going to start our account."

Now that she's here, I notice about six things I forgot to tidy. "Yeah, I figured this would be good for the time being. I have no idea what Mia has planned for us."

Andie looks around, no doubt wondering where Mia is. "Hopefully she can help us not make fools of ourselves."

"I wouldn't count on that. I think being a bit foolish is what people are going to expect." Not knowing exactly what to do now, I make my way to the kitchen. "Can I get you anything? A drink?" *An orgasm?*

Bad Milo. Bad boy.

"Water, please."

I watch as Andie wanders around my living room, making her way over to the windows that provide an excellent view of the park where we first met. It's different having her here, but I feel a sense of joy at seeing her smile as she turns her gaze to my bookshelf.

We both jump when there's a crash from Mia's room. I move toward her door, Andie's water glass in hand. "Mia?"

"I'm good! I'll be right out."

Andie joins me, taking the water from my hand. Our fingers brush against each other, sending a shiver through me. These tiny touches are killing me; a glance at her flushed face tells me she's at least somewhat affected as well.

My hopes are up.

She clears her throat. "Thanks."

I catch a whiff of her shampoo and the scent of sunshine on her skin. It takes effort not to lean in, bury my nose in her hair, and take a deep breath. I want to lose myself in that glorious smell, memorize it so I'd recognize Andie's presence even in the dark. I must make some sort of noise, because Andie looks up at me, her eyes wide and lips parted.

God, I want to kiss her.

Mia's bedroom door opens, and I find myself pulling back. Andie also seems to give herself a shake as she downs her water in one large gulp and sets her glass down. Forcing my attention away from the way Andie's throat moves as she drinks, and on my daughter, I realize she has her hands full. Overfull.

"What the hell is all that stuff?"

Mia smiles, her gaze darts between me and Andie. "A tripod, ring light, and a few props to use." She shrugs. "I mean, if you want to."

I look closely at Mia, trying to gauge if she's nervous, anxious, or if I'm going to have to jump in and do something to help her. I can't tell if she's using the things she's carrying as a barrier to keep anyone from getting close, or if she's trying to drag everything into the living room at once to save a trip.

"Hi." Andie takes a half step forward, holding up her hand in a small wave. "I'm Andie. You must be Mia."

"Hey. Yeah." Mia looks down at the array of items in her hands. "I liked your picture of Dad."

"Thank you." Andie doesn't make a move to get closer to Mia, I see her shoulders relax as she slides her hands into her pockets. "I wish I could say I'd put a lot of thought or effort into the setup for taking it, but it was a lot of luck." She pauses for a moment before pointing at the tripod. "That's a good one. It has the angle arm so you can make some great closeup shots if you have the right lens."

The tension seems to bleed out of Mia's shoulders. "Cool. I've been practicing some different angles with my phone, but I can't quite get the look I want. It's been fun though."

"I'd love to see some of your work. I'm always interested in how other people view the world."

I don't know what I expected, but this easy back and forth isn't it. A strange sensation of tightness in my chest as my stomach churns catches me off guard.

Am I jealous? What the holy hell do I have to be jealous about? Andie is used to talking to people and setting them at ease. She's doing what comes naturally to her, a skill that I've had to work hard on most of my life.

Mia lets out a little huff as she strides quickly over to the couch, her equipment jostling as she moves. "I know this is supposed to be about the two of you, but I had some thoughts about your account."

That tiny bit of jealousy instantly morphs to panic at the idea that Mia has had *thoughts*. "I think we wanted to do different things around the city," I say. "Ah, like escape rooms and stuff."

"Oh yeah, that's great. But you should also do some of the trending stuff. Not everyone knows who you are, so it will help.

Especially if you want to get on people's For You page, then you'll need to catch those trends."

I glance over to Andie who is slowly nodding but has the same confused expression that I know full well is on my face. She runs her hand through her hair, her frown wrinkling her forehead. "Seeing as your dad and I don't know the first thing about TikTok —" She looks over at me. "You don't, right?"

"Not a thing."

Andie smiles at Mia . "We're going to have to rely on you to guide us through this. If you want." There's something so genuine about the way Andie speaks to Mia, my concern and tension drops off.

Maybe this isn't going to be the nightmare I feared it would be.

"Awesome." Mia has my optimism surging to life. "I'd suggest we start with the 'tell me without telling me' challenge."

"I know that one!" Andie quickly moves to help Mia set up the tripod. "That would be a great way to announce the channel."

"That's what I was thinking. And then you could do a second video talking about what you hope to do in a more straightforward Q and A way."

I honestly don't care what we were going to do. Seeing Mia this excited, watching her converse so easily with Andie, means that even if this TikTok thing falls flat on its face, I'll still consider it a success. Mia is smiling, relaxed, with no hint of the anxiety I feared would creep out.

I'll love Andie forever simply for giving Mia this one moment to shine.

It's easy enough for me to sit back and let the two of them take over, get everything organized and placed where it will give us the best space for recording. Mia snatches my phone from me, typing in my not-so-secret passcode.

"Dad! I though you installed the app?"

"I did. Didn't I?"

"No." That earns me a disgusted groan. "I have to do everything."

"Baby, you know I'd be lost without you." Just to annoy her, I pat the top of her head. "You love me."

"Maybe." Mia points to the couch. "Move over there please. I need to give you two a crash course on how to use this."

That's how I find myself sitting side by side with Andie on my couch, our legs touching at the knees as Mia stands behind us, leaning over to hold my phone between us to see. I have a solid attention span, but it's next to impossible to focus on what Mia is saying about recording, pausing, adding songs, stickers, texts, and pictures when all I'm painfully aware of is Andie touching me.

And my daughter between us.

"Does that all make sense?" Mia is clearly excited, and I don't want to discourage her by asking her to repeat everything.

"Sure does, baby."

"I think it will help to actually film something after we set up our account." Andie shifts on the couch, turning to better face us both. Her knee presses harder against mine. "What are we going to call it? We need something catchy."

"It should reflect the two of you." Mia stands up.

"Wait, you're not going to do this with us?" Andie says, crossing her arms. "I don't think we'll be able to pull it off on our own."

Mia's eyes grow wider before she bites down on her bottom lip for a moment. "I mean, yeah, I'd love to. I didn't want to ... you know." She shrugs.

Knowing Andie is on board makes this easier. "Baby, we need you."

"Oh. Okay." She grins. "We could call it MAndM. For our names."

"Ah!" Andie chuckles. "I love that."

"Me too." I reach for Mia's hand and give it a squeeze. "MAndM it is."

Now, all we have to do is make a video and see what comes of it. Maybe we'll get a sponsorship that will help Andie. Maybe nothing will happen at all. We'll probably just end up being idiots online, clowns for everyone to look at, laugh at …

Shit.

What have I gotten us into?

SIXTEEN

Andie

Standing beside Milo, pointing at an imaginary spot between us initially feels funny. But every time Mia has us redo the shot, the tension bleeds from me and I become more and more silly. Milo seems far less relaxed, which only serves to amp me up to tease him.

"Daaad! Man, do you know how to smile without looking like a creep."

"Come on, Milo." I bump my shoulder against his. "Don't be a creep, dude." I face him and point a bunch of fingers at his face. "Don't. Be. A. Creep."

"This isn't fair. Two against one." But his shoulders relax, and his smile doesn't look as tight.

Mia has us play around for a few more minutes before finally waving us over to the tripod that she set her phone up on. "Okay, now we do this for real."

"Wait." Milo holds his hands up. "You mean we haven't been doing this *for real* all this time?"

"Dad, you're a voice actor not an *actor*, actor. Besides, you always do warm-ups before you record anything." She sounds so exasperated. It's cute.

"Voice actors *are* actors." And doesn't that sound like something he's said more than once. "Regardless, what are we doing?"

Mia bites on her bottom lip, her arms tight against her body as she taps her foot. Her uncertainty has me wanting to hug her. Instead, I lean in a bit closer and point to the phone screen. "So how does this work? We record ourselves and then add the bits later?"

"Yeah." Her gaze darts from the screen to me and back. "This is what I was thinking."

In a flurry of finger movements, she uploads the image I took of Milo at the park, as well as some screenshots from the video that the women took of us during our first meeting. I haven't seen that video since the day it was posted, and I can't stop staring at how we looked, huddled close together in the rain.

The screenshot is blurry but unmistakably us. I was smiling at something Milo said, and he was leaning in close. If this had been one of my photos, I would have focused in on his expression, the way the rain rolled down his cheeks, getting snagged in his stubble. When Mia switches to another shot, this time of the two of us dancing a moment ago in the living room, I'm struck by how our bodies are bending toward each other. Like leaves of a plant turned toward the light.

"And now we add you two live."

I jump slightly at the sound of Mia's voice, not realizing how pulled in I've become to what I'm seeing. Milo drapes an arm across Mia's shoulder, giving her a gentle squeeze. "You're really good at this."

Mia blushes. "So basically, I want the two of you to come from opposite sides and meet in the middle. Go, like, back-to-back and cross your arms."

"That sounds cheesy." Milo straightens. "I approve."

A sudden rush of energy courses through me, and I bound over to my predetermined position. "This is our big announcement pose, right?"

"Yup!" Mia shoves her dad and Milo moves to his spot. "Ready?"

I look at Milo and grin. "I'm all set."

"Ready." He looks a bit nervous, yet I know there's no way he's going to back out. In the short time we've been working on this, I understand that there's nothing he wouldn't do to make Mia happy. Even if it means making a TikTok video he doesn't exactly want to. The fact that he's also helping me is a bonus.

We do the walk, spin, and back-to-back pose three times before Mia is satisfied with the end result. When she finally gives us the thumbs up, I laugh at the look of relief on Milo's face. "It wasn't that bad."

"I'm a fifty-year-old voice actor who lives a life equivalent to that of a mushroom. This is more exercise and stress than I've had in months."

"I guess that proves you really do need to get out into the city doing things. It will be good for your creative soul."

He opens his mouth to say something else but seems to think better of it.

"Do you guys want to watch me post this?" Mia's obvious excitement is contagious. "Come on, this will be anticlimactic from what you're expecting. Come see!"

Milo winks at me. "Well, if you're going to sell it that hard, how can we not?"

Spending most of these past two hours physically close to Milo is doing inappropriate things to my body. I could pick his scent—a mix of coffee, Old Spice, and mango body wash—out of a crowd with precision. I can only imagine what his naked skin would smell like after tangling in the sheets.

Bad. This is so very bad.

Mia plays the video for us, and while I half expected it to be full-on cringe, the result is funny and more than a little cute. After the montage of images, the two of us walk into the scene, do our little move, and the words We're Starting Our Own Thing! appear just over our heads between us. Somehow, Mia has taken the two of us and turned our dorky selves into something appealing.

Well, if I were a viewer, I would want to see more.

"Wait, that's it?" Milo leans over Mia's shoulder. "But we're not telling anyone what we're planning to do. How will they know if they want to watch us?"

"You don't need to tell them. They'll come back just to see." Mia turns to me. "You get it. Right?"

I really do. "Yeah. We want to tease things out. Build some hype, and if we're lucky, get some viral action going. It's smart."

Mia blushes, but there's no mistaking how pleased she is by my comment. "Can I post this? We all set?"

Milo straightens as he crosses his arms. "Do it. Let's see if anyone remembers who we are anymore."

"Dad, you went viral for a second time last week."

"Exactly. That's like a thousand years ago in internet time."

I haven't considered how unlikely it is that we'll be able to take our fifteen minutes of fame and make something from it. The odds of success are astronomically low. It's likely nothing will come of this and I'll have to go find another retail photo job far faster than I anticipated. Still, my heart skips a beat when Mia publishes the video and we're officially live.

When we get the first few views, I let out a little sigh. After about five minutes of standing there watching the "view" count inch up and a few confused comments appear, my disappointed creeps in. Mia's shoulders slump forward, and the look on Milo's face morphs from joy to concern.

I clap my hands together lightly. "Well, we didn't go viral immediately the first time either. No doubt this will also take a hot minute to see if we're going to have a following or not. That doesn't mean we didn't make a kickass first video or that our project isn't worth doing."

"Yeah." Mia closes the app and puts her phone in her pocket. "I guess we'll just have to see."

"Baby, you did good. We didn't look like fools, which is more than I would have been able to do on my own." He gives her shoulder a squeeze. "Like Andie said, these things do take time."

Mia nods but says nothing else. She heads to her room. My heart breaks for her, knowing how excited she was and how hard this sort of thing is to get started. Deep in my heart I know if we're serious about creating something successful from this, we'll have to put in a crazy amount of work. I left home hopeful that lightning would strike for the third time and we'd become an overnight success.

Reality begs to differ.

I nod toward where Mia disappeared. "Is she going to be okay?"

Milo isn't looking at me; his gaze has been pretty much locked on the door since Mia's departure, so when he turns to look at me, my heart sinks at the expression of sadness I see in his eyes. "I honestly don't know. Things are really hard for her. I don't know how to fix them."

It doesn't take a rocket scientist to see that not only is Milo a good dad, but that they've both been struggling for a long time to straighten their off-kilter existence. Seeing Mia's disappointment and Milo's exhausted frustration makes my heart ache.

All my life, I've wanted to travel, to experience life in other places and do my best to capture special moments, and share the beauty in our daily life. I now have an opportunity to take my skills and put them to use helping these two lovely people. Yes, I need this to work, or else I'll have to get a second job, but that seems small compared to the positive impact I might have on Milo and Mia.

And I *want* to help them.

A surge of energy rushes through me as I stride over to the kitchen counter and set my phone down. "We need to plan out our adventures. The first three at least. The more we do quickly, the more likely the algorithm will pick us up."

"I thought you didn't know anything about TikTok"

"Don't have a clue. But everything is run by an algorithm. Crack that, and we can make it work for us." When he doesn't say anything else, I clear my throat to pull his attention away from Mia. "You coming?"

His gaze shifts from my ass to my eyes. "Sure. Let's do this."

SEVENTEEN

Milo

The weight of the small sledgehammer pulls against my underused shoulder muscles, reminding me once again that I need to add more weight to my bench press routine. This is our first outing that Andie has planned for us, one I have to admit I've been incredibly excited for. I first heard about these rage rooms from my agent, Bruno. They're apparently quite popular in L.A., where he lives. Only a few months later I read that one popped up in Toronto. I've wanted to give it a go, to vent any unknown—or at the very least unacknowledged—frustrations on a bevy of inanimate objects. As usual, I came up with some excuse or another to avoid giving it a try, and then forgot.

Until now.

The room is about the size of a double car garage, the walls have thick gray padding covering them. It reminds me of when I go into a sound booth and the way sounds die a premature death. There's a strange array of items littered around the room, each one appealing in its own way. Computer monitors, empty bottles, old printers, sitting on makeshift tables and old bookcases.

Andie is unrecognizable, dressed head to toe in a protective outfit that includes gray overalls, a face shield, heavy gloves, and steel-toed boots. Mia is also dressed up and protected. The camera looks small and awkward in her hands. Andie suggested that Mia use one of her professional ones to record the video. She can edit and post the video once we get home. Mia agreed, but she's clearly nervous about holding such an expensive device.

It's been a long time since we went out together like this to do a fun social thing. If Mia goes out at all, it's with her one or two friends from school. Who wants to hang out with their dad when they're in high school? I certainly didn't, and I had a decent relationship with my dad before he passed. Still, she's been excited to try the TikTok thing again, and that alone made my day.

And then Andie showed up wearing a pair of tight jeans that hug her ass and thighs and all thoughts left my head. Her short hair is pulled into some sort of clip that exposes her cute ears. Can ears be cute? They have to be, because hers are small with little lobes that hang like small cherries from a tree. I want to lean in and suck on one of them, run my tongue across the skin to see if it's as soft as I hope it is.

Thankfully, the grey jumpsuit I was also wearing was baggy enough to hide my appreciation.

The rage room attendant gave us the lowdown of the rules within the room, and because we weren't the first people to ever come in with cameras to record something, gave some suggestions to Mia where she could stand to get some good shots. He was maybe in his early twenties and not bad looking, but I was still surprised when she flushed at his attention and muttered her thanks.

Instead of calling her out, I thump the sledgehammer against my palm, doing my best to mimic a thug from an action movie. "So, are we ready to bust some shit up?" I use the voice of a character I performed in a recent video game, which pulls a smile from Mia and a chuckle from Andie.

God, I love making her laugh.

Mia holds the camera up with the viewscreen out to the side so she can get a better perspective on what she's recording. "Umm, I don't think this is going to work."

"Is there a problem with the camera?" Andie is by her side in a beat, looking down at what Mia is seeing. "You've got it set up right."

"It's not that." Mia won't look at Andie, but she catches my gaze. "I got thinking about our first video and why it didn't do anything, really."

"What's that, baby?"

"It's kind of my fault. I made you do a bunch of poses and stuff. It was obvious that we were trying really hard to make it look professional." She let out a sigh, as she finally glanced at Andie.

Andie made a small adjustment to the camera's position as she spoke. "I take it professional is bad."

Mia hesitated before straightening. "Yeah, I mean it can be. The good uploads are quick and obviously not like a production and stuff, even if they are. We should just be doing things for fun and letting people see what you're really like. Everyone wanted to watch you because you were both relaxed and didn't think anyone was looking."

Andie makes a soft *huh* and gently takes the camera from Mia. "I trust your instinct on this. I'll take this outside so it won't get damaged, and you grab your phone to record instead."

"You're not mad?" Mia is focused on me, but she's clearly talking to Andie.

"Why would I be mad? I've never used TikTok before two days ago, and you're the expert. I figured out long ago to listen to the pros when I'm learning a new thing." Andie gently bumps her shoulder against Mia's. "You're the boss. I'll be right back."

In a flash Andie marches from the room with her camera, leaving me and Mia alone. "You okay?"

Confrontation, no matter how small, can trigger Mia's anxiety. Thankfully, she doesn't look upset at all. If anything, she appears a bit surprised. "I'm good."

I guess this is turning out to be a fun adventure for both of us.

The moment Andie returns, she picks up a baseball bat and says to Mia, "Ready?"

Mia snorts. "That's not intimidating at all." Lifting her phone, she points it at Andie. "Go for it."

Andie grins and marches close to the phone. "You know what? Going viral is stressful."

She takes a step back and swings hard at an old television set that's sitting off to the side. The smash of glass and pop of plastic fills the room, rivaled in volume only by the shout of joy that explodes from Andie and the squeak of surprise from Mia. But Andie doesn't stop. She turns and gives the TV another whack before moving to a bunch of old bottles lined up on a makeshift table. Bits of glass explode outward like an aggressive rainbow hell bent on destruction. Turning to me, she grins.

"Dude, you *have* to try this. It's awesome."

Her cheeks are already flushed, her eyes sparkling from the adrenaline that's no doubt coursing through her. I want to march over there, pull her face shield off and kiss her long and hard. Instead, I walk over to the giant photocopier in the corner and eye it up. The thing has seen better days, but it's about to see a lot fewer of them. Hoisting the sledgehammer up to my shoulder, I pick a spot on the photocopier and slam the head down as hard as I can.

The connecting shock vibrates up my arm and through my body, bringing my mind to focus on the present. The rush of release dispels the anger and frustration I've been holding deep inside. It's euphoric. I repeat the motion, letting the heavy head connect again. Then a third time. Finally, I stop and turn, shocked to realize that I'm smiling.

"This is far cheaper than my therapy."

Andie laughs and the two of us start smashing everything in sight. She sets up another row of bottles to break. "I was so freaked out about going viral." She knocks two bottles against the wall at once. "It was creepy and weird."

"I was worried about my privacy being exposed." I set the sledgehammer down and pick up a lighter bat. "People forget about that stuff when you go viral."

"I lost my job!" Andie bounces the bat against the side of the copier.

Mia moves around us with her phone held out. I'd forgotten for a moment that she's recording us. What she should be doing is taking a bat and venting some of her own frustrations. "Hey, let's trade."

She hesitates.

"You have to try it, Mia." Andie holds out her bat. "You'll love it."

She doesn't move immediately to take it. Instead, she holds her finger up. "I'm going to post this first. Hang on."

Andie glances my way and smiles. Sweat has stuck a strand of her hair across the side of her cheek beneath the face shield. Her skin seems to glow under the fluorescent lights, making her eyes sparkle with the humor I associate with her now. Andie is funny, kind, and despite saying she doesn't see herself as anything special, I can't help but see her as anything less than amazing.

"There." Mia nods at the phone as though in some sort of strange communion.

"Ready?" Andie holds the bat out once more but makes no other move toward Mia.

My jaw drops as Mia lets out a little huff taking it from Andie. My baby doesn't have an aggressive bone in her body and seeing her with a bat as she slowly makes her way over to the line of bottles freaks me out. Eyeing them up, she takes a half-hearted swing. Two of them tumble, one breaking on the floor while the second rolls away. I have to laugh. "You can really hit it. No rules."

She nods, narrows her gaze, pulls back, and takes another swing. This time, shards of glass fly against the wall and bounce off. Instead of the smile I expect to see creep onto her face, Mia looks determined. Another swing, this time accompanied with a shout that might have been a battle cry or one of pain.

"Mia?"

I step forward, but she doesn't hear me. She turns to the photocopier. Time after time, swing after swing, she connects with the sides of the derelict unit, and plastic shards scatter everywhere. All I can do is stand here and watch my baby girl vent what I can only surmise is every pent-up emotion she's been holding onto for … God only knows how long. I'm so fixated on Mia, I don't notice Andie beside me until she takes my hand in hers and gives it a squeeze.

There are no words for what I feel; every emotion I have is colliding inside me. Had I been here alone—not that I would have ever come here without Andie's prodding—I would have been lost as to what to do. Or worse, I would have rushed to Mia to offer support for whatever anger she's clearly working out. Andie's hand gives me the strength to stand here and watch.

To bear witness.

The sound of the metal bat clanging to the floor makes me flinch. Mia turns and pulls her face shield off to push her hair away from her eyes.

"You good, baby?"

Mia cocks her head to the side and gives me a nod. "I'm done. I'll wait outside for you guys."

She leaves us standing amongst the chaos.

"Is she okay?" The concern in Andie's voice is obvious. "It looked like she was genuinely working out something."

My instinct to brush things off, to flippantly say *Of course, she'll be perfectly fine* evaporates from my tongue. "I don't know. She's been in rough shape for over a year now. I hoped this year of high school would be better, but so far it doesn't feel like much has changed."

Mia has a birthday coming up in a few weeks, her seventeenth.

Maybe this has to do with her reaching another birthday without her mom. Maybe she did poorly on a test. Or maybe she's having a bad day. Despite how close we are, Mia always holds a piece of herself back. That's her right as a person, but I still want to know what she's thinking and feeling.

Andie gives my hand another squeeze and starts to let go. I tighten my grip and face her. The gloves we're wearing are thick, to protect our skin from any flying debris that might cause us harm. It means I can't feel her skin—the warmth or softness. But the connection is there, and I don't want to let go. Not yet.

"For years now, my life has basically been focused on Mia and making sure she's okay. I'm starting to realize that there's only so much I can do to make things better for her."

Andie's gaze fixes to mine. "I don't know what it's like to have the level of depression or anxiety she clearly has. And I'm not going to presume I know either of you well. But from the little bit I've seen, and how I've heard you talk about her, you're doing the best you possibly can."

Am I?

Most days it doesn't feel like I'm doing the right thing. Mia swings from mood to mood and all I can do is stand by and pray she'll be okay. I hate feeling incapable of fixing her and the problems that started when Rachel left us. I hate thinking that Mia might not get better, but that if we're lucky, she'll learn how to manage these churning emotions.

I hate ...

Letting go of Andie's hand, I adjust my hold on the handle of the sledgehammer and heft it up. Careful not to trip over the glass and metal on the floor, I approach another bunch of old office equipment. The ball of dread that long ago took up residence in my stomach threatens to grow with each thought that creeps through my brain. Lifting the hammer, I swing low and connect with a large chunk of yellowed plastic. It splinters and goes flying along the floor.

"Milo?"

"Rachel left us. I knew she'd been unhappy for a long time, but I didn't think she'd walk away from Mia. Me, yes. But not her daughter." I pull the hammer back and slam it down again, harder. "I really hated her for that."

There's a label on the side of a monitor; I line up and hit it dead on with the hammer. The physical ache of my muscles from the impact begins to overwhelm the ache in my stomach. The knots are still there, but somehow they've loosened. I'm about to smash it again when the *thunk* and *crack* of reinforced glass being hit has me turning around to face Andie.

Her breath is coming out ragged, fogging up her face shield. Her gaze is locked on a smashed television screen several feet from where I stand. "I hate that I never got to be an artist."

I want to say something, to encourage her or tell her that she *is* an artist, but my throat has tightened, and I can't speak. Instead, I bear witness to her anger as she pulls back and clobbers the screen with the bat.

"I put so much work into my show. So many photos that were really fucking good." *Smash.* "And not a single person came." *Smash.* "Only my mother, who made her disappointment known." *Smash.* "No one gave me a chance, and I hated them for that." *Smash.*

Andie stumbles backward, panting, and drops the metal bat to the floor. Without thinking, I set the sledgehammer down and move to her side. Something is happening in this room for each of us. And while I don't fully understand what she's been through in her life—and I suspect she feels the same way about me—I know some type of connection is forming between us.

"Andie?" My voice is hoarse, and I have to swallow to try and build up enough moisture to speak.

She finally looks at me, her eyes full of emotion. My hands twitch as the urge to pull her into my arms strikes me. I can't look away from her, from the rich hazel of her irises, from the look of confusion and relief that shines through.

I want to kiss her.

I want to strip her naked and feel her body pressed against mine.

I want to feel something other than anger and fear and loneliness.

Andie's lips part and my gaze is drawn to the plump skin. Two plastic barriers are the only things stopping me from leaning forward to see exactly what she tastes like. I pull my face shield off and let it fall to the floor, my gaze shifting back to hers. I know my intentions are clear from the way the blush spreads across her cheeks. I wait for her to decide if this is something she wants as well.

Her tongue darting out licking her lips, has my breath catch. She removes her face shield tossing it to the floor beside mine. My heart skips a beat, my hands grow sweaty in the gloves.

It's as though we've become living magnets, each pulling toward the other. I know I should close my eyes, but I don't want to lose sight of her face for a second. Finally, all my nights of wondering, of fantasizing what it would be like to be with her, is going to be reality.

The door bangs open, sending Andie jumping away with a gasp. Mia stands in the doorway, her phone held out in front of her, her screen on and flashing. "Oh my God! It's working. We're a hit!"

EIGHTEEN

Andie

Look, I've never been a prude when it comes to sex. I like sex an awful lot, despite it not being something I often get to share with another person. And I'm old enough not to give a shit about what anyone else thinks about me or who I want to sleep with.

So why my soul nearly leaves my body when Mia interrupts what I can only imagine would have been a spectacular kiss, I can't tell you. Probably because she's his daughter, but mostly because I don't want to be the thing that comes between them.

Maybe. I don't know.

That kiss would have been amazing! Instead, we pack up our things and I try to keep a small physical distance between myself and Milo so I'm not tempted to throw myself into his arms and encourage the kiss regardless of Mia's presence.

Not that I think she'd notice, given how excited she is about our numbers. Squished in between us in the backseat of the car, all she's focused on is her phone screen with the looping video of us smashing the crap out of things and the view count.

"It's only been up for half an hour and we're already into the tens of thousands. Shit, over a hundred of thousand!"

"Absolutely amazing, baby!"

Sweat fills the air, and I'm thankful the SUV has large vents in the back blasting us with too-cold conditioned air. I'm also thankful for the small water bottles that the driver has placed in the cup holders on the doors. My throat's been dry since the moment I realized that Milo wanted to kiss me. Cracking the seal, I swallow down most of the bottle, letting out a tiny groan when it's gone.

Milo glances my way and smirks.

Because I'm apparently a horny asshole, I hold his gaze and lick a bead of water off the bottle opening. He looks away instantly and I suppress a laugh when he awkwardly shifts in his seat. The Uber pulls up in front of their condo building and Milo opens the door, practically leaping from the vehicle. Mia clamors out after him, still staring at her screen.

When I don't get out immediately, Milo leans against the side of the SUV to look at me. "You want to come in?" His gaze snaps to my breasts and back so quickly, I'm not certain he's aware he even looked.

I have no other plans for today, but I know there's no way I'll be able to simply hang out at his condo given my current state of arousal, knowing his daughter is there. "I think it's probably best if I head home."

Is that disappointment on his face? "You sure? We can get a pizza."

God, it's so tempting. *He* is so tempting. "Yeah." I glance at Mia. "You two have a good evening."

Milo pats the top of the vehicle. "Okay. I'll talk to you later."

As we drive away, the driver looks at me through the rear-view mirror. "Date with the kid, eh? How'd that go?"

"Oh, it wasn't a date. We were filming a video."

"Really?" he says skeptically. "There's some traffic on our way. It will take a bit longer than normal."

"No problem." I pick up the untouched water bottle from Milo's side and crack it open.

Today's been ... not at all what I expected.

I mean, yeah, it was cathartic smashing the hell out of objects. And I'm thrilled, surprised the video caught traction and is doing well so quickly. Mia was clearly right when she said people wanted to see the two of us relaxed and being dorks, rather than in some put-on production. And really, thank God for that. I don't think I'd have been able to handle performing that way and kept my sanity intact.

The more time I spend with Milo, the more I realize that there's a connection growing between us. An undeniable spark that charges my body up and makes it ready to explode with the briefest of touches. The phantom sensation of his fingers caressing the inside of my wrist makes my skin tingle. I wanted the middle seat on the way to his condo, to be as close to his side as I could manage and still maintain public decency but wasn't about to ask Mia to switch with me when she climbed in first.

I should have gone in with him.

Even if that meant I wouldn't have been able to do much of anything about the heat between my thighs and my urge to grind against the seat. Why I feel this way with him, I'm not certain. It's nothing more than the result of reading too much fan fiction about us and my undeniable curiosity as to how close to reality it would be.

The moment the Uber pulls in front of my place, I bolt inside. I'm not sure if I should grab a shower or my vibrator to deal with my current horny state. Hell, maybe I'll use my vibrator *in* the shower. I'm a single, healthy woman after all. If I want to do that, I totally can.

My apartment is warmer than it was when I left this morning. I open a window and try to catch some of the cooler air. The last vestiges of summer are trying to hold on, but the change in temperature the last few days tells me it will soon be time to dig out my fall jacket. Given how many hot flashes I randomly get these days, I'm going to thoroughly enjoy the cooler weather. Not that any of that matters one iota right now.

Toeing off my shoes, I reach under my shirt and behind my back to unhook my bra. With speed, little grace, and without taking my shirt off, I pull the straps down one at a time and pull my arms free. I groan as my breasts swing free from their prison, my nipples instantly hard against the cotton of my shirt.

I don't remember the last time I was this aroused. Everything inside me aches, wants to be touched, to feel the press of another person against me to find release. Not that I necessarily need someone else, but it would be nice to not have to rely on either my hand or a vibrator. I start for my bedroom, but at the last second change direction for the bathroom. Flipping the shower on to let the water heat up before I strip. To avoid the embarrassment of seeing the flush of desire across my body, I try not to look at myself naked in the mirror.

The water, once it's just the right temperature, blasts some of the insanity I've been feeling from my head as it washes over me. I catch my breath as my head falls forward, the water caressing my overly sensitive spots.

This is nuts. Why the hell am I so turned on right now? Milo hasn't done anything directly to have me this amped up. He didn't touch the inside of my wrist or anything this time. He just smiled, teased me, and adjusted himself when I licked the top of my water bottle. Had we been alone, would he have leaned over to touch me? To kiss me?

Maybe all this emotion and horniness is the fallout from the physical relief that hit me after I smashed the ever-loving fuck out of the television. I didn't anticipate the well of emotions that connecting the bat to the glass yanked from deep inside me. Milo's acknowledgment of his anger at his ex-wife felt intimate, private, and something he cautiously chose to share with me. Seeing the change in his body as he brought forth and let go of his dark feelings sparked something in me.

I never realized how angry I've been. Not until I hit the TV and something inside me snapped. With each crack of damage I inflicted, the weight on my shoulders seemed to lessen. For the first time in a long while I feel more settled in my skin, alive and ready to seize the day.

To seize Milo's face and kiss him hard on the mouth.

My hand, slick from my bath wash, brushes against my nipples, sending another burst of pleasure through me. Okay, I'm clearly on this path and there's no sense trying to delay the inevitable. With my eyes closed, I slide my fingers through my pubic hair, lightly touching my clit. That single brush is nearly enough to push me over the edge. I pull back, let out a little huff, and try to calm down enough to make this last longer than ten seconds.

And yet when I start again, all I can see is Milo's blue eyes as they roam down my body. The cord of muscles in his forearms that flex when he reaches for something. I wonder how it would look if it were his hand between my legs instead of my own. I increase the pressure on my clit and with one final stroke, I gasp as pleasure rolls through me. My muscles tighten, and I have to press my free hand against the shower wall to keep from slipping. And as quickly as I began, it's over.

Opening my eyes, I stare at the white tiled wall and the beads of water trickling down as I come back to reality. Now, normally I'm a one and done kind of gal. When I was younger and my sex drive was far stronger than it currently is, I'd come once and then I'd be fine. I've never felt bad about that, mostly because my orgasms are quite excellent. A girl needs a chance to recover and all that.

But after cleaning myself up, getting something to eat, and slipping into my pajamas, that old familiar tingle starts to build once again. It's after seven, and I find myself wondering what Milo is up to. Have they eaten supper? Is he helping Mia with her homework, or is that something he has to do with her? Given how smart she seems to be, I doubt it's a problem.

I pick up my remote and navigate to Netflix. I have a bunch of shows on the go—two documentaries, the latest season of *Nailed It*, and some nineties comedy that I can't remember the plot of—but can't focus on any of them long enough to choose one to watch. Blindly, I pick something, toss my remote to the side, and pick up my phone. There's a TikTok notification, which has me clicking.

Wow, that's a lot of views.

I'm about to read the comments when our video loops and I see Milo's smile shine out from behind the protective face mask. It doesn't matter that we're head to toe in the most unflattering protective gear possible, there's no hiding how handsome he is. My heart does a little flutter and the next thing I know I'm squirming on the couch.

Shit.

There's no way I'm going to get myself off again.

Is there?

No.

Why didn't I take him up on his offer to come back to his place? I mean, not that we would have been able to do anything, given how engaged Mia was the with video at that point. Not that we would have done anything *after* that, given that Mia would be there too, in the next room at the very least.

What I should have done was invited him over to *my* place. That isn't crazy, is it? He's not exactly someone who wants to go out, be social; he's said that on more than one occasion. And really, it's not like we've been on a date or expressed any sort of desire to have a fling. As far as we've both been concerned, getting together has to do with the TikTok channel, finding a way to make some money from this, and maybe, *possibly*, developing some sort of friendship.

Flipping over to my texts, I look at the last one from him. We were making the plans to go to the rage room and the last thing he sent me was a smiling emoji. It was cute, totally appropriate for the moment, and not at all horny.

Unlike my current self.

I figure I can approach this one of two ways. I can find my vibrator and finish myself off once again in hopes I'll be satisfied with the resulting orgasm. Or …

My thumbs start moving of their own volition as I type out just my address. I don't hesitate—I press send before my brain catches up and tries to stop me. Letting out a little huff, I stare at the screen, waiting for some sort of response.

I mean, he might not understand what I'm asking for. He might not have his phone with him or be able to leave, depending on how Mia is feeling. He might not be interested in me *that way*, and I could be massively embarrassing myself. Or—

Bloop!

Or he is. I burst out laughing at the very Miloesque response— an eggplant emoji with a question mark. There's still time to change my mind, to pull this strangely spontaneous booty call back and continue on as though nothing happened. Knowing Milo the way I do, he'd make a joke about my silliness and we'd continue on.

Horny.

And more than a little lonely.

I scramble for the spurting emoji, biting down on my lower lip as I press send. I'm half hoping for a thumbs-up emoji, or maybe a blushing face. Something.

Certainly, I don't want the *absolutely nothing* that I get. No *Hey maybe this isn't a good idea,* or *I don't like you that way so let's stick to the TikTok thing.* Just dead air. Groaning loudly, I toss my phone to the side and let my head fall back against the couch.

Great.

I should have realized going that far would push him out of his comfort zone. Milo barely leaves his condo on a good day, and if something is up with Mia, he certainly won't leave her home alone.

Even if that's probably something he should do more frequently than he does.

Fine, I'll go in search of my vibrator later. Right after I sulk-watch *Nailed It*.

I get halfway through my second episode and I'm feeling better about myself when there's a loud knock on my door. Without bothering to stop the show, I leap from the couch and scurry to the door, pausing long enough to confirm that it's who I hope it is through the peephole.

Then Milo is standing in my doorway, his hands braced on either side, half out of breath. He's still wearing his outfit from earlier, though the scent of shampoo and fresh deodorant is strong.

"Sorry. I didn't want to wait. I mean I didn't want you to wait. When you texted I was in—"

I grab him by the front of his shirt and yank him inside.

NINETEEN

Milo

I'm just getting out of the shower when I hear my phone *ding*, letting me know that Andie texted. Yes, I personalized her in my contacts, despite not getting many phone calls from people. It's being a good business partner, not wanting any of her texts to sit longer than necessary. My fingers are wrinkled from the hot water, which makes biometrically unlocking my phone a challenge. Frustrated and still wet, I finally get my phone unlocked only to blink at her message.

Seeing her address typed out looks odd, and my brain doesn't quite register what she's implying.

Well, my head doesn't register. My cock on the other hand ...

Oh.

Oh ...

Because it's been a stupid long time since I've had anything remotely close to a booty call, I send her the eggplant emoji to confirm.

Like an adult.

Her spurting emoji sends me into an aroused panic as I stand still wet from the shower. Am I really going to do this? It's one thing to go on a date with someone, but this feels different. Andie is my friend, and now my partner in our strange project to become famous online. Having sex could screw up the relationship we've been building.

Or it could be a good time with no strings attached. We're adults, after all.

I have to be extra cautious drying *him* off because if things are going where I hope they are, he needs to be at the top of his game. Still damp, I quickly throw my clothes back on, ignoring my internal voice screaming at me that this is a terrible idea and that I should put on my pajama pants, a clean T-shirt, and crawl into bed to watch TV.

Fortunately, my cock is currently steering the ship.

Mia went into her room as soon as we got home and fell down the YouTube rabbit hole of meme compilation videos. Knocking quickly, I opened her door just wide enough to stick my head inside. "I, ah, have to go out for a bit."

"Umm, 'kay." She turns her face and smiles at me, all without taking her eyes from her phone.

"Are you good? I can cancel if you need me to stay." This should be a signal to her that the end of the world is happening or something, but she doesn't even look at me. A part of me hopes she'll say yes if she has any hesitations about being alone. The last thing I want is to go do something sexy with Andie, then get a frantic call from Mia.

"Took a clonazepam."

"Why? You okay?"

She nods. "Got anxious after the numbers spiked on the video. Good now."

"Baby, if you're not feeling well, I can—"

She waves and rolls onto her side. "Have fun."

Well, okay then.

At least a dozen times from the moment Andie sent me her address, to the moment I'm standing on the sidewalk looking up at her building, I've questioned whether I'm making a terrible mistake. And really, I knew all along I might arrive and find out she's come to her senses, changed her mind and she'll beg me to leave. I mentally prepared something funny to say, something self-deprecating and light.

No, no, you're right. I wouldn't want me to have my home address either. No dorks allowed!

Hey, at least you won't need to worry about me leaving my condo to come here again. Way too much outside for my liking.

Well, there we go. I DO know how to use Google Maps. Now to find my way home.

I close my eyes and try to catch my breath after taking the stairs two at a time up to her apartment. I knock far louder than I probably should have. Needing the extra support, I brace my hands on either side of the doorframe. Shit, she's going to think I'm someone here to harass her or something. Some obsessive fan who found out where she lives. If I were her, I wouldn't come close to the door, let alone open—

Thunderous footsteps on the other side, followed by the rattling of a door chain and the loud click of a dead bolt sliding open shocks me into opening my eyes.

Andie yanks her door open. Her eyes give me a once-over that I can only describe as hungry. My brain short-circuits when I realize I didn't misinterpret her intentions.

"Sorry. I didn't want to wait. I mean I didn't want you to wait. When you texted I was in—" The next thing I know, she's yanking me into her apartment, and everything feels amazing.

I might be an introvert by nature, but once I get to know a person it's as though a switch goes off in my head and everything becomes easier; I can be myself. The second I cross the threshold to Andie's place, that switch flips and my body relaxes.

Well, not *relaxes,* relaxes. I'm still quite horny.

"I didn't think you'd come." Her voice is breathy, her tongue moist as it darts out to lick her bottom lip. "You didn't say anything."

I really want to kiss her. "I thought if I said something, the universe would conspire to keep me from making it here."

"Mia?"

"She'll be asleep for the night."

The familiar pang of guilt threatens to chase away my desire to do something purely for myself. Instead of going down that path, I take a beat and give myself permission to be selfish. I'm allowed to want this, to need this. I'm taking this moment to do something for myself, and there's nothing wrong with that. Right? Just because I fled my home to come halfway across the city and take advantage of what is essentially a booty call, that's fine, right?

Something must show on my face because Andie frowns. "We don't have to do this. If you want to go back home."

My mom once said the greatest gift one person can give another is that of understanding. I always questioned that sentiment until this moment. Reaching up, I cup her face and get a bit closer.

"I'm a single dad with a teenage daughter who needs a lot of extra support. I've pushed myself to the back so frequently, I forgot that it's okay to do something just for me." I stare at her mouth, knowing exactly what I want to do.

I hold her gaze as I lean in, announcing my intentions. Unless the world suddenly explodes, aliens arrive, or Andie changes her mind, this kiss is going to happen. Thankfully, Andie closes her eyes as our lips touch.

It's been a long time since I kissed a woman.

My chest tightens as a shiver rolls through me at the soft, tentative caress of my mouth against hers. I rub her cheeks with my thumbs, my pinkie resting against the pulse in her neck. The rapidly increasing thump and patter of her excitement serves to encourage me to keep going. Deepening the kiss, I tease her tongue with my own, taking greedy gulps of air whenever we break apart.

Andie's hands find my hips, then my ass as our bodies press completely together. There's no hiding my painful erection now.

Not that she seems to mind whatsoever, given the way she bucks her hips forward.

I could stand here for hours, kissing her like this, feeling her body come alive against mine. Maybe I'm more than a little touch-starved after years of solitary living. I focus on every sensation all at once, making the kiss somehow larger than I remember one being. My shirt, rough against my skin, serves to dull the electrified sensations across my skin. That is until Andie worms her hands beneath the bottom of my shirt and scrapes her fingers across my stomach.

Shit.

Shit. Fuck and damn.

Stepping back, I let go of her face and take a moment to calm my breathing.

"God, are you okay?"

I hold up my finger, silently asking for a second. I chuckle. "I nearly came in my pants."

Andie blushes as she smiles. "Now if you'd told me that I possessed that kind of power before, I wouldn't have believed you."

It breaks my heart that she lacks self-confidence. "You're a fucking goddess. Any man would be privileged to be allowed a toe into your world."

Her mouth falls open and before the denial she's about to speak emerges, I pull my shirt off, drop it to the floor, and scoop her into my arms. "Bedroom?"

She points, her mouth still gaping.

That's fine by me. There are many things I'd love to do with that mouth.

The small bedroom is exactly the way I imagined it. Photographs in dollar store frames cover the walls, each one beautiful and unique. If I wasn't so fucking horny, I'd stop and look at every one of them. Later.

Setting Andie on her bed, I stand over her and look down, taking in every inch of her. She's beautiful in every way a middle-aged woman can be. Her thighs and ass are thicker, her breasts full, and her hair is streaked with occasional gray strands. Small wrinkles have begun to form around her eyes, no doubt from all the smiling she does. Andie is sunshine and joy, and I want nothing more than permission to bask in her glow.

Why the hell don't you ever take my feelings into account? Rachel's voice rips through my head, making me twitch.

I haven't lived the life of a monk since my divorce; I've had the occasional one-night stand when Mia visited her grandparents. Those had nothing to do with relationships, and I like to think the women involved left happy and satisfied. But this thing with Andie, this is different.

"Milo?"

I shake my head. "Yeah, sorry."

"You okay?" She pushes herself up on her forearms to look at me.

"Just a little rusty." Rachel is so far in the past, she doesn't deserve the mental space she clearly still has. Andie is here and she deserves a show. By God, I'm going to give her one.

Unfortunately for her, I'm not much of a dancer. Still, I put my hands on my hips and give my ass a little wiggle. She smiles. I turn around and ... I'm not going to claim I can twerk, because middle-aged white guy. But I attempt it.

That has her laughing.

I take her small distraction as an opportunity to unbutton my jeans and open the front. My cock is already peeking up from beneath my boxer's waistband. When I turn back around, there's no hiding my current state from her. The laugher peters away as Andie's gaze latches on the prize before her.

Me. I'm the prize.

"Well, sir. Is that a banana in your boxers or are you just horny?"

"Definitely the latter." I wiggle my hips again. "Like what you see?"

My breath is pulled from my chest when her gaze moves to mine and she smiles. "I do. I really do."

All remaining reservations evaporate. Gone in a blink. Nothing else matters in this moment than me, Andie, and the fact we're about to have sex. I push my jeans to the floor and step out of them, grabbing each sock as I pull free. I keep my boxers on, wanting to preserve a bit of modesty until I'm able to get her equally naked.

Andie lifts her hips as I reach for the waist of her soft, plaid microfiber pajama bottoms and pull them down. She's wearing neon pink panties, a stark contrast to the thinning gray sleep shirt she has on.

I stop to take in the sight of her. "There's nothing sexier than a half-dressed woman."

"Sure there is." She sits up and pulls her shirt off.

She's not wearing a bra. I should have noticed that her breasts were free from their confines. Now all she has on are those neon panties.

When she lies back down and lifts her hips up to take them off, I put my hands on her knees. "Wait."

She cocks an eyebrow at me but lowers her hips.

Her bed is thankfully not very tall, which means I have some room. Dropping to my knees, I pick up her feet, one after the other, and place them on the edge of the bed. Her skin is prickly from the unshaven leg hair, but that doesn't stop me from running my palms from her ankles, along the inside of her thighs, to her knees and back down. I can smell her arousal, can see the damp spot on her panties.

From this vantage point, it's hard to see her face, so I gauge my actions on her body's jerks and the intoxicating sounds spilling from her lips. When I spread her thighs apart and move my mouth to the inside of her calf, she sighs. When I lick small circles, letting my tongue tease the sensitive spot behind her knee, she giggles. The scrape of my nails against the inside of her thighs pulls a gasp.

And when I finally shift forward and press my open mouth to the deliciously dark wet spot on those beautiful neon pink panties, she groans.

I'd forgotten how much I love this. Teasing a woman, bringing her pleasure, losing myself completely in another person. Andie's fingers find my head, teasing my hair and scraping my scalp. In turn, I use my teeth against her still-hidden clit. I'm not going to last much longer, knowing how badly I want to taste her. I give one long, hot exhale against the fabric before I pull back. "I need to see you."

Together we shift. I pinch the thin barrier between my fingers and pull it slowly down her hips and ass, peeling it free like the very best present. The sight of black curls also tinged with gray makes my mouth water. God, I hope she isn't expecting a marathon session or anything, because at this rate, I'm going to come before I get off my knees. Well, there is one way to distract myself from that outcome.

Sliding my arms beneath her legs, I pull her ass to the very edge of the bed, putting her core directly in line with my face. Andie throws an arm across her eyes. "God, I ... been a while."

"I saw the vibrator on your nightstand. Couldn't have been that long."

"Before I texted you, actually."

The mere thought of Andie masturbating is utterly erotic to me. "And you still texted?"

"I couldn't get you out of my head."

Wait, what? "You thought about me while masturbating?"

She laughs. "Yeah."

"Shit, I've stopped myself from doing that thinking it would be weird." I lower my face and lick a quick swipe across her soft skin. "At least I know I have permission now."

"All the permission." She groans again when I give her another quick lick. "Milo, please."

I can't deny her anything at this point. I take my time, wanting to ensure Andie feels every bit of pleasure I can provide. With each moan I pull from her, I narrow my focus, trying to do exactly the right thing, wanting to keep her happy.

You're so selfish, Milo. All I've ever wanted was to be treated like you love me more than your stupid job.

Andie holds me in place as she comes. I do my best not to move, scared I'll ruin the moment for her. When she finally gasps and her hand falls back to the bed, I pull away. She's flushed from her face, down her throat, to the tops of her breasts. With her eyes closed and her chest rising and falling from her panting, I can't help but stare at how beautiful she is. I don't move until she opens her eyes. Her gaze meets mine and she smiles.

"Condom?" We both ask at the same time, which in my experience means neither party has one.

Andie lifts herself onto her forearms again to glare at me. "You came to a booty call without condoms?"

"It's been a long while. I'm rusty." Well shit, there goes that idea.

"It's fine. We're smart. We can figure this out." She gets to her feet, stumbling briefly before she reaches for me. "On the bed."

I can still move impressively fast for a fifty-year-old. When my ass hits the bed, I don't immediately lie back. Andie is standing there naked, smiling at me, her skin glowing. She turns and looks through her nightstand drawer, no doubt searching for condoms. "I might have an old box somewhere."

God, Milo, only you can screw up a sure thing like sex. This isn't Rachel's voice in my head. Nope, this is all me. This time, the bite of guilt hits me harder. *You passed three pharmacies on the way here.*

"I can check the bathroom. Hang on." Andie leaves the room before I have the chance to stop her.

First, it's this, but later it will be something bigger. Important. It's better to keep my distance. That way I can't let Andie down when I fuck up. I've mentally decided to leave when she finally reappears, a battered condom box in her hand. It must show on my face because her demeanor changes from happy-excited, to immediate concern. "What's wrong?"

Why can't I be normal? Why couldn't I have sex with a woman who I genuinely liked and it not become this weird thing in my head? Andie sets the condoms on the nightstand and sits beside me on the bed. She places her hand on my thigh, giving me a gentle squeeze. "Milo?"

"I've...I..." I let out a sound that was supposed to be a chuckle, but sound more like a half sob.

She squeezed my thigh again. "We don't have to do this."

"I want to." How the hell can I put into words the torrent of *things* inside my head? "I really want to."

"Milo, I don't pretend to understand everything you've been through. It was obvious today that both you and Mia have been hurt badly." She's facing me, but I can't meet her gaze. "I...my mom and I don't have a great relationship. Not like you and your ex, just...I know how it makes me second guess everything sometimes."

As she's speaking, I look up and at her. That tiny bit of understanding somehow eases my rising anxiety. When my eyes meet hers, she smiles. "I have an idea." Her gaze drops to my groin. "If you're game."

"Sure." I'm sitting mostly naked on her bed, my cock half-hard in my boxers.

Instead of reaching for the condoms, Andie picks up her tube of lube and squeezes some onto her hand. "Lay down."

I do, even as my embarrassment at how foolish everything suddenly feels threatens to take over. "Now what?"

Andie pushes her hand into my boxers, pulling a gasp from me. "Now, I want you to close your eyes and be selfish. I want you to enjoy this. I want you to know that I'm going to do this because I want to make you feel good. You deserve to feel good."

With each sentence, she strokes me. It doesn't take long to relax and begin to revel in the intimacy of her touch. Instead of listening to the negative voice in my head, I focus on the sounds coming from Andie. Her sighs, the rapid rate of her breathing. It's enough to push me past my block and into my release. I cry out, my hand finding her hip to squeeze, needing to hold her until I'm spent.

Despite the intensity and my body's reactions, I never once lose sight of the fact that I'm here, doing this with Andie. Until sex exhaustion slams into me. Groaning, I try to keep my eyes open. I can't fall asleep. I can't be the typical dude and pass out after having the best orgasm ...

Maybe just a tiny nap.

TWENTY

Andie

Have you ever been so tired that your brain won't shut off, resulting in you being wired and staying awake for twenty-four hours? No? Just me? Well, it's an unpleasant feeling, despite it working to my advantage on more than one occasion. It's easy to get a lot done at three in the morning when there's no one around to bother you. In the past, I've finished marking assignments, tweaked my photos—done just about anything in the wee hours. I inevitably crash the next night around seven, but I've rarely regretted the burst of manic energy.

Except tonight.

Milo left hours ago, needing to get home to Mia, but I can't sleep. So I get up and try to distract myself with work, hoping it will burn off my energy. It doesn't. I keep replaying the look of panic and pain on his face when I came back from my successful condom scavenger hunt. I knew he wanted to be here with me, that whatever was happening in his head wasn't necessarily about me. I could only assume it was about his ex.

We didn't really say much after we recovered enough to get dressed. I mean, yes, we got each other off and probably could have cuddled or something in bed, but that didn't feel right. He needed to deal with whatever was going on in his head. And while the impulse to help him was strong, I didn't have a clue how. Instead, I smiled at him, watching the way his naked body moved and flexed as he slowly covered it up.

I didn't bother dressing; I threw on my housecoat and slippers. "We still on to film before Mia goes to school tomorrow?" I was hoping that what we did wouldn't ruin the TikTok thing. That he wouldn't be too embarrassed to want to continue.

"Are you up for being at the café for seven?" He reached out and tucked my hair behind my ear. It was the gentlest of touches, and it made me feel cared for. "It's a long way for you to come for a short video."

"I'll be there. We need to promo that lemon loaf."

His smile had my heart doing a little dance. "If this keeps going the way it feels like it is, we'll be able to get some sponsors or something soon. Maybe."

Milo had leaned in, his mouth moving toward mine as he held my gaze, but he stopped before he got within kissing range. "I have to go."

Please stay. "I'll see you tomorrow."

And then ... that was it. He left.

The rage and lust that powered me for most of the afternoon and evening is gone. It should have been easy to curl up in bed and crash, but instead I'm walking randomly around my apartment, cleaning up the piss-poor tidying job I did earlier. Coffee cups have multiplied next to my laptop, and I have to carefully balance them along with two plates to get them safely to the dishwasher in one trip.

When I realize there's nothing left to clean and I'm still not tired, I go back to my computer to look again through my recent batch of photos. Maybe it's the modicum of success my picture of Milo has received, but I begin to see my photos in a slightly different light.

They're good.

I'm a great photographer.

Picking one at random, I start playing around with the color balance in Photoshop, tweaking the settings until I'm satisfied with the result. The image of the fog-draped red and gold maple tree I snapped last fall looks ethereal, magical. It's the sort of image I enjoy capturing. Abandoned houses, reclaimed spaces, moon shots behind buildings—discovering the beauty in the world that people are often too busy to stop and enjoy themselves. This is what I hoped I could explore with my art—the hidden emotions that can be evoked by photography. I wanted nothing more than to do this in art school, but I was forced to produce an art portfolio that wasn't reflective of my goals instead.

It's not this tree. Or Milo sitting on a bench trying to make his world better. Or the decaying remains of a farmhouse long abandoned when the family had no choice but to move away. It's capturing a fleeting moment in time, a blink in the history of the world. Something that shouts *Hey, I'm here and I'm a witness to this reality.*

Me. Andie Matheson. Present on this planet.

I know if I really want the canvas size big enough to impress, it will need to be massive—far bigger than what I'm capable of producing on my own. That leads me to falling down a rabbit hole of print shops I could send it to for production. The next thing I know, my alarm is going off telling me it's time to get up.

Shit.

Frantically saving my work, I get dressed and bolt for the door. My view of the world needs to wait. I have a TikTok and lemon loaf to attend.

"OH MY GOD, this is the best!" I'm drooling as I pop the last bite of the still-warm pumpkin spice loaf into my mouth.

Apparently, being sleep deprived hasn't done anything to dull my enthusiasm for food.

The staff insisted we try their new fall treat, wanting to drive up additional business. We were more than happy to assist. Milo and Mia are also moaning their appreciation as we stand outside The Pear Tree, ensuring their sign is prominent in the shot. Milo stands next to me so our arms are pressed together, sending my already overstimulated body into hyperdrive. I mean, about eight hours ago we were both naked on my bed. The scent of his deodorant and the black coffee he holds in his hand are quickly becoming how my mind conjures Milo. I now know that his body is far tighter than I assumed when I saw him at the park. Still dad-bod territory but leaning heavily toward the sexy-fit side on the dad-bod scale of hotness.

Mia shoves most of her loaf into her mouth and walks franti-cally around filming us. "T-Dot peeps, come to The Pear Tree café and get yourself some pumpkin spice loaf!" As quickly as she started filming, Mia stops. "Okay posted. I have to run."

"You have everything you need?" How quickly he switches from being-filmed Milo to dad-mode Milo is impressive. "You good on your own?"

"I'm meeting Steph and Luna at the corner." Mia waves him away, snagging his coffee as she marches past. "I'll see you later."

It isn't until she turns her back to Milo that I realize how tense he is. "Everything okay?"

"She took her anxiety meds last night and wasn't herself this morning. She's been spending a lot more time online than normal." He doesn't look away from her, and I can feel the anxious energy flowing from him. "I shouldn't have left her last night. I knew something was wrong."

Being on the outside of their relationship, it's hard to fully appreciate the challenges they both face daily. The fact that he left her to come to my place to have sex only to have what I assume was an existential crisis? Well, that makes me feel like a giant asshole. "Do you want to go after her?"

I can tell he's genuinely considering the idea before he gives his head a shake. "She's almost seventeen. At some point I have to show that I trust her enough to come to me if she needs help. It makes things worse if I ride her too much. Pressuring her to do things when she already knows she needs to."

That makes sense, despite it not sounding easy to do. "So, we've filmed our TikTok and eaten our loaf. Now what are you up to?"

Milo's gaze keeps darting to Mia's retreating form as he turns to face me. "I have to record some lines for a video game."

"That's ... wow. I forgot that you're a voice actor." I'd forgotten that he has an entire career and life beyond his daughter. "Do you enjoy that? Voice acting?"

The dark cloud that descended on him vaporizes when he smiles. "Oh yeah. I'm getting paid to be the class clown."

"So, if a girl wanted to get to know your body of work," I say, totally emphasizing *body*, "where would she start?"

Yes, I'm overtly flirting.

Despite his hesitations, I got the impression he enjoyed himself last night. And sure, maybe sex adds a layer of complication to our relationship, but that doesn't mean it's a bad idea. I like him, like us together, and I can't help wanting to see where this might go. Hence the flirting.

Milo is a smart dude; he picks up on it. His gaze drops to my breasts, lingering there far longer than he would have even a day ago. When he sighs, I know I'm about to be disappointed. "I really must record these lines. I've been putting it off for a few days now, and the deadline is uncomfortably close."

"Shit, yeah, no, don't worry about it. Go do your work. I should probably get ready for class tonight or something."

I finished my lesson plans for the rest of the semester days ago.

He takes my hand in his, brushing the inside of my wrist with the pad of his thumb. "Call you tonight?"

"I'm in class until nine, but I'll be home by ten."

"I'll talk to you then."

For a moment, I think he's going to kiss me. Right here in the middle of the sidewalk in front of his normal café where anyone who might know him can see. My body is instantly ready for this, wants it. So when he drops my hand and pulls back, I know there's no hiding my disappointment. I should have known it was too much for him, especially after what happened last night. I'm a fucking idiot. "I'm sorry."

The look on his face tells me he's going into panic mode. "Andie, wait—"

"It's totally fine." Nope, I can't deal with his anxieties right now. Best to get the hell out of here and lick my wounds in private. "I'll talk to you later."

"Andie, I'm sorry. Wait."

I spin around and bolt in the opposite direction Mia went. If I walk fast enough, I'll catch the next bus home before I die of embarrassment.

TWENTY-ONE

Milo

"Dee, she wanted me to kiss her, and I totally froze."
I've never been so thankful for a regular therapy session in my life. I didn't lie to Andie when I said I had work to do —I am, in fact, behind schedule. But there's no way I can focus on playing a creepy demon who's hunting the faceless protagonist of whatever generic role-playing game contracted me until I figure out what the hell is going on with this thing between me and Andie. Best to put everything out there so I can work through why I'm such a trash romantic partner.

Dee doesn't immediately respond, and for a moment I think we've been disconnected, leaving me sitting alone in the darkness of my recording office. It was so quiet, the only thing I could hear was the beating of my heart. "Dee?"

"Why do you think this is a problem?"

I pull my phone from my ear to look down at the screen for a moment before answering. "I repeat, she wanted to kiss me, and I could. Not. Do. It."

"That happens with new relationships."

"Yes, but I've kissed her before. We basically had sex, Dee."

While she doesn't sigh, I can tell from her tone that she really wants to. "What you're describing—kissing her on the street; if you were to rate that on your intimacy scale, where would it fall?"

I immediately want to claim that a kiss is far less intimate. That I'd kissed her during sex. That I had never been opposed to the idea. But I know in my heart this was different. It isn't about the kiss, but about the change in our relationship that specific kiss would imply.

The fact that we'd have a relationship and not simply a social media partnership. One with occasional benefits that we both took pleasure in.

Oh.

"Milo?"

"I see what you're getting at."

"You're finally coming out from under the emotional weight left by your ex-wife. Maybe give yourself permission to take things slowly with Andie. If you do, in fact, want to have a relationship with her that goes beyond TikTok."

"Yeah. Thanks." I'm regretting taking this call in my office, being surrounded by the dampened quiet and smell of my cold coffee. Being outside in the park, fresh air in my lungs might have made this conversation a bit easier. Maybe.

Who am I kidding? My office with its lack of windows, insulated from not only the rest of the condo, but the rest of the world is my sanctuary.

"Milo, you're a good man who deserves to be happy. Cut yourself some slack."

I'm going to do this because I want to make you feel good. You deserve to feel good.

"Easer said than done."

"If you put the effort into some of the CBT techniques we've talked about in the past, this sort of thing will become easier. You'll be better able to handle stressful situations."

Whenever Dee brings up cognitive behavioral therapy or any other techniques she wants me to put into practice, my skin crawls and I get annoyed. I've tried the exercises off and on, but I always feel stupid, and they don't get me through when I need the help. "Those things don't really work for me. You know that."

"They will if you give them a chance."

"I have given them a chance." Why the hell does she always come back to this stuff? I squeeze my phone hard enough that I could have cracked the casing. "More than once if you remember."

"Yes, but before now, you didn't have someone else in your life to get better for."

I suck the air through my nose. Anger sits in my mouth like a sour candy, making me want to spit. "Mia. I have *Mia* to get better for."

"You've been coming to see me for a long time now." Dee is obviously choosing her words carefully; her tone has gone flat. "If you meant that, you would have put these things into practice. You would be further along than you are."

Never, in all the years we've been meeting, have I felt this angry at Dee. She of all people knows exactly what we've been through, what I'm still going through. "What the hell does that mean?"

"It means that therapy isn't working for you. It's not for everyone. There's no shame in that."

It's been ages since I've been as angry and frustrated as I am right now. "If this isn't working, then maybe I should cancel our future appointments. Best to not waste your time and my money."

"Milo, you've been my patient for years, so I'm going to say this to you bluntly because you need to hear it." She pauses. "Pulling back is what people do when they're scared, when things are hard and they don't want to face that pain. Yes, you're still hurting. But until you're able to acknowledge what's wrong, are willing to step up to that essential pain and deal with it, you're never going to get unstuck. If that's the choice you make, then fine. You're an adult who understands the consequences of his actions. But realize that it will impact your relationships with others. With Mia and Andie."

I rub at my eyes, angrily wiping at the sudden tears. I want to argue with her, but I can't.

"Milo, you're a good man."

"No, I'm not." The words hurt to say.

"Why do you think that?"

I don't need any soul searching to know the answer to that. "Because I was the reason Rachel left us. I made her miserable and was too selfish to see she was hurting. Mia is hurting now, and I can't fix her. I hurt Andie when I couldn't give her what she wanted."

When she doesn't jump in and say anything else, doesn't fill the silence, doesn't stop me from continuing, I close my eyes and say out loud the thought that echoed in my head in the middle of the night.

"Dee, I'm not okay." It's barely a strangled whisper, but it feels good to speak it. "I'm not okay. But I ... I want to be better."

"Oh, Milo." I sense her relief. "We can help get you to a better place. I'd like to keep working with you, but only if you're ready to try and take this to the next step."

Boy, I don't want to. Because what I need to do is going to suck emotionally. "Yeah. I think so."

"Okay then. Our next session, we're going to start over and see where we can end up."

"Yeah."

"Is there anything else you need before I let you go?"

I can't help but try and lighten the mood a bit. "Dating advice? Any ideas how can I make this better with Andie?"

Dee chuckles. "I know you'll think of something."

Great. I guess there are some things a therapist can't help you with.

We hang up, I toss my phone on my desk and press the heels of my palms against my eyes. I haven't felt this mentally or physically exhausted after a call in years. Being in the dark helps, like being wrapped in a cocoon.

Maybe my instinct to take things slow with Andie is the right one. I mean, we don't really know each other that well. And yes, there is clearly some mutual sexual attraction between us, but that doesn't mean we need to act on it or move beyond what we've done. This is something we'll clearly have to talk about tonight.

For now, I need to find my inner demon.

I open my recording software and get to work on the line readings. I long ago gave up trying to figure out what some of these games are about based on the lines. Sometimes I'm right, but when I receive a description of the game's plot, it doesn't always make sense until I see the final product. I provide several different readings to give the game developer some options based on the atmosphere they choose for the scene. I've fallen deep into the well of my work when I notice the time.

Shit, Mia will be home any minute now.

Saving my latest recording, I close everything down and step out into the living room, cringing at how bright it is, just as the front door opens and Mia races in.

"Hey, baby."

"Dad, I had the *best* day!" She drops her backpack at the door where she kicks off her shoes. "I was going to go to the library at lunch to watch videos on my phone like normal, but then I had three girls from drama ask me to come hang out. They've seen our videos! And they were asking me all sorts of questions and want to hang out online later. They even gave me the link to their Discord server." She flops down on the couch and giggles. "I think they actually like me."

Mia has friends—not a lot of them, but some good ones. She's never been super popular in school, which is something I know she's talked about in her therapy sessions. And while I'd like nothing more than to believe these girls are genuine with their interest in Mia, I'm skeptical.

"What do you mean they've watched our videos?"

"Dad, we're like, crazy popular on TikTok. They wanted to know if you and Andie were dating, and where we're going to film next and stuff. I don't know and didn't want to lie to them, so I tried to be coy and said I didn't want to give anything away. They think you two are super cute together and think you're like a real couple and everything."

It's strange seeing Mia this excited, and more than a little concerning. "Baby, are you okay? You're not going on an up-swing, are you?"

She waves me away but doesn't look me in the eyes. She pulls out her phone and starts scrolling. "I'm awesome. Why can't you just be happy for me?"

Sunlight streams from the window and streaks across her body, washing away the blue of her shirt. Her face is pale, and her lips are a tight line. Shit, I'm screwing everything up today.

"I am happy for you." I add extra enthusiasm in my voice. I've been down this road with her before. It's best to accept what she says at face value, though I know her mood will likely take a turn for the worst later. Is that the right thing to do? No idea. But it's how we manage this rocky road together. Right now, I'm too exhausted to do anything else. I head to the kitchen and pick up the stack of old take-out menus we've collected over the years. "What did you want for supper tonight?"

"Can we get Thai?" She looks up from her phone and smiles.

The tightness in my chest loosens, making it easier to breathe. "Sure. The usual?"

"Yup."

Someday I really need to learn how to make some of these dishes myself. "So, what do you think we should film tomorrow?"

Mia doesn't respond immediately, and I worry that her good mood is already starting to crash. It's brutal not knowing if these swings are a part of her depression and anxiety, or if she's behaving like a normal sixteen-year-old with all the struggles that come along with that.

Pulling out her phone, she starts scrolling. "I was thinking maybe we should record a bunch on Andie's camera like she suggested and then I can upload them one at a time later. Then we won't need to run around everyday recording."

"Practical. I'll mention it to Andie tonight when I give her a call."

"Or the two of you can go and record some stuff. I don't always have to be there."

"Well, our channel is called MAnd*M*. It's not as fun without you there."

She shrugs. "I'm in school, and you two can do some when I'm not available."

This is starting to feel more like a trap, but I'm not in the mood to prod her and potentially start a fight. "Only if you're certain."

Mia sits up and finally looks my way. "Do you like her?"

"Yeah, of course I do. I wouldn't bother running around the city filming things with her if I didn't like her."

"You know what I mean. Do you *like* her?"

"I ... I don't know, baby." Ah, I should have realized this would come up sooner or later. "Would it bother you if I did?"

Where she was previously excited by the prospect of me showing a romantic interest in Andie, I hope she still feels the same way. Instead, Mia shifts awkwardly on couch. "I don't really need another mom."

"We're nowhere near that particular option."

"You should pretend that you're both into one another though. It's great for the views."

Whoa. "That sounds like pretty cynical thing to do."

She shrugs again. "Lots of influencers do it. People like to speculate about you two, so you should do more of that."

"I won't do it if it upset you, baby. You're far more important to me than any online account."

"I know." She gets to her feet, but instead of heading to her room, she comes into the kitchen and gives me a hug.

Wrapping my arms around her, I squeeze her hard, kissing the top of her head. I hate that her life is so difficult, that I can't snap my fingers and make everything better, smoother for her. But I know I won't do her any favors by constantly coming to her rescue. Life needs some edges to help us become resilient and able to navigate the rocky roads that we inevitably travel on.

That doesn't mean I want to see her struggle.

When she finally pulls back, the tension in her body seems to have faded. "Seriously, you two should do some videos without me. It's hard to flirt with a third wheel around. And ... you two *are* cute to watch together."

"I'm going to talk to her tonight when she's done teaching. I'll mention it."

"Okay." Mia smiles.

"Are you sure you're okay? That was quite the emotional rollercoaster we just took."

"I'm ..." She lets out a huff. "Yeah. It's just I spent all day with Brianna and her crew—they're like the girls everyone wants to be around. And they kept asking me all these questions and stuff. I was also talking to some ... people online about the account. It was a lot."

"You don't owe them anything. Anybody. Remember that, okay?"

"Okay." She steps back and turns toward her backpack. "I better go do my homework. Don't forget to order supper."

"Calling now. You sure about Andie?"

She sighs dramatically. "Love you."

"Love you too." I go in search of my phone to order food, ignoring the fact that having Mia's kind-of blessing to spend some alone time with Andie eases some of the tension I hadn't realized I've been holding.

While she might not be ready for Andie to be a mom figure, she clearly likes her. And maybe, just maybe, having Mia's blessing is what I need to allow me to take that next step with Andie.

This time, I might even kiss her.

TWENTY-TWO

Andie

Lucy is sitting front and center in the classroom when I arrive for class. She isn't giving me her normal mischievous smile, nor are Fatima or Ronald sitting with her. She has her laptop open, arms crossed, and her gaze locked on me.

I should probably say something, but everyone else in the class seems to be fine, and the vibe isn't off. The air isn't stifling for a change, even with all the computers turned on. While I like to think I have a close relationship with all my students, I'm also not their friend or parent. Letting them have some space on the rare occasion when they need it has worked well for me in the past. There's no reason to change things up now.

The chatter begins to die down when a few people notice my arrival. Chairs scrape, and someone's sneakers squeak as everyone drifts to their chosen locations. I'm aware of Lucy's glare, but I keep from directly looking her way, not wanting to add fuel to whatever fire is burning inside her.

"Good evening, everyone." I begin unpacking my laptop and mouse, plugging in the charging cable and making sure I connect to the school's wi-fi. "I have your self-portrait assignments marked and uploaded into the system. I'm also nearly done with your landscape assignments. There are three of you who haven't uploaded your final files into the portal. Just giving you a heads-up that I'll be finishing the markings by Friday, so you have until then to—"

"Why didn't you tell me you were starting a TikTok account?"

I'm so shocked by Lucy's outburst, I lose my train of thought and stumble against my desk. "Lucy?"

"You and Milo. You started a TikTok account. Doing things around the city."

"This isn't the right time nor place to have this discussion." Given how easily this class gets distracted, I have to keep on track or risk losing another night of instruction. "Tonight, I thought we'd do something a bit different and talk about what settings, gear, and accessories we'd need to take successful astrophotography—"

"You've only posted five videos, and you're already on the main trending page!"

I have to briefly close my eyes to keep my frustration inside. "Lucy, could you please step into the hallway so we can discuss this?"

The words are barely out of my mouth before she's on her feet and halfway to the door. Everyone looks surprised except for Mrs. Babineau, because nothing fazes that woman. All I can do is sigh. "Sorry, folks. Please open the document I uploaded in the portal for tonight's class and start reading. I'll be right back."

Lucy is sitting on the stairs across from our classroom door. For the first time since I walked into my classroom in September, I remember how young she is. She told me on day one that she wanted to take my class while she figures out what she wants to do with her life. Photography seemed to make sense, given her online presence and how many photos and videos she takes. I'm sure coming to school at all had to do with pressure from her parents to get a formal education. Not that she talks much about them, but the occasional comment from her makes it obvious.

"Hey." I shove my hands into my pants pockets and hope I don't look too dorky or too intimidating. "What's going on?"

I half expect Lucy to go off on one of her energetic tirades, so I'm surprised when she laces her hands together and bites down on her lower lip. The unshed tears in her eyes have me moving to sit beside her on the step, close but not touching. "I'm sorry." I'm not exactly sure what I'm apologizing for, but it feels like the right thing to say.

Lucy swipes at her eye with the palm of her hand. "I've spent the past two years building my following and putting out videos that are perfect. I've never hit the trending page. Not once."

God, I want to jump in and tell her how amazing I think her videos are, how funny she is, how talented. Instead, I keep my mouth shut and let her talk.

"You put, like, five videos up and you're already on fire. It's just ..."

"Not fair?" I know Lucy puts every fiber of her being into everything she does online. It breaks my heart that she feels this way. "I'm sorry. I honestly never thought we'd get this popular this quickly."

"It's because you're so cute together." She makes it sound as though it's the worst thing in the world. "You're going to get a shit-ton of sponsorship requests."

"I sure hope so." The words leave my mouth before I have a chance to think about it. When I see Lucy's eyes widen, I know I have to fill her in. "I lost my photography job at Walmart. Because we went viral, I'd developed some young stalkers overnight who showed up at the store and caused trouble. I got fired as a result. If we don't get some sponsorships soon, I'm going to have to find another retail job so I can pay my rent. And I'm not sure how that's going to go."

She leans back and looks at me as though she's seeing me for the first time. "Shit. I'm sorry."

I shrug. "It's not your fault."

"It is. If I'd never posted your picture on TikTok, this wouldn't have happened."

"But I also wouldn't have met Milo, so it wasn't all bad. Besides, we could be a flash in the pan that will disappear tomorrow. You have a huge and loyal following. Mia, Milo's daughter, loves you and your posts."

"Really?"

"Oh yeah!"

Lucy nods, a small smile spreading across her face. "Cool."

The chatter of voices from the classroom gets louder. "We better get back. Mrs. Babineau will take over teaching, and I'll be out of my second job."

"Can't have that." Lucy gets to her feet and bounds back into the classroom without a backward glance.

Well, okay then. Problem solved.

I'm about to stand up when she reappears in the doorway. "Ms. M?"

"Yeah?"

"You and Milo are adorable."

"Thanks." I think?

"You should totally date or something."

"I don't think we're at that point." *I wish we were.*

"You should. When you're with him, you actually look happy." She smiles. "You deserve to be happy."

And with that, she leaves me alone in the hallway, stunned.

MILO TEXTS me about ten minutes after everyone has gone. The janitor is standing outside my classroom waiting for me to go home so he can get to work. I pile everything up, shove what I can into my bag, and unlock my phone to read his message.

You free tomorrow at lunch? We can film then have something to eat?

I don't know if it's because of what Lucy said or if I merely want a repeat of his visit to my place, but my heart begins to pound at the thought of us getting together without Mia present. Standing on the steps to the next main floor, the weight of my messenger bag pulling me off kilter as I clutch a book under my opposite armpit, I fumble thumbing out a response.

> Sure! Thoughts on whale to film? Meat?

His response comes fast.

> ???

I groan.

> Stupid autocorrect. Thoughts on WHAT to film? EAT?

> LOL! I thought maybe I should put myself out there a bit and do something scary.

> Scary? Am I going to like the sound of this?

> The CN Tower.

Every person who's grown up anywhere within a few hours' drive of Toronto has been to the CN Tower on more than one school trip. Being originally not from Toronto, I still find it to be quite the impressive sight whenever I get close. Holly, on the other hand, always makes fun of the "giant concrete phallus" by the lake whenever we go out. At night, they display light patterns up the side of the tower, casting magnificent colors across the sky. It's beautiful.

But scary?

Milo, are you scared of heights?

Terrified.

Oh, this will be interesting.

This will be amazing. I can't wait!!!

Is that too many exclamation marks? I delete one and hit send, hoping I don't come across as cheering on his doom. A group of students from another class comes clamoring up the stairs behind me, a reminder that I still have to get home tonight. I move to the side and continue to type.

Mia okay?

The last thing I want is for him to feel any more guilt about spending time with me when he needs to be there for his daughter.

The pause stretches on to the point of being uncomfortable, without the benefit of any bouncing dots to indicate that he's typing. When it doesn't look like he's going to say anything else right away, I shove my phone back into my purse and trudge up the stairs to the main floor and out the doors to the street. The evening air had taken a turn, several degrees cooler than when I'd arrived. Pulling my coat closed I head for the bus stop, my mind wandering as I walk.

I don't want to be selfish with Milo's time. The longer I spend with him, the more I realize how hard it must be to care for someone with mental health challenges. Harder for Mia, being the one living that life, but Milo's struggles are equally apparent.

I pull my phone out again once I get onto the bus that will take me home. I missed the notification of Milo's response. The words nearly break my heart when I read them.

Rough evening. I'll see you tomorrow.

There might not be much I can do to help him with that, but at the very least I can be there for him as a friend. And I have to accept that while I want to see where things go between us, it might never happen. His commitment is to his daughter; it's something I admire and respect. But he might not have the time or inclination for a relationship beyond that.

Sighing, I look up and find the CN Tower glowing in the distance.

TWENTY-THREE

Milo

For once, I'm not late. Not that I'm stupidly early either, which would be hell, standing beneath the giant red tower entrance sign waiting for Andie to come. I mean, being here without Andie as people pass by is almost more than I can handle already. I've been outside of my condo way more in the past few weeks doing TikTok videos with Andie than I've been in the last year. Sometimes I feel as though every eye in the city is on me, judging me for some reason or another.

He's too creepy.

Too fat.

Too weird.

I know guys are supposed to be super confident about this sort of thing. Toxic masculinity and all that. I rarely care about other's opinions of who I am as a person; they're not friends or family, so their opinions are irrelevant. But given that I'm now apparently a recognizable online person, I worry more about those perceptions and how they might impact my life.

Really, I'm anxious that Andie won't show up.

Worst case, Mia and I go up the tower together. We look around for a bit before coming down and getting food to bring home. That's literally the worst thing that can happen. And yet I'm still concerned that something more important has come up for Andie and our recording time will be pushed aside. That would be disappointing.

Yup, that's what it would be.

Mia has wandered away from the ticket booth and over toward the Ripley's Aquarium doors. It's getting cooler now that we're into October, but Mia insisted she's fine with a T-shirt and yoga pants. I wasn't about to argue with her, once again tamping down on my parental instincts to wrap her up in a jacket. I let her do her own thing.

Last night with Mia was rough. After dinner she went into her room to do her homework, and everything appeared to be fine. But then I was texting Andie and the next thing I knew, I heard Mia sobbing in her bedroom. I went in and found her laying on her side on the floor, a blanket pulled up over her head. I crawled onto the floor behind her and held her while she cried. Once she calmed down, she wasn't willing to tell me what was going on. Sometimes there isn't a reason for her anxiety to spike, but the crying always crushes me.

All I want to do is make things better.

This morning, she came out of her room and gave me a hug. "Sorry."

"Baby, you have nothing to apologize for. What was going on?"

She shrugged. "I had some intrusive thoughts. I'm just stressed with midterms and stuff."

High school is brutal for most kids, worse for those who have mental health struggles. She's a great student, and I knew this morning she'd be better served to have a mental health day and come with us to film than she would sitting in a classroom. What I didn't do was tell Andie that Mia would be here. Not that I think she'll care, but after everything we shared in the last few days, I feel like we've lost an opportunity to build on this thing between us.

I'm pacing when I see Andie come down the stairs next to the Roger's Centre toward me. My shoulders relax and I wave when she looks in my direction. "Hey!"

"Hey back."

She's wearing black jeans and a loose-flowing green shirt that hugs her breasts perfectly. Her black jacket is open, her ever-present camera bag slung across her body. I don't know what it is about her, but every time I see her for the first time after an absence, I just stare at the glow that seems to envelop her entire being. We're out in the daylight, but it looks as though a higher power has taken a magical highlighter and colored her so she stands out from the rest of the crowd shifting around us.

I'm little more than a moth hovering around her.

"Is that Mia over there?" Andie nods in the direction she wandered off. "Is she okay?"

"Rough night, so I thought it best if she took a mental health day and came with us." I wonder now if it was a mistake not mentioning it sooner. "That's okay, right?"

Andie's eyes widen. "Oh my God, of course. We're a trio! The Three Musketeers and all that. You never have to worry about her coming with us. I'd be more worried if she wasn't here."

"It's just—" I take a step closer to her, my gaze sliding to her hand that's clutching her camera bag strap across her chest. "The last time I saw you in person, things didn't ... I didn't ..."

"Hey." She lets go of the strap and presses her hand to my chest. "It's okay."

Her gaze is soft, and I desperately want to believe her sincerity.

"Andie!" Mia comes bounding over, her brown ponytail bouncing and swinging. "Are you ready for the elevator? Dad's going to freak."

"So he mentioned last night." Andie looks between us. "Are you really that scared?"

Mia starts cackling. All I can do is sigh. "I have to hire someone to go up stepladders for me."

Andie's mouth falls open as Mia continues to laugh. "But you live on, like, the fourteenth floor of your building. You have massive widows that I've seen you look out of."

"What you haven't seen him do is go near them." Mia bumps my shoulder with her own. "He gets bad vertigo."

My legs go numb, my head spins, and my stomach threatens to empty its contents is what really happens. "This will be fine."

"It will make for great content." Mia pulls out her phone with her e-ticket on it. "I'm going in."

Andie looks horrified. "Why are we doing this again?"

"She's right, it will make great content. Plus, I'll get bonus points from my therapist for going out and doing a thing that scares me. I like to make Dee happy." It's only sort of a lie. I spent hours last night lying in bed thinking about how I can take some sort of control in my life. Face the various fears that sway me. This might not be what Dee has in mind, but it's a place to start.

Andie hesitates, clearly trying to process the insanity I just laid out for her. "Well then, let's go make Dee happy."

We fall into step. I show the attendant our e-tickets and we walk inside. I came to the CN Tower once before on a school trip. While my friends excitedly chatted as the long line for the elevators wound past signs on walls talking about the history of the tower and how it was built, I'd stood there with a growing sense of dread. Cramming the maximum number of junior high kids into an elevator with a window that showed the entirety of the city the higher up you went, sent me into a panic. I never went beyond the inner room of the tower once we reached the top, and I came back to the ground the moment the teachers said it was okay. I swore once I got back down that I'd never, *ever*, do that again.

And here I find myself once again marching toward my doom. This time willingly.

Mia jumps in front of us when we reach the line, her camera in our faces. "So, you two, are you excited about going up to the top of the CN Tower?"

"You know, I've never actually been up." Andie laughs at Mia's surprised gasp. "I've lived in this city for years now, and I've just never gone. I'm really excited to see what it's like and what pictures I can take from so high up."

"I'm pumped." I smile as best I can, but I have no doubt the entirety of TikTok will see my lies.

Mia hits pause on the recording and turns to look around and get some other shots. "I think we can probably get a few videos from here that we can post. The more content the better."

"Great. Everyone will be able to watch my emotional breakdown in multiple parts."

Andie bumps her shoulder against mine. "It will be okay. I'm here to help."

Strangely, that does make me feel better.

True to her word, Andie keeps me engaged in chatter as we make our way through the line. It isn't as busy as it is in the summer months, but there's still a steady stream of people coming to bear witness to Toronto from very high up. We're doing well until a group of students comes into the room. Their shouts echo against the concrete.

The sound draws Mia's attention, and she takes a step closer to us. "School trip," she whispers.

"You're here with parental permission." I glance over. "I'm willing to lie and say we're from out of town."

"Dad, most of them are probably on TikTok. They might recognize us."

As much as I hate seeing her like this, there's a hard truth we all have to acknowledge when it comes to what we're doing with this account. "Baby, that's kind of the point."

"Yeah." She doesn't sound convinced and keeps glancing their way as we move along.

Thankfully, none of the students are put into the elevator with us, which means Mia is able to fully focus on the fact I'm about to lose my shit. She pulls her phone out and holds it up to my face. "Scared yet?"

"No."

"Liar."

"I'm a bit nervous."

Mia swings the phone over to Andie. "Scared?"

"Hell, no. I'm excited! I've always wanted to come up here." She gives the camera two thumbs up.

"Dope."

"Welcome, everyone." The attendant controlling the car smiles and we all quiet down. He points at the floor. "If you look down, you'll notice the transparent panel in the floor so you can see just how high up we're going as we move. This is North America's first and the world's highest glass-floor elevator."

"Oh God." Everyone turns to look at me, but I'm too freaked out to care.

The attendant doesn't look surprised when the elevator starts with a small jerk. "Here we go. It's quite the sight."

My racing heart tightens my chest. It becomes difficult to breathe. I go through every trick Dee had taught me to keep myself calm, but they don't work. Sweat beads on my forehead as my head spins. My gaze is involuntarily drawn to the retreating ground beneath my feet. We were rising so high so quickly, I want to black out.

The feeling of Andie's fingers sliding through mine help ground me, and for a moment I'm able to catch my breath.

She leans in close, her voice soft as she speaks. "I find it helpful to pick a point outside and focus on it. Just one thing to look at. That way your senses don't get overwhelmed by everything out there."

"Okay." I pick the top of an office building that's visible through the narrow elevator side-window and lock my eyes on it. "It's easier when I don't look down."

"Yup. Just keep focusing on that and everything will be okay."

"Promise?"

"Promise." She gives my hand a squeeze. "I don't mind looking down so I can describe it for you. Oh cool. They've put two outlines of sharks on the roof of the Ripley's Aquarium. That's smart. The side of the tower makes it look more like we're getting squirted up a concrete tube. You can really see the cars on the road, but they almost look fake from this height."

The longer Andie speaks, describing what she's seeing, the easier the trip becomes. Seeing the ride from her perspective, having her hand laced with mine, somehow feels more intimate than the night I answered her booty call. Before I know it, the ding of the doors opening sends a wave of relief through me. I step into the room and am immediately assaulted with people standing around, and the loud din of talking. Sucking in a deep breath, I skirt around everyone in my path and beeline toward the nearest wall. I currently can't see out of the tower, which makes it easier to calm down.

I laugh as my face heats. "Well, I survived the elevator."

Mia's phone is pointed directly at me. "Your followers are super proud of you." The tell-tale sound of her posting the clip makes me want to cry. "And so am I," she says.

That feels nice to hear.

Andie is a few steps away leaning against the bright yellow sign that fills most of the opposite wall. Despite the distance and steady stream of people walking between us, it's obvious she's keeping an eye on me. No doubt she wants to know if she'll have to drag my ass back home after this. "We don't have to go outside quite yet. There's lots to see here first. They have a bunch of facts about the tower we can read."

"I'm going to look around. Maybe see how expensive the restaurant is." Mia's grin looks genuine. "I'll be back in a few."

Andie dodges a group of school kids and comes back to my side. "She looks excited."

"It's been a long time since we've done something like this."

Not exactly a great parenting move on my part. "I've been so wrapped up in making sure she was okay, I kind of forgot that we both need to live our lives."

"COVID screwed a lot of us up."

"We were screwed up long before that."

What's scarier? Talking about your ex-wife and failed marriage, or facing your debilitating fear of heights? "Hey, let's go outside."

Andie cocks her head to the side. "Are you sure?"

"I can see that it's screened in, which is somehow less terrifying than looking out the window. And if I do that, then I'll feel like I've accomplished something." She nods, but before she moves away, I grab her hand. "I'd appreciate the support."

Her entire demeanor lights up when she smiles. "Of course."

I trail a bit behind her, texting Mia so she knows where we went, as we walk toward the door that leads to the outside walkway. For safety reasons, it's enclosed so no one will fall, but that does little to slow down the wind that whips around us. There's no way I can walk to the edge and look down, but I get close enough that I'm able to look out across the city. "You can see so much of the lake."

Andie pulls out her camera and snaps a few pictures. I don't blink when she turns around and takes a few of me as well. "To commemorate the occasion of your brave excursion."

"I'm not brave."

"Of course you are. You're one of the bravest people I've ever met."

I think she's going to stop there, but instead she looks down at her camera, her thumb rubbing the top of the button.

"You have been chasing a better life for yourself. You go to therapy. You help Mia do what she needs to do to become a more confident woman. You've found a career that clearly makes you happy, and that's just so amazing to see."

The wind blows her hair wildly around her head, as though she's a superhero flying to the rescue of some poor soul who needs her. My heart breaks for the pain I see. I reach out and cup her face in my hands. When she looks into my eyes, I make sure to hold her gaze long enough for her to see my sincerity.

"You're not too old to follow your dreams."

Unshed tears pop into her eyes. "I'm forty-five."

"*Only* forty-five."

"I'm ..." She closes her eyes, but I won't let her pull away. She swallows hard. "I'm actually terrified about what will happen if I try."

"You can't be scared of failing."

She laughs. "I'm more scared of succeeding."

"What?"

"It's—" She gently takes my hands from her face and waves at something over my shoulder. "It's a conversation to have later."

"There you are!"

Turning from Andie, I smile at an excited Mia. "Hey, baby."

"I want to film you on the glass floor."

"And now I think it's time to leave." I manage to get two steps away before both Andie and Mia catch my arms.

"Dad, look." Mia can't quite hide her amusement as she tugs me toward the group of people standing on what I assume is the aforementioned floor. "It's not as bad as you think. You can see through, but there are people below us as well. Look."

In my panic, it hadn't registered that there are two floors to the observation deck. Mia stops me close to where I can see the glass and points. People are walking over the glass. One less brave man is standing on the small section of tile floor between the glass panes. Another younger person is sitting fully on the floor, phone out, taking a picture of whatever is directly below him.

My heart races and my palms sweat as my brain makes up its mind to do this. My life has been a seesaw of emotions and events, none of which I've been able to predict. I logically know the CN Tower isn't about to fall apart simply because I finally made the trip. I hadn't expected my marriage to fall apart or my that daughter would be faced with steep mental health challenges either.

Andie and Mia are standing in front of me. Life isn't easy, and if I don't try to push myself on occasion, then what kind of man—or father—am I?

Sucking a deep, not-so-calming breath in, I close my eyes for a moment before letting the words spill from me. "I will go down there. I will stand on the glass. You can get a video, but be warned that I will last about three seconds and I won't do it twice. Make sure you're recording."

Mia squeals. "Oh my God, Dad. This will be amazing!"

Andie grins. "Want me to hold your hand?"

If that question had come from my ex-wife, it would have been mocking. From Andie, it's genuine and comforting.

"Fuck yes." I grab hold and yank her toward the steps to the lower level, not wanting her to back out.

In case *I* back out.

The students who were behind us in the line are now all rushing around the observation deck. Their buzzing chaos is an adequate distraction that allows me to mentally distance myself from what I'm about to do. The entire floor isn't glass, which also gives me time to pump myself up, build the huge measure of courage I need to make this happen.

I check to make sure the way forward is clear. Closing my eyes, I move forward. Nausea rises up my throat and it feels as though my legs are rubber. One step, two steps, three, until I'm sure I must be standing on the glass floor.

To her credit, Andie never loosens her grip on my hand. She follows me until I come to a stuttered stop. "You okay?" Her voice is comforting.

"Are we standing over my doom?" I have my eyes squeezed shut so hard, my vision is red tinged and filled with floaters.

"We sure are."

"Is Mia recording?"

"I sure am!" Her voice is directly in front of me.

It doesn't matter that I haven't opened my eyes yet; the weakness in my knees has already started. Rather than fight it, I sit, dragging Andie with me. "Tell me if I'm in anyone's way."

"Ah ... that's not a problem."

Sucking in a breath, I wait a few moments before I think I won't faint and tilt my head down. "Okay. One, two ... two and a half—"

"Go, Dad!"

"Three."

My stomach turns at the initial vertigo of seeing the roof of the aquarium below us. "So. High. Up." My voice is so shaky it doesn't even sound like me.

I nearly jump out of my skin when a rousing cheer explodes around me. The students are all watching, applauding my accomplishment. It takes a moment to realize that a bunch of them are recording me sitting on the glass floor, no doubt looking as though I'm about to vomit.

"I didn't want to add more stress by letting you know about our audience." Andie's whispered confession against my ear sends a tingle through me. "You're far braver that I've ever been."

Ignoring our observers, I look into her eyes. There's been something bothering her—certainly not the height—and I wish we'd been able to talk about it.

She cocks her head slightly and gives me a knowing look, like she somehow heard my thoughts. "Maybe another time."

"Okay." I glance around and force a smile. "I'm not sure my legs work."

"I'll get you."

Andie stands and holds out both her hands to take mine, yanking me to my feet. The momentum gets me going and I don't stop until I reach the elevator and hit the button.

"Aww are we going?" Mia genuinely sounds disappointed.

"Baby, you can stay up here as long as you want. I need to get back to solid ground."

Mia looks back over her shoulder at the kids running around. "Naw, it's fine."

The elevator doors open and another group of people steps out. We wait for them to exit before the three of us filter in. The attendant smiles. "Have a good visit?"

"It was awesome. Thanks," Andie says as she pulls up her camera and snaps a few photos of the city before we begin our descent.

Mia spins around and rests back against the window. "Dad, we should totally go to Canada's Wonderland and ride some of the rollercoasters next."

"God, no." I thought my daughter loved me.

"Oh, come on. You managed this—going there won't be any worse."

Andie's shooting me an amused expression, but she clearly has no idea how big a problem that single request is. I somehow hold in my sigh. "Rollercoasters have three things that I hate. Crowds, heights, and the possibility of getting trapped someplace you can't easily escape. I just ... no."

"Dad, how is that any different from what we just did?"

"I'm in a building here. With spots I can pretend I'm safe."

Mia drops her head back and lets out a frustrated groan. "Sometimes you suck."

"How about we let him recover from this traumatic experience before we encourage him into another," Andie says, putting her lens cap back on her camera.

I don't like how she said *encourage*. "Maybe next time we can do something that terrifies you instead."

"Yeah! What are you scared of, Andie?"

She's still looking over the city when she says, "Nothing."

And that's the first time Andie has lied to me.

TWENTY-FOUR

Andie

W*hat are you scared of, Andie?*
    I lie awake in bed with Mia's question turning over and over in my head to the point of near insanity. I hadn't intended to lie, and truly, I didn't … But that isn't the truth either. There are tons of things that terrify me. No, not heights, bugs, or anything like that. I might not be a huge fan of spiders, but we've at least come to an agreement of sorts over the years.

Yes, there are things that scare me. I just don't know what they are.

Shit, that's not true either.

I know when something scares me, I just can't articulate exactly how it makes me feel in the moment. Seeing Milo sit down on the glass floor, his eyes screwed shut—that was difficult for him. Not just confronting his fear of heights, but doing it in the most bad-ass way possible. The moment people recognized us, I had to force my attention on Milo to drag it away from the gnawing dread that crept up inside me.

Everyone was watching, gauging, and recording our every action. I tried to ignore them and keep Milo front and center while we sat there. My irrational internal voice though, oh, she had a fucking field day yelling at me, telling me how much I was screwing up the video, or was making this worse for him. That I shouldn't have allowed his moment to become a spectacle, making him the center of attention when he didn't want to be. A part of me expected him say he was over all of it and ready to deactivate our TikTok account so he could go back to his normal life.

And everything was going perfectly fine!

I haven't checked out the account to see how well those videos are doing, but I have no doubt our followers are eating them up. Milo was so brave, his face so animated—no wonder everyone was looking at him. Terrified, he literally walked right up to his fear and faced it. Here I am, sitting in bed and moping because I'm unwilling to even *acknowledge* what scares me, let alone face it.

A tear escapes the corner of my eye and slides into my hairline near my ear. "Idiot."

So far, we haven't received any offers for sponsorships. That means I've gone nearly a month without receiving enough income to stay afloat. My rent is due, which means my bank account is about to take another hit. I won't be able to continue this way much longer before the need to get another job smacks me squarely in the face. The problem of being recognized is only growing with each successive video we post, which means my original concern of being stalked at my job—no doubt it will be in retail—will likely end up the same as what happened at Walmart. I'll soon need to take the chance, get a second job and hope for the best.

The alternative is giving up and moving back home.

I mean, the thought of having to go home after all these years makes my stomach bottom out and my chest tighten to the point of pain. But it's not so much about moving home as it is finally admitting that my dream of becoming an artist, a world-renowned photographer who's respected by her peers, has failed. That I have failed.

Have I?

Like Milo said, I'm only forty-five years old. It's not like my life stopped when I became middle aged. I have way more life experience, and I like to think I know myself better now than I did back before I left for college. Even if I sometimes don't want to admit it. Lots of people restart, bound gracefully into a second phase of their professional lives at ages far older than mine. I'm not so different from them. All I need to do is make a choice.

And that's terrifying.

In the morning—I'll worry about it then. Rolling on to my side, I pull my blankets up to my ears, screw my eyes shut, and stubbornly don't move until I finally drift off to sleep.

MY PLAN for self-reflection is sidelined by an email from Dean Robichaud's office. He's scheduled another appointment with me later this week and the reason has been left blank. I fire off a text to Milo the second I see it.

> Dude, my boss wants to see me again.

Rarely anything good comes out of a meeting with Mr. Robichaud.

Milo doesn't immediately respond, which means he's probably busy helping Mia before she goes to school. If she's able to go today. My heart breaks for her and all the challenges she faces on a daily basis. I wish there was something I could do to help them. Anything. But life isn't that easy, and mental health challenges are some of the hardest things in the world to deal with.

I get dressed, have breakfast, and sit at the kitchen table to check my emails while I wait for Milo to get back to me. I've set up a fresh email for our account, not wanting to blast my personal account with spam but wanting to ensure that we catch anyone who might want to sponsor us. There are tons of people reaching out to us, most of them obviously bot accounts.

What I didn't expect to see are the copious amounts of fan mail. The first few confuse the hell out of me. *Hey, I love the two of you! You're so cute together! OMG plz keep posting!!!* Some of them are adorable, others border on creepy. More than a few have opinions on what they perceive our relationship to be and want to know incredibly personal details.

Dear God, some of this is out of line.

I'm nearly through the first two pages of emails when my phone buzzes, and Milo's name pops up as an incoming call.

"Hey!" *Jeeze, calm down. You're going to scare him off.* "How's it going?"

"Ah, okay. I think. Weird morning with Mia."

That's never good. "She okay?"

"Yeah. She was really excited about going to school today. Which isn't something I'm normally faced with." He pauses. I can hear him pouring what I assume is his morning coffee. "I hate that her being happy is so foreign that I get worried when she is."

"You know her better than anyone. I guess you have to trust your gut with this."

"Maybe. Or maybe I've been focused on doom and gloom for so long I've forgotten what joy looks like." He chuckles and it does something pleasant to my insides. "What's going on with your boss?"

I look around my apartment, annoyed that I let piles of stuff build once again. "No idea. He booked a meeting with me for Friday but didn't say what it's about."

"That's not a normal thing, I take it?"

"No. He terrifies me."

The fridge's compressor turns on, startling me. It's no louder than normal, so it shouldn't have made me jump. Maybe I'm more freaked out than I realize.

Milo laughs. "Hey, you were the one who said nothing scares you."

I groan, lean back in my seat and run my free hand through my tangled hair. "Well, nothing that's normal." The last thing I want to talk about is my ongoing existential dread about failing as a human being. "I mean ... of course there are things that scare me."

"Really? What?"

"Spiders."

"Andie ..."

It's my go-to answer whenever anyone asks me this question. It's not exactly a lie—they're just not my favorite—but I know that it isn't what he's looking for. "And maybe I'm terrified that I'm not as good a photographer as I think I am." Tears instantly pop up in my eyes and my throat constricts, forcing me to swallow several times. "Wow, I don't think I've ever said that out loud before."

"That's impostor syndrome talking." His little huff doesn't sound dismissive. No, if anything, it sounds like he's experienced this feeling himself. "I know that this won't exactly mean much coming from me, but I think you're an amazing photographer. You see the world in a way that I can't. And you're able to capture moments that make me see exactly what I think you're feeling. That's ... that's a major talent."

My cheeks are hot, and I have to smear away the traitorous tear that escaped. "Thank you."

"You're welcome." I hear a soft clunk on the other end. "In fact, I think our next TikTok adventure should be you and I going out and you showing me how to take photos."

"I don't think anyone would want to see me do—"

"One of your photos is how everyone discovered us. It only stands to reason people would love to see you teach me. Maybe you can do promo for your college program and make your boss happy with you before his mysterious meeting."

It's a really good idea. "Ah, sure. Did you want to wait for Mia and do it later?"

"She mentioned this morning she's been invited to a study session with some girls from her English class. We'll be on our own."

As much as I enjoy our times with Mia, the thought of having some one-on-one time with Milo is immensely appealing. "Okay."

"Yeah?"

"Yeah." I take a quick peek out the window for a weather check. "I'll come to your place and we can walk around the park?"

"Excellent. I have some meetings this morning, but we can start after lunch."

We chat a bit longer before he has to run to his meeting. By the time I put my phone down, I feel beyond emotionally drained. I've never been to therapy before, but I imagine the aftermath of a session would feel a bit like this. I said *the thing* out loud—that I don't think I'm very good at my job. And Milo acknowledged it before telling me how my photos make him feel.

It's a gift I hadn't realized I'd needed.

So, I'll get my camera, mentally pull out my beginner lessons, and share my love of photography with the man who's quickly becoming the most important person to me.

And that's a realization almost as terrifying as my fear of failing.

TWENTY-FIVE

Andie

I shouldn't be surprised when Milo texts me saying he wants me to come to the condo instead of meeting at the park. While we've been doing a lot of *outside* activities, I know it's probably quite hard on him to be constantly on the go. Both Holly and my sister are more introverted than I am, so I'm used to sometimes changing direction on the things we've had planned.

The smell of something baking wafts down the corridor the moment I step out of the elevator. Each step I take toward Milo's place only reaffirms that whatever the amazing smell is, its origin is his condo. The moment he opens his door, the scent of baked bread hits me, making my mouth water.

"I thought you didn't cook."

"I don't. Not really. But I do bake." He makes a beeline toward the counter, leaving me to take my shoes off and hang up my coat in the small closet by the door. Milo cleans up the remnants of spilled flour off the island counter. "Cooking is art and baking is science. At least that's how I always think of it. When my brain is stuck on something, baking helps me push it away so I can focus on the very important task of making bread."

The sun fills the entirety of the condo, giving everything a warm glow. Between that and the bread, being here feels like a warm hug around my heart. Setting my camera gear by the couch, I quickly join him at the island and slide onto one of the stools.

I take a deep inhale and hope I'm not drooling. "Bread is very important. Vital." I'm going to die if I don't get a chunk of it right the hell now. "You've been holding out on me."

He shrugs. "It's just bread."

"My mom always bakes her own. One of the few things she and I could always agree on was homemade is better than store-bought." As he bends down to check the oven, an idea hits me. "Wait!"

I pull out my phone and open TikTok to record. "Today, Milo has revealed that he has a secret talent for baking bread! I'm excited to try it."

The moment he knows I'm recording, he straightens and the goofy grin that I now associate with him appears. "Bread is vitally important to a lot of people. Baking is an excellent skill to learn."

"Was this a pandemic talent you picked up?"

"Nope. My grandfather taught me when I was a teen. He told me it would help me pick up chicks."

"Did it work?" I ask, laughing.

He has his oven mitts on, long ones that come nearly up to his elbows. It looks adorable and ridiculous at the same time as he reaches in and pulls one of the loaves from the oven. "Of course. Guys, learn to bake."

I stop recording and post the video as he puts the bread on the cooling rack. "There we go. Upload for the day."

"Excellent."

"What is your brain stuck on today?"

He hesitates, and I can tell that whatever is going on with him is important. The urge to pepper him with questions threatens to overwhelm me. So I bite down on my tongue and wait for him to continue.

"I had quite the email last night after we texted. My agent,

Bruno, sent me a script for a big triple-A video game. I've worked with the company before, mostly doing secondary characters, background sounds and the like. This time they wanted me to give them a sample for the main character, and I've been struggling to find the right voice."

We rarely talk about his job or anything he does outside of our account or Mia. It's nice to see this other part of him—a far more confident Milo than the man who baby-stepped his way across a glass floor for online clout. "What's the character like? How do you normally go about figuring this out?"

"I have my normal default range based mostly on the character's role in the game or show." He rattles off a bunch of random lines in different voices. Had I not been watching him say them, I wouldn't have realized it was Milo. "This guy will need to be different. Unique." He pauses to grab the second loaf from the oven, setting it down beside the other one on the rack in front of me.

Leaning in, I inhale deeply and let the magical smell fill my head. My mouth is watering and I'm strangely at peace. I find myself looking at him in an entirely new light. "You're amazing."

"It's nothing special."

"Are you crazy? I tried to imitate the Kermit the Frog voice for my sister once and it was so bad, she made me swear I'd never do anything like that ever again. You. Are. Awesome!"

"Thank you?" He chuckles. "I've been doing this for so long, I sometimes forget that this is a special skill. Kind of like you and your photography. We take the hard work we've had to put in over the years for granted."

"The problem with being middle aged. We see all the younger people doing cool things and think we're too old to try ourselves, but we're too young to ride off into the sunset."

Milo nods, frowning as he takes off one of his oven mitts. He throws it at me. "You're not too old to try something new. No one is."

The temptation to throw the mitt back is strong, but I instead clutch it to my chest. "I mean, I know I'm not. Not really. But it seems like unless you're in your twenties, or somehow starting over when you're ninety, no one cares."

"Do they need to? Care?"

"No?"

Milo hums. "See, this is the problem with us creative types. Whether we like to admit it or not, a part of our self-worth tends to come from how others receive our art. They don't need to necessarily love it, just acknowledge it."

"I ... ah. Yeah. That makes sense." When no one came to my school art show, it felt as though my heart was rent to pieces. In a small way, it would have been better to have my photos seen by the world and harshly critiqued. That would at least have given me some feedback to work with.

Though at the time, I'm sure I would have seen the criticism as mean.

"Do you ever worry about companies not wanting to work with you any longer? Have them go after a younger talent?"

"Not really. My profession is a bit different in that regard. I'm not reliant on my appearance so as long as my voice fits the character I'm good. But the types of roles I'm being offered have changed over the years." He frowned. "I guess I hadn't thought about why."

Reaching out, I poked the cooling rack with my finger moving it slightly. "What's made this role different then?"

Milo braces his hands along the edge of the island counter and leans closer. "When this role came my way I realized I had a choice. I could keep doing the same thing over and over until I retire, or I could push myself, evolve to the next logical step as a voice actor, and see what I can do. This role is kind of the first step to see if I can make that work."

That makes sense and it explains his creative block. "You're stuck because you're scared that you're going to make the wrong choice and lose the part."

He nods. "Hence, the bread."

I might not know the first thing about character voices, but I know Milo. I get up, toss the oven mitt to him, and retrieve my camera bag from the couch. "Okay, let's try this then. I'll record you doing some voices, playing around as the character. And after, you can watch it back and see which versions you like." When he grins at me, a tingle of pleasure surges through my body.

I look around the open area trying to decide the best place to setup. With as much light spilling in from the windows as there is, I don't need to worry about adding more. Three large Ikea bookcases line the wall beside the windows, books haphazardly arranged within and the occasional frame holding a picture of Mia as a child dotting the shelves.

"I thought you were going to show me how to take pictures?"

"We can still do that. If you want. But it might be difficult for you for learn a new skill if your brain is fixated on something else." I've taught enough classes to realize that.

Milo pulls the apron from around his waist and lays it beside the cooling bread. "Okay. A different approach is exactly the sort of thing that might help."

I didn't bring my tripod with me. Mia has one in her room, I'm not about to invade her privacy by asking Milo to get it. Instead, I grab some books from his bookcase, stack them on the island counter, and set my camera on top. Not perfect, but it will give him ample space to move around.

"Okay, I'll hit record, and you can tell me about the character and try out some voices." I flip the video display around to ensure he's in frame and take a step backward. "Whenever you're ready."

Milo hesitates for a moment. He rubs his hands down the sides of his jeans and steps into the camera's frame. "This character is for a new game. It's an old series that they're trying to reboot, I guess. I played the game when Mia was a toddler and I couldn't get back to sleep after one of her feedings. His name's Max but goes by the moniker Painbringer in the game. In this version, he's a broken man who's trying to rescue his son from demons."

It should sound ridiculous, but he speaks so seriously, so earnestly, that I'm sucked in. "And you're going to play Max?"

"If I get the part. They wanted me to read a monologue from a key moment in the opening scene." He blushes. "I was so excited by the idea, I memorized it last night."

"Now I really want to hear this." I lean with my back against the island counter, the camera to my side, and motion for him to move. "Stand in the space behind the couch. Come forward a bit. There you go."

He follows my directions until he's framed perfectly on the camera's display screen. "Do I get to say action?" Now I'm getting excited. "I've always wanted to say that."

"Go for it."

"Action!"

Milo shakes his head but is clearly amused. "Alright. Just to set the scene a bit, Max is talking to his wife, who has come to tell him that their son is missing but that she doesn't want him to go fight the demons."

Milo drops his chin to his chest and takes a deep breath. He tilts his head to the side and lets out a low rumbling noise that's far deeper than anything I've ever heard come out of him.

"No one else will fucking help us."

My mouth falls open. That can't be Milo talking. The harsh bitterness laced with desperation rips from his throat. He opens his eyes and looks directly at me. A shiver races through me as I hug myself.

"Lani, I promised you ... both of you ... that I've left that life behind. The killing. Chaos. But it's like a fucking blight, stuck to me. Hate and murder and death chase me into the darkness. I'm terrified I'll get lost." His voice cracks slightly. "But I won't let fear stop me. They thought I wouldn't take up my swords again when they took Bastion from us. They were fools."

I don't know who Max is or who he was before now, but by God, I'm on board and ready to dive into battle with him.

"I would have been lost forever in the darkness if it hadn't been for you." Milo swallows hard but doesn't break the intense eye contact we're sharing. "You're my light. My beacon. My love. I love you, Lani. I promise you, there's nothing that hell can throw at me that will keep me from you. I'll be back. With our son. I swear this to you. I swear."

I have never been so aroused by anything before. In. My. Life.

Milo stands straighter, running his hand through his hair, sending the strands this way and that. "That was one voice. I'm still not certain if it's dark enough for him or if they want something more unhinged."

You know the first time you realize your parents are people and not superheroes, or the first time someone you admire makes a mistake? Or the first time someone you previously thought poorly of turns around and does something amazing and recontextualizes their entire being to you? Or when something magical happens and you see someone in an entirely new light?

I'm having that moment with Milo.

Now look, I'm not saying I haven't found him sexy—obviously I have—or that I haven't seen any sort of strength in him. I totally have. But that voice and those words coming out of his mouth? Combined with him having the internal strength to face one of his fears head on in a public manner?

Well, yeah. New eyes.

"Andie?"

I give my head a shake. "Sorry. I ... ah. That was amazing. I ..." The embarrassed laugh that erupts from me is like a pressure valve going off. "I'd buy the game, watch the movie, or anything else involved if that's the voice you're using."

"Really?" A grin splits his face, and any sign of Max disappears. "You don't think I needed to be more menacing? Painbringer is a nasty guy in the previous games, but I think their intention is to humanize him a bit this time around."

I step closer to Milo, shoving my hands in the back pockets of my jeans. "Not at all. I mean, he's talking to the woman he loves. If anything, maybe you need to soften it a bit. Make it a bit more earnest."

When I get about half a foot away, I look up at him. "Say it again."

Milo's gaze roams across my face, stopping on my mouth. He cups my face in his hands then looks directly into my eyes.

"No one else will fucking help us. Lani, I promised you…both of you…that I've left that life behind." Milo swallows hard. "I would have been lost forever in the darkness if it hadn't been for you."

His face inches closer as my heart beats manically in my chest. "That's not the next line," I whisper.

"I know."

My eyes close the moment I feel his breath across my mouth. I open to him, to the press of his lips against mine, to the brush of the tip of his tongue on my bottom lip. The moan that escapes me would be embarrassing if I'd been with it enough to stop and think about it. But the only thing I'm aware of is how gently he's holding my face in his hands, the smell of his aftershave and baked bread, the barely contained desire in his kiss.

I want more. I want to soak in this moment for eternity in case it never occurs again.

Wrapping my arms around his waist, I close the remaining distance between us to feel the warmth of his body. Unlike the character he was pretending to be moments earlier, I know this is the real Milo. His hesitation before every touch, the small gasps of wonder, soft moans of pleasure, all speak of the man who I saw sitting on the bench in the park.

Sliding my hands up his back, I deepen the kiss until my brain no longer seems to function. That's why I don't immediately process the sound of Milo's door lock clicking. He clearly does, stepping away so suddenly I stumble forward. It then registers that there are multiple voices in the outer hallway.

Mia is home. And she brought friends.

I race over to the camera, which is—*shit,* still recording and turn it off as the door swings open. Mia is there with two girls who look far older than the highschoolers I know they are. She's obviously nervous as they follow her in, though that changes to curiosity when she sees me.

"Hey. I didn't know you were over."

"Andie was helping me with some voice work." Milo clears his throat. "Why are you home so early?"

"Ah, it's a half-day today. I told you that this morning." Mia frowns. "We were going to work on our English assignment."

One of the girls with Mia, a tall brunette who has that high school athlete appearance I used to envy back in school, steps past Mia. "Wow, is that bread? Did you bake that for a video?"

Milo has already moved to stand behind the island, his hands on his hips. "Yeah, we ended up doing a quick video. But we should do more. I could do a bunch of baking and Andie can taste test everything."

I felt his hard-on pressing against my belly moments ago, so I have to assume the tremor in his voice has to do with the residual effects of being interrupted.

Sex. We really need to have sex

The tall girl twirls her fingers around a lock of her hair as she kicks her hip out to the side. "You guys are so funny together. I've been watching your TikToks since day one."

"Me too!" The other girl, a slightly shorter version of the first, chimes in. "Your CN Tower vids were amazing. I wish my parents would pull me out of class to do videos."

Mia's eyes widen. "That's ... ah ... not why—"

The tall girl interrupts. "You guys should really have a meet and greet. Or promote other people in your videos."

"Or you can have like a flash mob event or something. I know I'd come to something like that," the other adds. "Really anything where you can have some of your fans meet up. That would be so cool."

Milo laughs, but I can tell he's a bit uncomfortable with the attention. "Thanks for the enthusiasm. We're still figuring some things out. But Mia will let you know if we decide to use any of your ideas."

I watch as Mia practically deflates. "We should probably get to work. The project is due tomorrow."

The taller girl lets out a sigh. "Yeah, I guess we better."

The two girls hesitate to follow Mia to her room; she stands in the doorway waiting for them to come in. The taller girl smiles at us as she turns. "You let me know if you need any help. I have two-hundred-and-eighty thousand followers on my TikTok." She turns and strides past Mia, who glares at us as she shuts the door.

This isn't good.

"If nothing else comes from this, seeing Mia with new friends and getting out there socializing makes it worth it."

Now, I'm not a parent. I don't even play one on TikTok, but I know in my heart that those girls aren't going to be any sort of friends to Mia. "Does she have many friends?"

"Yeah. Well, one or two. I've always encouraged her to get out there and try to meet some other people. It's hard for her, and I can't tell you the last time someone other than her best friend Luna has been over."

Shit. He looks so happy, and I know there's no way he wants to see the bad in the two girls we met for all of five minutes. But I've been on the receiving end of comments from girls like those two when I was in school. So did Cara. While it bothered me, I was too wrapped up in working to earn enough money to buy a camera and afford film for it to care. Cara, on the other hand, came home on more than one occasion sobbing because of some mean girls.

Stepping closer to Milo, ignoring the flare of desire that

blooms inside me due to simple proximity, I lower my voice. "Just keep an eye on them. The tall one could be trying to use Mia to increase visibility on her own account."

Milo recoils. "That's pretty jaded."

"You were one of the popular kids, weren't you?"

"I was the class clown."

"So, you were popular." I roll my eyes. "Just, keep your eyes open. Okay?"

He takes a step back. "She's my daughter. My eyes are always open."

Whoa. "Sorry, I didn't mean to imply that you don't. I just ..." *Time to shut up, Andie.* "Hey, did you want the recording of your monologue? I can send it to you as soon as I get home."

Milo's attention has shifted over to Mia's closed door and the muted sounds of the girls chatting. "Yeah, that would be great. Thanks."

I snatch my camera from the book pile, move around the island, and shove it into my camera bag. The moment brought on by the speech is gone, and I need to give him some space while I get some fresh air. "Maybe we can do our camera lesson another day."

"Andie, I'm—"

I shake my head as I throw on my coat and shoes. "I overstepped. And now I'm mortified, so I'm going to leave before I say something else stupid. I'll talk to you later."

I open the door; his hand touches my shoulder. "Here. Take this." It's one of the loaves of bread.

"Thanks." Hugging the warmth, I retreat home.

TWENTY-SIX

Andie

Friday morning comes far faster than I anticipated. Once again, I'm sitting outside Dean Robichaud's office, and once again the pit of dread has opened in my stomach. While there've been no comments from anyone at the college about my little TikTok side project, that doesn't mean my job isn't at risk. Though, I reviewed the code of ethics on the bus ride here, just in case.

If he brought me here to give me an ultimatum—TikTok or teaching—I honestly don't know which one I'll pick. I mean, teaching has become important to me over the years, not to mention that it's my only source of income. But TikTok has opened so many possibilities, opened my mind to things I could be doing in my life. I don't want to walk away from that either. I don't want to walk away from Milo, despite his current annoyance with me.

I hope he isn't still upset …

No, that's a problem for future Andie to deal with. Right now, my goal is to do my best to sit still and not look like the nervous mess I feel like on the inside. Carly isn't in this morning, which makes everything more intense than my previous visits. I miss her calming presence and ability to set me at ease with a simple smile.

The door to Dean Robichaud's office opens to reveal the man himself. Unlike every other time I've seen him, his tie isn't exactly straight, and his hair is a bit wild. If I didn't know better, I would think he spent the night sleeping in his office. He looks at me with those cold blue eyes of his and motions for me to follow him.

The guest chair is already pulled out, so I sink down on it and try not to implode from nerves. "Good morning."

"Thanks for coming in first thing." His tone is as crisp as ever. "I appreciate you doing so outside of your normal working hours."

"It's not a problem." *Unless you're about to fire me, then it's a serious problem.* "What can I do for you?"

"It's been brought to my attention that you've become a bit of a minor celebrity due to the photo you took. I don't pretend to understand everything, but your social media presence has increased?"

"Yes, it has." My nerves get my mouth moving, and I unload the entire story of what's happened with Milo and myself since the last time I spoke to the dean. "Our TikTok account is apparently quite popular, and we're starting to get some minor promotion requests trickle in every day or two. Nothing much yet beyond local businesses. I checked the school's Code of Ethics and Business Conduct policy, and so far, nothing I've accepted violates my conduct as an employee." My cheeks and lips tremble as I force my smile to remain on my face.

For his part, Dean Robichaud only nods. "I assumed as much, but I appreciate the confirmation. It's good to know you're at least aware of potential conflicts. That's more than I can say about some other staff."

When he runs his hand through his hair, the illusion of the frigid man shatters. I lean forward slightly. "Are you okay?"

"I'm fine." And the mask snaps back into place. "The reason I asked you here today is, quite frankly, to take advantage of your rising celebrity."

"Oh?" The honesty is a bit of a shock. "For what?"

"The college is having a fundraiser in three weeks, and the board has insisted that we bring in as many big-name celebrities as we can muster. Alumni, local politicians, social media personalities ..." He looks at me from across the top of his glasses.

"I see." At least he's upfront about it. "What is it exactly you'd want me to do?"

"You and your partner would come and mingle at the event. Lots of people will want their pictures taken with you. You can promote your program, the school, encourage the attendees to donate as much as they can. You'll get a fancy meal and lots of wine as payment."

I've always wanted to attend something like this. The school's fundraising events are the stuff of legend with the staff, and very few of us ever get invited. Certainly not part-time photography instructors. "I'd love to come. I'll have to check with Milo about whether he'd be up for it." Mingling in a crowd of strangers is no doubt Milo's definition of hell. "He has some family obligations that might prevent him from coming."

"Fine. But you're coming. Make sure you dress up. I'll have Carly send you the rest of the details." And then he turns to his computer.

Standing, I frown. "Thanks." He doesn't say anything else, so I take a step backward toward the door. "Are you sure you're okay?" I know it's dumb to ask, to stick my nose where it really doesn't belong. And yet, there's something so off with him, I can't help wanting to know.

His fingers stop moving. They hover above his keyboard. He doesn't look at me, but I can tell he's thinking. "I ... maybe." He clears his throat. "Thank you for asking."

I nod and leave, knowing there will be nothing further coming from him. He's a grown man, and I have no doubt whatever is going on, he'll be able to work it out sooner or later. For now, I have an exciting opportunity for us. All I have to do is figure out how to present it to Milo in such a way that he doesn't completely freak out.

THE BUS RIDE home is interrupted by two equally exciting things. First, Holly inviting me to her house for a tasting. She's in the process of expanding her menu and wants my opinion on a few of her new dishes. She seems particularly proud about a kaya tiramisu creation. That means I have to hop off the bus and switch to the subway to backtrack. Not that it's a problem whatsoever.

There's free food involved.

The second and arguably more exciting thing is an email. I re-read the message as I make my way up the stairs to the restaurant. It's from a potential sponsor for the channel!

"Hey, you!" Holly's voice is right in front of me, but I'm unable to look up at her. "Are you okay?"

"One sec."

I have to read the words a third, then a fourth time to make sure I understand what they're asking and what they're offering.

"Andie?"

"We've just been offered a sponsorship." I finally look up at her and realize I stopped in the middle of her walkway. "Shit, sorry."

Holly rolls her eyes. "Come inside, sit down, and tell me what the hell's going on."

I kick my shoes off by her front door and reach down to scratch her cat Rupert when he rubs against my legs. "Hey buddy."

"I have five dishes I want you to try." Holly is already around the corner in the kitchen.

Rupert is already trotting ahead of us, so I follow him in. Holly's kitchen isn't huge, but it has an island workspace I know is the reason she chose to rent here. The large stove is one she bought special to accommodate her cooking needs and takes up a large section of the room.

There's already a place setting ready for me at her island, as well as a glass of water. Normally, I'd be bubbling with excitement over the food I'm about to try, but I can't get my mind off the email.

Holly knows I'm not all here; she's pulling something out of the oven while I let my brain sift through my emotions. When she finally places a small pizza in front of me, the aroma rich with garlic and spices pulls me back to reality.

"Now, you eat one slice of this. Then I want you to tell me what's going on with your sponsorship, and secondly what you think of the pizza."

I lift the slice halfway to my mouth before stopping and looking at Holly. "I was just offered fifty thousand US dollars to produce some videos for *Travel Now* magazine."

"What?"

My hand falls back down to the plate. "They reached out before, but it looked pretty sketchy at the time. This time they've sent paperwork for me to review. They recommend I get a lawyer to look it over."

"Open it up and let's see! Fifty grand? That's fucking amazing!"

"What about the tasting?"

Holly stands straight and crosses her arms. I pick the slice up again and take a massive bite. The moan that escapes me is near instant. "Garlic white sauce, kale, and what's the meat?"

"Bison jerky. From within the province."

"Amazing." I shove the rest into my mouth and speak around my chews. "Ten out of ten."

"Awesome." Holly claps her hands before coming around the island to lean against me and read over my shoulder. "Now your turn. Open that file."

My email client is a bit slow opening the attachment, but it doesn't take long for me to see exactly what is on the table. "They … Oh shit. They want me to come down to the US, travel around a bit, and take photos. They also want me to make promotional videos."

"Andie, hon, that's amazing."

"I mean, it's kind of my dream job."

I keep reading the document; I'm surprised when I get toward the end. "Oh no."

"What? What's oh no?"

"They've made it clear that this is an opportunity only for me. A trial position with the chance to expand to a full-time position."

"Oh." Holly straightens. "*Oh*."

The realization of what this means hits me like a truck. "I'd have to move away. At least for six months for the initial contract while I did this. And it wouldn't involve Milo or Mia."

Holly visibly cringes. "Shit. But this is your perfect job. Milo would understand if you wanted to pursue it."

"Yeah." If he knew about it, he'd probably push me to take it on, regardless of what it means for the future of MAndM.

What it would mean for us.

"I can't accept this." Sighing, I close the document and put my phone away.

"Dude, that's a lot of money to walk away from," Holly groans, shifting to lean her hip against the island. "Maybe they'll negotiate with you? You can't just give up."

"Maybe." I scan the email, my heart sinking when I start to read the fine print. "It says due to the work visa I'd need to have they can't negotiate terms."

"Shit." Holly taps her fingers on the counter. "Are you going to tell Milo?"

In my heart, I know I should. Anything that has to do with our account is important for each of us to know. And yet I don't want to have the conversation that will come as a result. "No. If I'm not taking it, then there's no reason to bring it up."

He and Mia are becoming far too important to me, and I want more, not less, of them in my life.

"He'll be mad at you if he finds out."

No doubt. Glancing up at Holly, my face flushes. "Did I tell you that he and I ... ah ..."

"No, you did not." Holly punches my shoulder. "When did that happen?"

"After the rage room."

"You haven't gotten together again?"

"Not because I didn't want to. I thought something might happen the other day when he was practicing for an audition, but we were interrupted."

"Damn." Holly chuckles. "That must have been quite the role play."

"Dude, you have no idea." I'm not about to admit that I masturbated shortly after rewatching the video on my camera. "I've never really been one to feel that if I didn't have a boyfriend or partner, my life was missing something. But the more time I spend with him, the more I want to make our relationship something ... I don't know."

"Real?"

Holly is one of those friends who knows how to say exactly what a person needs to hear. How she's still single, I'll never know.

"Is that wrong? We didn't start this as a dating thing." Propping my elbows on the counter, I drop my chin into my hands. "I took a stupid picture of him in the park and our lives have been flipped upside down."

"Or *maybe* you took a picture of him in the park and you both got shaken out of the routine that wasn't getting either of you anywhere. Ever since your art show all those years ago, you've always seemed to be treading water. This TikTok account is the first time I've seen you take charge of your professional life, and I think it's the best possible thing. It also means that perhaps you see a path forward that involves being with someone else. There's nothing wrong with wanting to try."

That's an emotional gut-punch I hadn't anticipated. "I ... wow. Yeah, maybe you're right."

"Damn straight, I am." She slides another dish in front of me. "This is a kaya tiramisu. Try please."

I shove a heaping spoonful into my mouth and moan. "That's amazing. And so are you. What did I do to deserve such an awesome friend?"

"You helped me get a B plus in second year English literature."

"God, that class sucked."

"Never go to office hours alone!" We both say at the same time and laugh.

Holly shakes her head. "Man, she scared me half to death."

We chat and eat for a while longer, but I can't get rid of the little voice in the back of my head whispering that I need to go see Milo. Because if I don't, the small rift that has formed between us might grow into something much wider. And that's something I don't want to happen. Holly is right; maybe what I really want is to make a life with Milo. I just need to figure out how.

TWENTY-SEVEN

Milo

It's been five days since Andie called out Mia's friends, and things are still fucking awkward between us. We met yesterday afternoon at an indoor trampoline park and had fun bouncing around while Mia filmed us. The minute the camera was off, though, Mia left to go hang out with her new friends, leaving the two of us standing there trying to figure out what to say to each other. There were tons of families at the park, and at least two after-school programs that had arrived to burn off their energy. Screams and shouts of joy quickly became sensory hell to me. I couldn't handle the chaos any longer and needed to get out of there.

"I'm going to walk back home. I need the cold air on my face." What I should have done was ask her to come with me. What I ended up doing was waiting to see how she'd respond.

Andie looked around the minute we stepped outside. "Ah, I can catch the bus home. This stop will get me close."

We said a few more things, barely even chit chat, before each of us drifted away.

I hate this. Hate that the easy back and forth we've shared from nearly the moment we met is fading. It's the reason I set up a call with Dee outside of our normal schedule. Rather than sit in the darkness of my office, I sit on the living room couch and stare out the window. Gray clouds blot the sky, giving the horizon a gloomy tinge.

"Dee, I don't understand what the hell is going on. I mean, I know I probably screwed up or overreacted or something. But Mia's been hanging out with these girls for the past two weeks now, and she hasn't had a single panic attack. She's gone to school every day without an argument. How can I not like these kids?"

The pause from Dee immediately gets my hackles up. When she finally speaks, I can tell she's choosing her words carefully. "What are their names?"

"Ah, I ..." *Shit.* "They've been over to the house only once, and Andie was also there so I didn't think to ask. I know the tall one has two-hundred-and-eighty thousand followers on TikTok."

"You don't think it's strange that this girl has all of a sudden started hanging out with Mia?"

"Maybe she didn't think they had anything in common before now. It's not like Mia is great at putting herself out there."

"Milo, that's not fair."

"But it's kind of true."

"I don't know exactly what Andie said to you, and of course I would love to be wrong about this. However, I would keep an eye on Mia and her new friends. Andie got a feeling from them, and sometimes those instincts can be right."

Rarely do I get angry at Dee. But here I am, ready to explode at her for the second time this month. "I think I know my daughter, and we have a good relationship. If there was an issue with these girls, or if they were trying to take advantage of her, I'd know."

"Milo, you're a good dad, but it's not always possible to—"

"You know, I think I'm going to cut this session short."

"Milo."

"I appreciate you fitting me in. I'll see you at our normal

appointment time." I don't wait for her to respond before I end the call.

Like an asshole.

I stay on the couch for a half hour, glaring at the sky before I finally find the strength to get up and head to my office. I spend the rest of the morning trolling social media and half-reading my emails, sitting uncomfortably in my anger. Mia was in a fantastic mood this morning when she left. She said something about staying late to finish work on a project for History class, but I'm sure that was just an excuse to spend time with her new friends. Not that she needed one; I'm on board with highly social Mia.

Andie might care for Mia, and Dee might know all about her based on my sessions, but that doesn't mean either of them understands her the way I do.

I'm about to push away from the computer when an email from Bruno appears in my inbox.

Hey there.

Dude, you nailed the Painbringer audition! They loved your take on the character and the "simmering rage and love" that you brought to the monologue. Unless you've changed your mind, I should be getting a contract next week. I'll set up a call and we can go over the details then.

Congrats.

B.

I whoop as I jump from my chair, accidentally smacking my arm on the edge of my boom mic, sending it spinning against the wall.

"I can't believe it." My dream role is mine.

I'm the Painbringer.

Looking out the door of my tiny recording office into the empty condo deflates some of my excitement. I'm alone with some of the most amazing news of my professional life, and I don't have anyone to share it with. I should text Mia. Maybe she'll come home instead of going out to the movies with her friends and we can celebrate.

Shit, what am I thinking?

Still, I grab my phone and fire off a quick text to her.

I got Painbringer!

There's a far shorter delay than there should be before I get her response.

OMG dad! Grats!!!

Mia and I played the original games when she was probably too little to be exposed to them. Well, I played and she sat beside me, cheering me on. And now I'll be the voice others hear while they play the game. Me.

My mind will never be un-blown.

Did you want me to come home after school?

Looking down at her message, I know I have to decide between the right choice and the selfish choice. There's no way I can tell her she needs to come home, not when she's finally starting to get things going in the right direction for herself.

We'll celebrate later.

Sure?

Not at all.

Of course. The Pain won't be going anywhere.

There's another pause.

You should tell Andie. Maybe film a video about
it if you can.

That's an excellent idea. Though I can't say
anything publicly yet. Contract has yet to be
signed.

Fair. Okay, I'll see you at after the show.

My excitement fades as I stand alone in my office. My relationship with Mia has always been so close; we've always been there for each other through thick and thin. But she's a teen, soon to be graduating from high school, and no doubt will want to move on to university or college. Why would she want to come celebrate with me when there are history papers to write with friends? I know I wouldn't if our positions were reversed.

I don't have many friends I can hang out with. Most of them are industry professionals—at least three who also auditioned for the role, so I can't exactly celebrate with them.

"Call Andie, you idiot."

She was so dejected after the jump park yesterday, and that was totally my fault. I wouldn't blame her if she wants to end the entire TikTok thing and cut ties with me completely. Still, she was the reason I got the part in the first place. When I recorded the audition lines, I closed my eyes and pictured Andie standing there like she did that day. The look of awe, the unshed tears in her eyes, the kiss we shared afterward all rushed back, fueling my performance. She deserves to know.

I'm about to call her, my thumb hovering over the speed dial for her contact, when I stop. I should thank her properly. Buy her a bottle of wine and bring it to her place and offer a proper apology.

Before I change my mind, I throw on my coat, grab my stuff, and tear out of my place.

I pick up the Portuguese red she really likes from an LCBO

near her apartment before striding down her street and taking the stairs to her apartment two at a time. It's not until I get to her door that my brain clues back in that she might not be here. Andie does have a life outside of what we do together, and I didn't text her to see if she's home. Or if she wants anything to do with me ever again.

I could, quite possibly, be making a terrible mistake.

Fuck it.

My knuckles ache as I rap them against her door; my blood pounds in my ears as my anxiety spikes. I hear the little patter of her jogging to the door. When she opens it, her look of surprise is almost enough to send me packing. But then her gaze drops to my mouth and I'm done for. I push the bottle to her chest and she takes it.

"I got the part!"

"Oh!" Her eyes widen in excitement for me. No need for further explanation or conversation. She knows how desperately I wanted this.

Rachel would never have cared.

I could be saying or doing many things: apologizing for implying Andie had no idea what she was talking about when it came to Mia and her friends; thanking her for helping me find the creative space I needed to get the part in the first place; or appreciating her existence as someone important in my life.

Instead, I reach up to cup her face in my hands.

I hesitate, giving her time to stop me if this isn't what she wants. When I feel her breath hitch and her body sway closer to mine, the last of my defenses fall.

And I kiss her.

Andie

The kiss is frantic and needy and everything I've been fantasizing about since the last time I was at his apartment. Yesterday at the trampoline park I'd been ready to tell him about the sponsorship offer and about the fundraising party that's coming up in a week. That I've been considering doing both those things because my bank account is starting to get dangerously low, and I need to find an additional income soon. But the words refused to come when he seemed so annoyed with everything going on. All I wanted was for things to go back to the way they were—longing looks and stolen touches while we laughed our heads off at the ridiculousness of everything.

Then I open the door and find him standing there with the wine, and everything slots back into place. I'm still holding onto the bottle as he deepens the kiss, a small barrier between us as we make out in my doorway. As much as I like my neighbors, the last thing I want is to provide gossip for the people in the building.

With my free hand, I yank Milo's arm and step backward, leading him into my apartment and away from prying eyes. He's on board, walking with me without breaking the kiss and using his foot to shut the door behind him. I toss the wine on the couch as we draw close—no doubt I'll forget it's there and end up sitting on it later—giving me use of both my hands to do what I want to Milo.

Like take his shirt off.

And undo his pants.

Awkwardly, I try to yank off his shirt, but he's still holding onto my face, which God, that is hot. I don't want to pull away, so I leave it on and do the next best thing. I slide my hand across his stomach, using my nails to scratch at the soft skin as I make my way deliberately up to his nipple. Milo sucks in a sharp breath when I circle his nipple, teasing the hair close by.

He finally breaks the kiss but doesn't let go of my face. "You're evil."

"I'm fun." I flick his nipple with my fingertip. "And you like it."

"I do. I really do." He lowers his face again, but this time it's to the side of my throat where he bites down gently.

Whoa, and welcome to my sex drive; thank you for roaring back to life far more aggressively than before. While we should probably have a conversation about what happened between us, I'm old enough to know there will be plenty of time to sort that out after orgasms have been procured by both parties.

Multiple, if luck is on my side.

I'm about to snag another kiss from him but I pull back instead. I make sure he's looking right into my eyes because I need to know there's no hesitation in his response. "Are you sure?"

He nods. "Last time I was ... still figuring things out. I'm sure about this." He reaches up and cups my cheek. "About you."

Oh hell yes. "Condoms?"

For a moment he looks panicked, but then he smiles. "I went old school and put one in my wallet after the last time."

"Just one?"

"It's not a big wallet."

"You're fortunate that I bought a new box." That was an

embarrassment I'm not willing to live through a second time. "The last ones were actually expired."

Milo sighs. "See, this is why you're perfect."

Before my brain has time to register what he said, he kisses me. I start moving backward toward my bedroom, only stumbling twice over things I left where I shouldn't have.

Clothing is pulled off to land on the floor as we walk. Milo is warm, his skin soft, and the moment I fling my bra somewhere behind me and press my breasts against his chest, I let out a satisfied groan. We're kissing again as we move toward the bedroom, his chest hair tickling my nipples, bringing them to hard peaks.

The edge of the bed comes up hard against the backs of my knees, announcing our arrival. I've already opened the front of his pants, and now that we're no longer moving I'm able to push them down his hips and thighs until gravity takes over for me.

I kiss his chin before I look down. "Mr. Beechum, I forgot how lovely you are." I wrap my hand around his cock and give it a squeeze. "Or should I call you," I lower my voice, "Painbringer."

He chuckles. "Are you into that sort of thing? Not that there's anything wrong with it, but I'd need to learn a few bondage knots if we're going down that road."

"I'm not, though it's sweet that you'd be willing to try." I give his cock another squeeze. "I'm sorry to say, I'm more basic bitch than adventure seeker."

"It's fine. I'm not sure my back and knees could handle anything too extreme these days."

"Unless we got a sex swing. I've always wanted to try one of those."

Milo lowers his mouth to my shoulder and gives me a gentle bite. "Too much talking."

"Yup."

I sit on the edge of the bed and take his cock into my mouth. His skin is hot, and he smells aroused. I close my eyes and soak up the sensations. I've nearly lost myself in the feel of him when Milo drops his hands to my head and strokes my hair. His gentle touch sends chills down my spine. My skin becomes electric, a receptor to his every touch as he caresses the skin behind my ears, the hollow at the base of my neck. I groan with him still in my mouth, taking a moment to soak in the intimacy of the moment.

He sighs and tugs lightly on my hair. "Come here."

Pulling me to my feet and into his arms, he helps me remove what little clothing I have left. With each new inch of skin exposed, Milo dips his mouth and places a kiss there. The soft caresses are sometimes followed by the swipe of his tongue, which inevitably sends another shiver of desire through me.

I know what this man can do with his tongue.

In fact ...

I get on the bed and scooch up to the middle of the mattress and lift my hips. Thankfully, he gets the message and pulls down my panties. I'm so turned on, this is going to be the shortest trip from A to B imaginable. Spreading my legs, I give him a grin.

I've never seen him move faster; his clothing falling to the floor in a heap as his gaze locks onto me. "You're gorgeous."

Compliments have always been difficult for me, so instead of simply accepting it, I smile up at him. "Bring on the *pain*."

Milo laughs as he gets to his knees and lowers his mouth to me. The first few flicks have my eyes rolling back in my head as I dig my fingers into my thighs to kept them apart. Shit, this really isn't going to take me long. He hums as he increases the suction, teasing my opening with one hand while caressing my calf with his other. The muscles in my back tighten as the warmth from my oncoming orgasm floods my lower body. I tense as I cry out, the pleasure blinding my senses.

When I come back to reality, I realize Milo is yanking a condom from the box in my nightstand drawer. God, being prepared is amazing. His hands shake as he rolls the condom into place, betraying how far along he is in his own arousal. He climbs over me and shifts his hips to line his cock up and gently pushes his way home. Once he's all the way in, he stops moving and for a moment, I think there's a problem.

He huffs, his eyes closed and his face turned slightly away. "There was a time I could last a half hour. I'm currently terrified I'm going to come on the next stroke."

"You've already impressed the hell out of me." I run my nails up his back and feel the goosebumps rise. "Come on and show me what you've got."

Milo drops his face to my shoulder, giving me a little nip. He pulls his hips back to thrust forward once again. Like so much of his life, I can feel his restraint. I know he's focused on me and my pleasure and not himself. While that's admirable, sometimes it's wonderful to be the reason someone loses their shit.

So on his next thrust, I squeeze my inner muscles around his cock as hard as I can.

"Jesus fuck." He shudders and thrusts hard again.

His moans and gasps are followed by a soft noise that sounds like my name. Another thrust and Milo loses his precarious grasp on his control. When a loud growl explodes from him and he begins to thrust into me without hesitation, I know I've won that battle. His mouth finds mine and it's my turn to grab his head, to hold onto this kiss as long as I can. Pleasure builds up inside me again, and for a moment, I'm surprised that it's even a possibility. But when Milo swivels his hips, the added pressure on my clit is all I need to send a second orgasm rolling through me.

That's the end of Milo's resistance as well. With a final thrust, he pulls his mouth from mine and cries out as he comes with full-body shudders. Gasping, I wrap my arms around him and hold him tight as we both came back down to earth.

With my eyes closed, I listen to our harsh breathing. Trailing my fingers along his back, I turn my face and breath him in, letting his scent imprint on me. This is nice. Better than nice. This is damn near perfect.

Milo turns his head and plants a kiss on my cheek. "One of

these days, we'll have to actually get under your sheets before we have sex."

"Are you kidding? I'm plotting out how we can do this in all non-bed specific locations. The couch. Against the fridge. In the shower."

"We'll have to install those support handles if we're going to do that. Do you know how many people die from slips and falls in the bathroom annually?"

I laugh as he slides out of me, shifting his body weight to press against my side while he dealt with the condom. "You're right. Far easier to do things on a mattress."

"Think of my back, Andie." He nuzzles his lips against my cheek. "My chiropractor retired during the pandemic, and I don't want to have to find a new one."

"Oh nooooo. We don't want you to have to do that." I snake my hand down his side and to gently poke at him. "You might have to meet a new person."

He chuckles. "Hey, I raced across town for a booty call. I'm extending my boundaries."

"That's what I am, eh? A booty call?" I don't know why that causes my chest to tighten the way it does, but I'm too warm and fuzzy to question it here and now.

"Of course not." His face is still pressed against mine, so I can't see his reaction. But I feel the soft rush of air against my skin as he sighs. "Honestly, I don't know exactly what this is."

I want to scream *It's love! Romance! A perfectly comfortable relationship!* though I know neither of us are at that stage. But for the first time in my life, I feel that perhaps I'm at the point where maybe, just maybe, a grand romance is something I want.

In particular, with Milo.

You need to talk to him, Andie. Pull what he wants out from behind his anxiety. I turn my face a tiny bit, hoping to see him better from my periphery. "Do you know maybe what you want?" And then feeling like that might be too much pressure on him, I quickly add, "I mean, you seem to be at a crossroads. It can be hard to know what to do."

I don't immediately panic when he doesn't respond. I've started to recognize his patterns when it comes to what he considers important. He's quick to fire off a quip if he doesn't care about a thing or if he's trying to make someone else feel better. But if the matter at hand is personal to him, Milo slips into his head, no doubt looking at every angle before him. Rushing him will only add stress and cause him to pull away.

Finally, he rolls to his side, propping himself up on his elbow. I shift deeper into the quilt to get a perfect view of his blue eyes. Gone is the light-hearted air that clings to him like a second skin. Instead, there's a shimmer in his gaze, and it takes me a moment to realize that it's unshed tears.

"When I met my ex in college, I had everything figured out. I was going to be an actor; not a movie star, but a working character actor who would grace the presence of every CBC production set remotely close to Toronto. Rachel was in finance and had a brain for numbers like no one else I'd ever met. She loved the social life of the theater groups and being able to point at me when she saw me on a show, even as an extra."

I hold my breath, scared to move in case he stops talking. Since I laid eyes on him in the park and up to now, he's never talked like this about himself or his ex. I desperately want to know more about the woman who dented his soul.

Milo's pained smile tells me more than his words ever could. "When I was offered voice acting parts and found that I loved that side of the business more than I ever did being in front of the camera, my world shifted. That was around the time Rachel discovered she was pregnant. After Mia came, I thought Rachel was struggling with post partum depression. I did everything I could to help her, make things easier. What I hadn't known was that she wasn't happy being a wife to a guy who wanted to stay home, nor was she interested in being a mother."

"I'm so sorry."

He shakes his head. "I'm not mad at all for her leaving. If anything, she probably saved all three of us from years of fights and heartache. It was my fault for pushing her toward a life she never wanted. I don't regret Mia for a moment. She's amazing, and the best thing that has happened to me."

He cups my face. "You're a close second."

My mind short-circuits, and all I can do is make an *o* with my mouth.

"To answer your question, I don't know yet what I want. I feel like I've made progress in the past few months. I don't panic at the thought of leaving my condo quite as much. I don't spend hours worrying about Mia and what she's going to be like every morning when I ask if she's going to school. I have a tiny bit more hope now than I did before you took that picture of me."

I clear my throat and let out an awkward chuckle, needing to pop the tension rising inside me. "This is the most I think you've ever said to me in one direct go."

He shrugs. "You bring it out of me." With his head cocked to the side, he narrows his gaze. "What about you?"

"What do you mean?"

"I'm not the only one with baggage to unpack. What do you want from this? From us? Life?"

Man, why did he have to go and ask that? "I ... I don't know."

"I bet you do. You know everything, Andie Matheson."

Finding it suddenly difficult to breathe, I shrug and pat his chest. "What I do need is to go pee."

Milo hesitates, then nods and rolls away. "I should probably head back home soon. I want to be there when Mia gets back from her study session."

I pause before leaving the room. "The same girls from the other day?"

His nod is hesitant. "So far everything's been fine with the new group. I hope you're wrong about them."

I know in my gut that I'm not. "Me too. Mia deserves to have good friends." I smile. "I'll be right back."

Shutting the bathroom door, I catch sight of myself in the mirror. My skin is flushed, eyes bright, and I look as I feel—like I just had amazing sex. But something has stirred inside me. Milo asked the one question I haven't wanted to ask myself for a long while.

What do I want?

Not what are the dreams I've been clinging to since I was a kid. Or what do I think I should be doing as a forty-five-year-old woman.

What. Do. I. Want?

You know. You just need to say it.

I want to be a successful photographer. I want to have a relationship with Milo where I feel like a contributing partner and not someone who needs him for financial means. I want to have a better relationship with Mom, one that makes me feel like I can pick up the phone and talk to her about my problems without being judged.

I want to be further along in my life than I currently am. Terrified I'm not because I lack the skill at everything I do. Fear spikes through my body, and I shake my head to push it back down.

"Nope." I wash my face, retrieve my housecoat from the hook, and go back out to see if I can avoid reality a tiny bit longer.

TWENTY-NINE

Milo

I'm the first to admit that I'm not the best at picking up when someone aside from Mia is having an emotional crisis. Well, not in the moment at any rate. But afterward, when I'm alone and my brain is going through its cycle of winding down and sorting out the memories that are still clinging, that's normally when I have my lightbulb moments.

Sadly, I didn't clue in that something was off with Andie until this morning. When it eventually hits me, the guilt is sudden and sharp.

"Shit."

Mia glances up at me from what she's reading on her phone, cereal spoon halfway up from the bowl. "What?"

I'm not about to go into all the details with my daughter over a bowl of Cheerios. *Hey, last night after Andie and I had great sex, she might have been upset about something, and I only now clued in.* Instead, I smile and lean my forearms on the counter. "I just remembered that I didn't respond to an email. It's all good."

Mia narrows her eyes at me for a moment before turning her attention back to her phone.

"What are you reading?"

She presses a few buttons as she tilts her phone up, making it impossible for me to see her screen. "Nothing. TikTok."

"How's our channel?"

She shrugs.

Oh no. "Do you have any ideas for what we should film today?"

She shrugs again.

"You okay? Did something happen last night when you were out?"

Mia lets out a sigh that sounds so much like something I would do, I have to mentally check to make sure I didn't just make the same noise myself. "Dad, I love you, but I don't want to tell you every little thing all the time."

I straighten and take a step back from the counter. My eyes are probably bugged out because my mouth has fallen open and the shock I feel from that little set-down is keen. "I'm sorry. I never meant to pressure you."

Mia rolls her eyes, finishes her cereal, and gets up from the counter. "I have to go. I'm meeting the girls at Timmies for coffee before school."

"Okay." I watch as she gathers her belongings and heads out the door.

That was … a thing that happened.

It's also a painful reminder that my daughter is growing up. While she might have her mental health problems and those challenges color how I view her, she isn't a little kid who needs her dad to fight all her demons any longer.

My heart breaks a tiny bit.

I don't understand how my life has changed so drastically in such a short period of time. I've gained Andie, a TikTok channel, my dream job, and a new lease on an admittedly still-limited social life. But I feel that I've lost a bit too. Somehow, in the last few months the bubble that Mia and I have cocooned ourselves in has burst, letting in all manner of things. Dee would tell me that's the whole point of life—to let people in and see where those interactions take me.

All it does is makes me terrified that I'll disappoint someone else.

Grabbing my coffee, I check my phone one more time before I lock myself away in my office to review my notes on Painbringer. Everything else will have to wait.

MY VOICE IS a bit hoarse after recording four promo spots for the local radio station. I didn't warm up properly, and now I'm paying the price. Of course, I have an appointment with Dee and will be talking for another hour with her. Which isn't ideal. I pour myself a cup of tea in the kitchen before I wander around the living room to stretch my legs and ease the ache in my lower back from too much sitting. A glance out the window shows more gray skies. The weather is starting to turn cold, which means I feel far less guilty about not going out.

When my cell rings, I take a breath to prepare myself for Dee's session and head over to sit on the couch.

"Hey."

I nearly jump out of my skin when I hear Andie's voice on the line instead. "Hey! Did I get you at a bad time?"

It's never bad when I talk to you. "I ... ah, have a therapy call in a few minutes."

"Oh shit, I'm sorry."

"It's good. What's up?"

"Ah, well. I forgot to ask you last night after we ... yeah, I forgot to ask. The college wants me to attend a fundraising event. They want to use my clout, I guess."

"That's fantastic, Andie. Congrats."

"Technically, they want both of us to come. I wasn't sure if you'd want to, so I told them you were a maybe." She hesitates again. "Do you?"

Had this come up a few weeks ago, I would have said no. And while I want to support Andie any way possible, I still can't completely change the person I am. I hate parties and the need to make small talk with strangers who couldn't care less about you. I avoid them whenever possible. But I'll go anyway. Besides helping Andie, it's a good way to take charge and put myself out there. "Of course!"

"I know parties aren't really your thing, and you don't have to stay the whole time if you need to leave or something. I would have asked sooner. I was debating going on my own. But it didn't seem right going as the only member of MAndM."

God, she's cute when she's panicked. "Andie, it's fine. I understand, and I get it. When is the fundraiser?" Without thinking I drain the last of my tea, cringing at the heat the liquid still holds.

She makes a clicking noise and groans. "See, I didn't think you'd want to come to this, and then things got a bit weird between us, so I didn't—"

"Andie, I'm a bit on the clock here."

"Friday. The party is Friday."

"As in three days from now?"

"Yeah."

Well, shit. "Text me the details. I'll come to your place, and we can Uber from there."

"Really?"

"Really, really."

"Awesome!" She sighs. "I have something else I need to talk to you about."

There's a shout followed by a *bang* in the background. "What are you doing?"

"Ah ... I'm at a printer, actually. Picking something up."

"That sounds fun. What did you want to—" My call waiting

beeps, telling me that our time is up. *Shit.* "That's Dee on the other line."

"Okay. Talk to you later." She's gone before I have the chance to say anything else.

I'm sure whatever she wanted to discuss we can talk about later. I answer the call. "Hey, Dee."

THIRTY

Milo

I've been staring at my closet for the better part of an hour, when Mia drifts into my bedroom doorway. She doesn't say anything immediately, which isn't unusual, so I continue to look for something to wear. I haven't thought too much about attending Andie's party tonight until an hour ago. She sent me the details after our call—formal, suit and tie, food and drinks provided—and I promptly ignored them.

Self-preservation or simply forgetful, I can't tell you. The end result is me scrambling to find something in my closet that still fits. It's been a long time since I attended anything remotely close to formal. My brain passes through every fear I have about this event as I spiral down.

What if I get overwhelmed by everything and have to leave?

What if I say something stupid and embarrass Andie in front of her colleagues?

What if I say something smart and overshadow something Andie said, making her look bad? Of all my worries, this is the one that concerns me the most.

I toss the maroon shirt I picked out onto the bed and reach for a navy-blue button down. I hold it up to my neck and look at myself once more in the mirror. Shit, I need to shave.

"Not that one." Mia's voice makes me jump slightly. She comes into the room and pushes past me to dig through my closet. "What is this thing again?"

"A fundraiser. Fancy, lots of smart people talking."

"What pants are you wearing?"

"Black dress."

"Jacket?"

"Nope."

"Tie?"

"Probably should."

Rummaging, she retrieves a pale blue dress shirt with a barely perceptible pinstripe to it. Mia holds it up to me, cocking her head to the side. "There you go."

"Thanks, baby." Not that I'm not capable of dressing myself, but it's always nice to have a second opinion. "Now I just need to shave."

"Oh, don't fully shave. You look good with the scruff."

"I look old with the scruff. Too many grays."

"Naw, you're cute. Andie will like it."

"You think?" I glance in the mirror and try to picture myself the way Andie sees me. I'm so wrapped in my thoughts, I nearly miss Mia's giggle.

"Hey, are you trying to set me up?"

"Nooooooo."

"Jackass."

Mia rolls her eyes. "I have a question."

"Give'r."

"Well, since you're going out tonight, I was wondering if it would be okay if I went over to Allison's place to do homework."

I stop fussing with the shirt and turn to face her. "Allison? Who's that?"

"She came to our house a few weeks ago to study. Remember?"

"The short one or the tall one?"

"Short."

I narrow my gaze. "You honestly think I believe that high school girls do homework on a Friday night?"

Mia groans. "Fine. We're going to watch movies and talk about boys. Can I go?"

"Of course." I don't remember the last time she went over to a friend's place for fun. "I won't be home until late, but I'll have my phone on me."

"I know." She bites down on her bottom lip. "Maybe I could spend the night?"

"Aren't you a bit old for a sleepover?"

"Dad, come on. Please? I never get asked to this kind of thing."

The last thing I want to do is ruin her new friendships by being overprotective. Even if I'm not entirely comfortable with the idea of her being somewhere without me. "I want you to check in with me every so often. And make sure you have your clonazepam with you in case you have a problem."

"I will." Mia throws herself into my arms, giving me a body-crushing hug. "Thank you."

Kissing the top of her head, I squeeze her in return. "I'll drop you off on my way to meet Andie."

"You're the best!" And in a flurry of movement, Mia races out of my room to her own.

This is going to work out better than I expected. If Mia is with other people, I won't need to worry about something happening while she's alone. I'll be able to focus my complete attention on Andie and schmoozing at the party. Hell, I might enjoy myself.

Now there's a concept.

Grabbing the fresh clothing, I make my way to the bathroom to shower and shave. As I pass Mia's room, I hear her speaking softly but with obvious excitement. Yeah, this is going to work out perfectly.

I close the bathroom door and strip naked. I'm about to hop in the shower when my phone pings. It's Andie. A quick glance at the message tells me without a doubt she's worried I'll back out on her tonight.

> Hey! Just wanted to make sure everything was good at your place.

I know there'd be no judgments from her if I did have to back out. The best part is I wouldn't need to go into a lengthy explanation. Nope, I know if the situation called for it, I could type *bad night* and that would be enough. Andie is one of the few people who gets it. Gets us.

Ignoring the fact my cock has also taken an interest in the idea that I'll see Andie soon, I pick up my phone.

> All good! Need to figure out the car situation. Need to drop Mia off at friend's place, and coming to get you. Not sure on the order. Still on for 7.

She doesn't respond immediately, so I add,

> About to shower and shave.

> Don't shave! You look good with the scruff.

Shit, Mia was right. There's a fine line between when the scruff looks good and when it's obvious that I've just been lazy. I think I'm riding the line tonight, but can pull the look off.

> Fine. A clean up shave only.

Andie responds with a dead emoji.

Turning on the shower to warm up the water, I glance back at the phone. The three dots are bouncing, telling me she's typing, but nothing is coming. Either she's writing a book or she got interrupted. I can't justify standing here naked to wait, so I flip my phone over and dive into the water.

Whatever she wants to tell me can wait twenty minutes.

THIRTY-ONE

Andie

I stop halfway through getting dressed for the event tonight, as an unexpected hot flash hits me. Bracing my hands on the bathroom vanity I feel sweat spring up across my skin a few second before the internal warmth surges through me. I can live with the hot flash itself, but it's the sweat that builds in my cleavage and under my boobs that drives me nuts. My reflection shows the flush on my cheeks, despite the ghastly yellow glow from the light above the mirror. I knew I shouldn't have had that second cup of coffee this afternoon. At least I haven't put my makeup on.

I get a clean facecloth from under the sink and begin to wipe myself down when my phone rings. The ID comes up for Mom and I can't help but laugh. Of course she'd call while I had my hand down the front of my dress, wiping away boob sweat.

Tossing the cloth in the hamper, I press the phone to my ear and head out to the kitchen table. I never know how these calls will go and it's better to sit in a chair with good support. Plus, it's cooler out here than in my windowless bathroom. "Hi, Mom. What's up?"

"Andie. How are you, sweetheart?"

I stop dead in my tracks halfway between the fridge and the

table, and pull the phone away from my ear to look down at the screen. Yup, that's mom's number. I press the phone back to my ear as I lick my lips. "I'm good. Getting ready to head out in a few hours for a work event. Everything okay?"

"Oh, I should have realized you were busy. I can call back later."

"Mom, it's fine. Milo won't be here for another hour and a half. I have plenty of time to talk."

The pause is far longer than anything I expect with Mom. The fridge's compressor kicks in behind me, the low hum filling the silence. The longer it stretches, the greater my anxiety. "Mom?"

"You know, it's fine. I was going to ask you about your financial situation since you lost one of your jobs, but it sounds like everything's fine."

I cringe. "Did Cara tell you?"

"Of course she told me. She doesn't keep things from me the way you do."

"Mom, I didn't keep it from you intentionally. I just ... I didn't want you to worry."

"No, you didn't want me telling you that you should come home. Even though that's ..."

I can't remember a time in my life when Mom was hesitant in a conversation or didn't speak her mind. Knowing what Mom thinks about me, my life—hell, anyone's life—is as reliable as the sun rising in the morning.

For her to trail off, to not tell me that I should find a way to move back home where she can make sure I'm looked after, well, that's beyond weird.

It's downright terrifying.

"Mom, are you okay?"

"I ... will be."

Whoa.

"I'll let you go. You have to get ready for your work thing. I can't have you being late and losing the only other job you have.

Unless they've started paying you to make silly videos of yourself online."

"But, I—"

"Love you, baby." And she hangs up.

Mildy annoyed at her jibe about our TikTok channel being "silly," I stand in the kitchen, little black dress on and makeup half done, suddenly very concerned for a mom who's half a country away. And there isn't a damn thing I can do to make anything better. Well, there is one thing.

I hit speed dial for Cara and wait for her to pick up. "Yo."

"What the hell is going on with Mom?"

I feel my sister cringe from three provinces away. "What do you mean?"

"She called me, didn't try to convince me to move home, and then hung up without telling me something that she clearly wanted to tell me."

"I really don't want to be in the middle of this." I'm not certain if she's saying that to me or if she's talking to Mom, despite her not being able to hear us.

"Do I need to be worried? Or come home? Because if there's a problem and no one is telling me because I live in Ontario, I'm going to be pissed. Then I will come home. And I'll be home *and* pissed."

That's the one thing I hate more than anything. Sure, I might not want to live in my home province any longer, but that doesn't mean I want to be kept in the dark when it comes to what's going on with the family. Nor is it fair to Cara that she's the one with all the knowledge and responsibility, simply because she lives there.

"Hang on." I hear her moving somewhere followed by the click of a door shutting. "I didn't want Kyle to hear. She hasn't said anything to me directly, but I think Mom is thinking about leaving Dad."

"*What?*"

"I don't know for certain, but she's not happy. She keeps

talking about going on trips or moving to England. Telling me not to worry if I don't see her as much, and to look after Dad and all that."

"Should I call her back and ask?" What the hell am I supposed to do with this information?

"No. I did talk to Dad, and he doesn't seem concerned. I guess we just have to wait and see."

"Great." Something else for me to worry about half a country away. My alarm goes off, telling me that my prep time is starting to run out. "I have to get ready for a work event."

"That sounds like fun. Going alone or have a date?"

"I'm going with Milo."

"A date!"

"No, the school is using our clout to get donation money. We're using them for a fancy meal and free booze."

"That sounds like a fair trade. Maybe you can convince them to hire you on full time."

Wouldn't that make my life a thousand times better? "I wish. We're probably going to post a few TikToks while we're there, so you can see all the fun for yourself."

"I'll be enviously watching from afar."

But after hanging up with her, I continue to worry about Mom. She's always been a straightforward, does-not-mince-words kind of person. Knowing there's something going on that she's not willing or able to tell me throws my world off kilter.

I'm considering calling her back when I get a text from Milo.

I'm heading out soon.

Awesome.

The tree dots bounce for a bit and I can picture him carefully picking his words.

Everything okay?

If he'd asked that five minutes ago, I would have known the answer. I need to tell Milo about the *Travel Now* offer. While I am at it, I should tell him that my feelings for him have grown to be way more than friendship. That I think of him constantly and want nothing more than to spend the rest of my days with him and Mia.

Maybe Mom is right that there's a better time and place to drop a truth bomb on a person.

Yeah, I'm good. Mom called and I got distracted. See you soon?

With bells on!

Flipping my phone face down on the bathroom counter, I go back to the task of making myself presentable for a party where I know I won't quite fit in.

Hooray.

THIRTY-TWO

Andie

"Holy shit, you look stunning!"

I'd opened my door to see Milo, hair freshly washed and full of floof, wearing a perfectly fitted shirt and dress pants, his tie on and loosely knotted. He shaved, but only so much as to make the scruff on his face look intentional and incredibly sexy. He isn't wearing a dress coat, which gives me the perfect view of his torso.

I shake my head to clear it. "What?"

The grin on his face is adorable. "I said, holy shit. You look stunning."

"Oh, I thought I said that," I laugh, feeling my face heat. "Thanks. I'm surprised this still fits me. It's been a while since I've had to dress up." I lean out and look into the hallway. "Mia isn't with you?"

"Dropped her off first. I wanted to make sure I knew where the house was."

"Look at you, being a responsible parent and all."

He snorts. "Just making sure she wasn't going to a wild party or anything like that."

I'm not about to remind him that teens are very good at moving locations if they want. There's no reason to upset him for something that isn't likely to happen. "Let me get my purse and coat."

"It's a bit chilly out, so good idea."

Really, I need some time to catch my breath and focus my now spinning brain on what we're about to do. My nerves kick in and it takes effort to stop myself from drying my sweaty palms on my little black dress. I grab my three-quarter length coat with both hands, hoping the cotton will help, before slipping into it.

Milo hasn't moved from the doorway, but I can feel his gaze on my cleavage. "Do we *really* have to go to this thing?" he says, a bit of gruffness coloring his words.

His hunger is obvious and directed toward me. I stop in my tracks and look at him. It would be easy to not go. Dean Robichaud would be disappointed—he might fire me for not coming. I mean, I hope he wouldn't do that, but it's a possibility.

Still, the temptation ...

I sigh. "Yeah, we really should."

He lets out a little groan. "We don't need to stay the whole time. We'll find an excuse to leave early. I'll feign a panic attack."

"That's something people would believe." With my coat on, I pick up my purse and nudge him into the hall so I can lock my place up. "We could come back here once we're done."

I keep my back to him as I say that, scared that his look of longing is too much for me to handle, and we'll end up in my bed instead of the car. Because apparently, I'm a horny, horny girl, and Milo is more than willing to help me out. "Let's get going."

We walk in silence out to the street, our hands brushing occasionally as we move. The gentle contact does strange things to my body, making our closeness more intense than ever before. Milo takes a few steps ahead of me, and I'm more than a little surprised when he leads me to an Audi parked in front of my building.

"Is this yours?" It's black, with tan leather seats and looks like one that you might see in a TV commercial.

"Hell, no. It's a rental." He holds the door open for me. "I thought if we were going to be used for our online clout, the least we could do was play the part up."

"Fancy." I slide onto the seat, swinging my legs inside in such a way to provide Milo an eyeful.

The drive to the party is easy, as is our conversation. It's all surface stuff, small talk—flirty, even. I know I need to tell him about the offer from *Travel Now*, that I'm seriously considering packing everything up, quitting my job, subletting my apartment, leaving all my friends, and moving to the US for six months to see if I can make a go of being a travel influencer. But every time there's a small lull in our chatter, the perfect opportunity to say *Hey, so guess what's fallen on my plate,* the words won't come.

And when I think I've finally pumped myself up to broach the conversation, we turn the corner and the college comes into sight. "Here we are, madam. Your party."

It doesn't make sense to ruin the mood now. Not when we're about to go in and need to be "on." It will have to wait.

After we park, Milo holds out his arm for me to take, giving me some physical support to get me through the door. Social situations rarely bother me, so I don't know why I'm so nervous about attending this event. The butterflies have taken up residence inside my stomach and are threatening to explode. I'm about to run away when Carly comes over to us at the coat check.

"I'm so happy you both made it." Her hair is piled up neatly atop her head, and her makeup is flawless. Her dress is also black, but it's a tad more low-cut than mine, and her physique is slimmer. "Jean asked me to keep an eye out for you."

"Hi. Ah, Carly, this is Milo."

I don't know if I expected him to flirt with her the way he did with me back at the apartment, but when he gives her hand a simple shake and a small smile, I'm surprised. "Nice to meet you."

One glance at him and I can tell he's already uneasy now that we were here. Shit, that's the last thing I want. He's doing me a favor by coming, pushing himself out into the spotlight when I know it's something he despises. Carly must have picked up on his unease and turns her attention back to me.

"I know Jean wanted you here to help with the donations, but you're not obligated to stay the whole time." She leads us into the main hall, smiling and nodding at people as they pass. "We have an exhibit in the back, mostly art from students and alumni. We have student waitstaff circulating with appetizers and beverages. And there's a dessert bar along the side wall. Mingle, maybe get your photos taken a bit, post a TikTok promoting the school – that would be amazing." She then gives us another smile and disappears into the crowd.

I stare after her. "She's like this ethereal being who knows exactly what to say and then vanishes into the night."

"Yup."

When I turn back to Milo, I notice he's gone a bit pale. "Are you okay?"

He pauses, his lips drawing into a thin white line. "What *is it* about parties?"

Looking around the throng of well dressed people, I can't quite see things the way he obviously does. I mean, yes, I'm a bit nervous about talking with these people. Most of them live a life with means well above my own. But other than that, I'm fine. I know as soon as I'm introduced to someone, I'll slip into conversation mode and everything will click into place.

I look at a couple standing not far away and compare them to us. They're well dressed and laugh with one another as they pluck a glass of wine from a passing waiter. But there's a physical distance between them, not even a stray brush of body parts. To test a theory, I brush against Milo. He leans in.

A string quartet plays off to the side, their music a relaxing soundtrack to accompany a lively party. Someone has draped strings of lights above where we walk, giving the room a pleasant glow. I relax, taking it all in.

Milo, on the other hand, looks as though he's about to pass out.

I take his hand in mine. "Why don't we get a drink and then start with the art exhibit. If anyone approaches us between here and there, I'll do all the talking. Deal?"

He nods and lets out a little huff. "Let's do this."

Thankfully, we're only stopped twice on our way to the exhibit. Once is by Fatima, who's here as one of the servers. "Mrs. M!" Her excitement is palpable when she looks up at Milo. "Hey!"

"Milo, this is Fatima, one of my night students. Fatima, see? He's a real person."

"I knew he was." She rolls her eyes and holds the tray out for us. "The coconut shrimp are apparently really good. I don't know what the other things are."

Milo takes the gray-looking bite and pops it into his mouth. "I think it's supposed to be chicken curry." He makes a performance out of swallowing. "I think."

Fatima giggles. "I have to keep moving. Have fun."

The second time, we're almost to the door to the exhibit. An older man and woman stop us to chat about the school and my role as a teacher. Thankfully, the couple knows nothing about TikTok, and after a few minutes we grab some wine from a passing waiter and slip into the dim light of the exhibition hall.

The walls and floor have been painted black, that in conjunction with the low lighting makes it feel as though we've walked into a dead zone. Milo chuckles as we enter the quiet and nearly empty space. "Thank God, that wasn't as bad as I expected. At least the booze is good quality."

I hear him speak, but my attention is snagged by the giant photos and painted canvasses on display, making me think of the giant photo I'd printed off the other day, only to shove it in the closet. The sign announces that these are from some of our recent graduates, each one with a brief overview from the artist describing their influence. My feet move forward until I find myself standing directly in front of a photo of downtown Toronto in the rain. It's beautiful. I can feel the light rain on my cheeks simply by staring at it. It was shot in black and white but manipulated afterward to inject yellow from the streetlights to highlight a lone woman walking in the rain, her umbrella held at her side allowing the water to wash over her.

"That's really good." Milo's voice is right behind me, the warmth of his body pulsing against my skin. "Not as good as yours, but a lot of talent."

He's trying to be supportive, encouraging. But I have eyes in my head, and there's no denying the aptitude for lighting this graduate has. "She should be the one teaching my class. Not me."

You know that feeling you get in your chest when you have a painful realization about yourself? Like you're embarrassed, angry, and are about to sob at the same time? Just me? That's how I feel looking at that photo. I can see the skill this person has; I can practically see the techniques that were needed, what she used to capture the image the way she did. I could teach a whole unit using only this photo as reference.

Milo groans. "But it doesn't make me feel anything. Not the way your photos make me feel."

Turning, I cross my arms and glare at him. "You've only seen one, and you were the subject."

"Not true. You have a bunch of them on the wall in your bedroom. And there's that nice one of Casa Loma in your living room." Slipping his hands into his pockets, he rises to his toes for a moment before coming down with a soft thud. "I particularly like the one you took of the child and dog running across the grass in front of the abandoned house. The joy at experiencing that freedom for the first time ..." He presses his hand over his heart.

My mouth has fallen open and a weird nervous energy begins to buzz inside me. "I didn't know you'd noticed those."

"I looked when you were in the bathroom," he says with a wink. "I also love the photo of the storm clouds rolling in just behind the church with the newly married couple emerging." He looks at the photo behind me again. "I've been that couple, so it resonated. This one is pretty, but the Photoshop ruins it a bit. Like she didn't trust me enough to see the streetlight on my own."

I turn to the photo again. "Maybe. But she has tremendous talent that will only improve over time."

Milo moves behind me and takes my hand in his. "You do too."

I don't know if it's the sincerity in his voice or that I'm at a student art exhibit, but feelings that I've been ignoring for years begin to poke at the cracks of my ego. I try to speak, to make some self-deprecating remark the way I always do. But before I start to say something, my throat tightens, and tears spring to my eyes.

I do have talent. What I lack is self-confidence.

"Andie?"

Turning so my shoulder is pressed to his chest, I resist burying my face against him. I have to swallow once, then again, to get the words past the lump. "No one came to my exhibit." It's little more than a whisper, but the way he stiffens, I know he heard.

That single sentence is the first hole finally poked through the wall of denial I've built. I squeeze his hand hard, close my eyes, and let the pain of the last twenty years flow through me.

"I'd always wanted to be a travel photographer. I wanted to go to new countries and capture images to show others who weren't able to go. I wanted to look at the world in a new way, show beauty where others didn't see it. No one ever encouraged me. My parents didn't want me to leave home. My teachers never thought I was brilliant, just average. All I wanted was for someone, anyone, to look at the thing I made and say *Wow, you're really good at this. You've made me feel something with your art.* "Thank you for that."

Milo's grip on my hand is nearly painful. I know he understands.

Tears escape my eyes, but I don't move to brush them away. "The one time I took a chance on myself, put my art out there and was willing to accept praise or criticism, I didn't even inspire a single person to come. So I packed up my dreams, tucked them away, and resigned myself to working at Walmart. Not everyone is meant to live the fantasy life they wished for as kids."

I glance up at him. I'm not the least bit surprised at the anger on his face. He's mad on my behalf, which is sweet. Reaching for his cheek, I brush my thumb across the stubble, enjoying how it feels. "I gave up on myself. But you've made me wonder if maybe it really isn't too late to start again. That maybe I needed to live my life a bit before I was ready to live my dream."

"Andie ..."

I don't care if there are people around, or that I'm technically at a work thing. Turning all the way against him, I slide my hand to the back of his head and pull him down for a kiss. It's soft, gentle, like the light patter of rain before a storm. His body trembles against me, but I can't be sure if it's from desire or anger. When I pull back and look him in the eyes, I smile and hope he understands it's okay.

He runs his thumb across my lips before looking away and taking a deep breath. As he lets it out slowly, I watch his expression change, an array of emotions flickering quickly past. "Whenever I see the picture you took of me on the bench, I see how tired I feel. If that makes sense. I ... I've been trying to take care of Mia, help her deal with her mother walking out on us, deal with these unexpectedly horrible mental health problems. Shit, just dealing with her being a teenage girl ... I'm so ... tired."

It's his turn to swallow, emotions making his voice quiver as he spoke. It's my turn to listen, to bear witness to the surge of realization he's living. I take his hand again, to help ground him the way he did for me.

"I love Mia. I don't for a second regret having her or being a single dad. But I feel awful for the challenges she's forced to face. I wish I could give her more of what she needs to cope. I just want my baby to be happy, and I feel like I'm failing at providing her that basic need."

It's hard to keep from jumping in, from interrupting him to tell him what an amazing dad he is, or that he's doing everything he can to give her the life she needs. Instead, I lean against him.

He sets his chin on the top of my head. "When Rachel left, I knew I'd failed as a husband. I need to know I'm not a failure as a father too."

"You're not a failure. You're an amazing parent."

The huff of his breathing moves the hairs on my head. "I'm so tired."

"I know. You put your own needs on the back burner constantly, and that can be exhausting."

He chuckles. "Dee calls it caretaker fatigue."

"Maybe that's what I should call my photo of you."

The cloud that descended over us begins to lift. As I look up, he smiles at me as he clears his throat. "I'll allow it. If you ever have your own art display like this, you can use my photo and its title can be that."

The urge to say I'll never have another exhibit doesn't immediately spring from my mouth. There isn't that crushing dread, the retroactive embarrassment that comes with the thought of it. A tiny part of me might welcome the idea of trying again.

The sound of laugher echoes around us and the fleeting moment of privacy is over. Milo takes a small step away, his gaze moving toward the door. "I guess we should probably mingle."

"Yeah. I don't want to upset Mr. Robichaud."

Before I take a step, my phone that I shoved into my small clutch buzzes. Once, then twice, a small pause, and then three more times. Milo's phone also begins to buzz.

Dread fills me as I pull it out. "Oh no."

"What's wrong."

"TikTok notifications." I frown. "And a bunch of text messages from Lucy."

I click the text and my heart sinks.

Ms M, Mia's in trouble.

"What's wrong?" Milo tries to look at my screen upside down.

"Hang on."

I open the link Lucy sent. It leads to a TikTok video. It's from an account I don't recognize; the only person I know in the short clip is Mia. The video is muted, but I don't need to hear what's being said to recognize what's happening.

"Is that Mia? Is she at a party?"

Milo takes my phone and unmutes the video. It loops around. The pain I saw plays one more time, along with the auditory heartbreak. She's talking to a guy, who I have to assume is in on whatever is happening. The person recording is giggling, the camera shaking as they watch Mia speaking. The boy, laughs at her and shouts, "I'd never go out with a freak like you." The whole room laughs, and Mia runs away crying.

The girl recording the video snarks, "How's that for a viral video. Bitch." And the whole thing loops again.

Milo is stunned, angry, and upset all at once. Me? Well, I'm fucking pissed off. Snatching the phone from him, I shove it into my purse. "Let's go."

"I ... I don't know where she is. I ..."

Grabbing his hand, I yank him out of his stupor and toward the door. We pass Dean Robichaud, who is standing with someone I can only assume is a mega donor. He smiles at me; it feels odd. "There she is. This is Andie Matheson, the social media expert I was telling you about."

"I'm very sorry, Dean, but we have to leave."

I'm expecting him to be angry, but instead he frowns. "Everything okay?"

I glance at Milo. "No, we have a family emergency."

"Go, then. I hope everything works out." He steps out of my way.

"Thanks. Me too." And I race out, stilling clinging to Milo, hoping things aren't as bad as I fear.

THIRTY-THREE

Milo

I'm so panicked about what I witnessed with Mia, I nearly forgot about the rental. Thankfully, Andie is clear headed. She fishes the keys out of my pocket and gets into the driver's seat. "Call her."

Why that wasn't my first impulse, I don't know. Probably something to do with the dread at watching my baby get publicly humiliated. I hit her number and let it ring until her voice mail picks up. I hang up and call again. I call three more times before switching to texts.

> Baby, are you okay?
>
> I saw the video.
>
> Mia, hon, I need you to tell me you're okay.
>
> Honey, please answer me.

I switch to texting Steph and Luna, the only girls Mia hung out with before the whole TikTok thing blew up. Neither one of them has heard from her, but they say they'll start reaching out and will let me know if they find out anything. I'm so wrapped up in talking to them and texting anyone else I can think of, I don't immediately realize the car has come to a stop.

"I didn't know where to come, so I brought you home." Andie sounds angry, but her voice also feels small in the cabin of the car. She doesn't look at me as she plays with the rental company tag that dangles from the key fob. "What now?"

I look up at my building. This is my nightmare come to pass. I've been so involved with Andie, the TikTok account, and Painbringer, I let Mia's needs fall to the side. She's supposed to be the most important thing in my life, and I've ignored her to the point that I didn't even clue in she was going to a party. I should have known, should have realized.

"I need to find my daughter." I want to punch myself for failing her. "I should never have gone."

"Maybe we can make a TikTok video? Put the call out there to people to help us find her?"

"Absolutely not!" I exit the car and slam the door shut. Andie also gets out, but I can't look her in the eyes. "That fucking account is what caused this mess in the first place. I'm not doing anything on there again!"

"I …" She sets the key fob on the roof of the car. "Maybe I should go."

"Yes." Of course she wants to leave. That's how these things go. "That's probably for the best." I snag the key from the roof and move to the driver's side. "I'm going to park this then find Mia."

I say nothing else to Andie. She moves fully onto the sidewalk, allowing me to enter the building's underground parking. The anger begins to cool and morph into gut wrenching fear by the time I pull into my parking spot and make my way back up to the surface. I'm not surprised that Andie is nowhere to be seen.

All that matters now is finding Mia.

The first place I check is the condo. I pray she returned and is ignoring me. Or that her phone battery died and is charging. I know the second I step inside she's not home. My baby is hurting and alone somewhere in Toronto. I need to find her, pull her into my arms, and promise her that I'll never let anything bad like this happen again.

I change into my sneakers and get my jacket before heading out again. Stepping out onto the street, I look up and down the sidewalk, not knowing where to start. The muscles in my chest tighten, and my head begins to swim.

No.

No, no, no, I am *not* going to have a panic attack. Not now when I need to be at my best. Not when Mia needs me to be more Painbringer and less painfully mortal dad who didn't leave the house enough. I close my eyes, try to calm my breathing, and pull myself together. While I'd normally hear Dee's voice in these moments, running me through what I need to do to pull myself together, this time it is Andie's voice I hear. Andie's smile I picture in my head as I count back from ten.

It's Andie who I wish hadn't listened to me and had stayed to help me find Mia.

God, you're a fucking idiot.

"I need a plan." Opening my eyes, I know there isn't anything I can do standing in the middle of the sidewalk. I go back to the car and start my search.

THE POLICE COULDN'T DO MUCH of anything for me. Even after I show the woman at the front desk the video of the bullying, she doesn't offer much help. Mia can't be considered missing yet, and there's been no indication of her going anywhere not of her own volition.

The trip to the closest emergency room was the hardest one I've ever had to make. The triage nurse also can't tell me much, but thankfully, no one fitting Mia's description has come in. I go to the next closest hospital with thankfully similar results.

Falling back into the driver's seat, I press my forehead to the steering wheel.

What I should do is find the girls who've been pretending to be Mia's friends and see if they know where she is. The house where I left her is at least a place to start.

THERE ARE MORE cars lining either side of the street where I dropped Mia off than there were earlier. There's a parking spot a few houses down from my destination, which gives me a few minutes to get myself together. My heart races as I try to calm my fears and get a handle on my anger. The air is crisp on my face but does little to cool my heated skin.

As I get close to the house, I'm greeted by the low thudding of music playing inside. When I'd dropped Mia off, I'd been impressed with how nice the house was, with it's two stories and modern flat roof. This was a great area of Toronto and I'd foolishly assumed that meant Mia would be safe. Now, all I could see was a house of horrors.

A steady stream of people come in and out the front door, letting the music blast outside unfiltered. Pushing my way past a trio of guys standing outside vaping, they glare, one blowing a sickly-sweet cloud in my direction. I don't care what they think of me being here. All that matters is finding Mia and making sure she's safe.

I'll fall apart later.

Stepping inside, I stumble over the piles of shoes by the door, making the large foyer a danger zone to traverse. The music is deafening, with people laughing and shout-talking. The smell of spilled beer and weed makes my stomach turn, forcing me to hold my breath as I step through a group of teens dancing in the entrance to the living room. No one pays any attention at first, which gives me the opportunity to spot the girls who came to my house. The ones who hurt Mia. Marching over to the sound system, I turn it off and wait for the shouts of complaint to die down and everyone's attention to land squarely on me. Only then, when I know I'll be heard, do I speak.

"Where's Mia?"

The tall girl, the one I suspect was holding the camera, moves forward. "She's not here." She lifts her phone to record me. "What are you doing here? You need to leave."

I know when I'm being baited.

Several more people lift their phones and point them at me. No doubt they're all hoping I'll lose my shit and they'll get another viral moment. I couldn't care less about them, not when Mia needs my help. Ignoring everyone but the two girls who were in my home, I move to stand in front of them. Not so close that I pose a physical threat, but close enough to force them to look me in the eye.

"You used her. You came into my home and made her feel like you were her friends. And for what? Views? Clicks on a social media program? None of you bothered to get to know her. To know how smart she is, or funny. How talented she is. You wanted her to be a punchline to your sad little joke."

I look around the room, make sure each phone has a good view of my face. "You've taken this amazing tool and turned it into a weapon. You've hurt someone I love more than anything. But she's going to be okay. She's stronger than anyone here. I'm going to find her, and we'll continue forward." I turn back to the girls, looking them each in the eyes. "Mia will come out of this stronger. And you? You'll still be nothing more than bullies."

Knowing there's nothing else for me here, I walk away to continue my search.

THIRTY-FOUR

Andie

The Uber was just around the corner when I put the request in, giving me an easy escape. As much as I wanted to stay and help Milo, I know his fear, anger, and frustration are too high. I'd likely be the unfortunate scapegoat for those emotions, even if I know he would come to regret his reactions later. Mom is much the same way, and I realize sometimes running away is the best option.

But that doesn't mean I won't do anything to help.

I fall into the backseat of the uber, as the driver smiles at me. "Hi there. Good evening?"

"Not really. Do you mind waiting for a minute?"

She shrugged. "Sure."

I pull up my text messages and open the last one from Lucy. She's continued to ping me since the video of Mia went live, which gives me an idea.

> Hey, what's your address?

When she gives it to me, I ask my Uber driver to change my destination address and give her a huge tip when I get out. Lucy is standing at her front door, her Raptor's snapback nowhere in sight. Instead, her hair is pulled back into a neat ponytail at the base of her neck, and she's wearing jeans and a T-shirt.

"Hey, Ms. M."

"Hey." I make my way to her front door and stop before coming into her house, struck once again by how young she looks. "Thank you so much for helping."

"Yeah, no problem." She looks back over her shoulder. "Ah, is it okay if I introduce you to my parents first? They're watching TV."

"Of course! I'd love to meet them."

"I know we don't have a lot of time. I promise it won't take long."

"Lucy, it's fine. I'm a stranger showing up unannounced." I smile as I step into the foyer. "Besides, I love to meet your parents."

I follow her through the immaculately decorated house to a sunken living room just off a beautiful open kitchen. Her parents are sitting side by side on a couch, her dad watching the TV while her mom reads a book. Lucy squirms slightly. "Hey, ah. Ms. M—I mean, Ms. Matheson is here. She's my photography teacher at the college."

Both faces turn to look at me, their skin illuminated by the light of the TV. Her dad gives me a little wave and returns to watching the Blue Jays game, while mom immediately gets up to greet me. "Lucy, why didn't you tell me your teacher was coming over? I would have had refreshments out."

"It's fine." It's then I look at the clock on the wall and clue in to just how late it's getting. "I'm very sorry to intrude this late at night. I need Lucy's help with a time-sensitive problem."

The expression her mom gives her tells me she doesn't quite know how Lucy could assist.

"Right." Lucy keeps her gaze locked on mine. "Speaking of that. What can I do?"

I hesitate, not sure if there's any reason I shouldn't say

anything about her social media influence or not. But time really is running out. We need to find Mia as quickly as possible. "Mia's missing."

Lucy's eyes widen slightly. "I was worried something had happened after that video."

"What video?" Her mom is clearly invested now. "I assume you've gone to the police?"

"There's not much they can do. Her dad is out looking for her, and I know he'll call around. But I also know Mia follows your TikTok account. I was wondering if you could put a call out to your followers? Seeing how good they are at finding people." There's no way I'm about to elaborate on that particular matter.

Lucy hesitates for the briefest of moments before nodding and racing away. Her mom makes a clicking noise in the back of her throat that sounds so much like something my mother would do, the response it brings up in me is nearly visceral.

"That girl. She spends so much time on her phone instead of focusing on the real world. I worry about her. How is she doing in your class? Are her marks good?"

It's not my place to discuss Lucy's marks with someone other than her, but this isn't the first time I've had a parent want to know. Thankfully, I don't have to mince words. "Lucy is an amazing student. She's smart, picks up on concepts faster than anyone else, and is passionate about what she does. She's also kind, funny, and a good friend."

Her mom seems startled at first, then smiles widely. "Oh. That's good."

Lucy returns, her Raptor's hat on and her hair down. "Okay, tell me what you want me to share."

Her mom steps away, but I can feel her eyes on us. I join Lucy off to the side. "Can you tell people that Mia had a bad experience?"

"I can duet the video and tell them that she's hurting and we need to find her."

"You think that will be enough?"

"They found your guy, didn't they?" She grins, presses a few buttons on her phone and walks away from me.

"Hey all my T-dot peeps! See this bullshit? My friend Mia was bullied at a party by a bunch of jerks and now she's missing. I need you, my friends, to help Ms. M find her." She spins the phone around to face me, and all I can do is give a little wave before she turns it back to her. "Let me know in the comments if you've seen Mia. And Mia, I know you're a follower. If you see this, call your dad. He's worried."

And with the press of a few buttons, the video is live.

Not that it does anything to help ease my tension. Mia is out there alone, hurting. Milo is also out there somewhere, angry and hurting. There's little I can do to help either of them. They aren't my family. Milo and I are close, but we aren't a couple. And yet, in the few months that we've been together, that we've been running our channel, I've grown so close to them both that I feel like they're mine. They're a part of my Toronto family, and I simply can't picture my life without them in it. Even if nothing else comes about with my relationship with Milo.

Even if I never get to tell him that I might have fallen in love with him.

"Ms. M?" Lucy is still holding her phone in her hand like a type of shield. "Are you okay?"

"I ..." The urge to lie is nearly as strong as my urge to cry. "No. I'm not."

"We'll find her. My followers are good at this sort of thing."

"Don't I know it." I laugh past the rising lump in my throat. "I was offered a job in the US as a travel photographer."

I don't know who's more surprised by my confession, me or Lucy. She shakes her head as her gaze narrows. "Like a sponsorship?"

"No, an actual job. They liked my photos and think I'd be a good fit for their company."

"Are you going to take it?"

"I don't know." The words are hard to speak.

"Does Milo know?"

I shake my head. "I was going to talk to him tonight about it before we knew Mia was missing. Then it just didn't seem important."

"Yeah, that makes sense." She bites down on her bottom lip. "For what it's worth, I'll miss you if you leave. You're my favorite teacher. But I know you need to do the things that make you happy."

And there's the real crux of my problem. Would leaving Milo and Mia, leaving Canada ... would that make me happy?

It really is a problem to figure out, but not now.

Lucy's phone has been beeping off and on, but all of a sudden something she sees grabs her attention. She immediately begins to type away, her eyes widening slightly. I try to catch a peek at what she's looking at, to no avail. "What's going on?"

"Hang on. We might have something." The light from her screen casts dancing shadows across her face, highlighting her smile as it blooms. "Oh my God, I think we found her."

"No way! Where is she?"

"Hang on. Just getting confirmation."

My heart pounds and I feel nauseous as the seconds drag on. I want to scream at whoever is on the other end of the phone to hurry up and tell me that Mia is okay. That she's safe, and Milo won't have to grieve for a lost child. I turn my phone around and around in my palm, waiting to text Milo some good news. Hell, I think any news would be helpful at this point. The not knowing is gut wrenching.

"Okay, so, I'm talking to someone who is at the Canada's Wonderland Halloween Haunt. They're one of the custodial staff, and they see her sitting at a bench." Lucy flips her phone around for me to see a short looping video of Mia sitting down, clearly upset. "That's her, right?"

"Oh, thank God." The tension lessens.

"Do you want me to have them go talk to her?"

I honestly don't know what to do. Milo would know the best way to handle the situation, would know if she needs a hug or to be left the hell alone. "Have them just keep an eye on her for the time being. I'm going to call her dad."

"You got it."

Stepping outside into the cool late-October air, I dial Milo's number. He answers almost immediately. "Andie?"

"I know you said not to, but I had Lucy reach out to her TikTok people."

"I don't care about that. I've been walking around downtown for over an hour. Where is she?"

"Canada's Wonderland."

"Shit." His relief is palpable. "Okay, ah, I have the rental. I'll drive out there and get her." He pauses, and I can hear him walking faster, no doubt having turned around to head to the car. "Do you want me to get you?"

He still wants you. "It will add too much time for you to swing around to pick me. I'll order an Uber and meet you at the entrance."

"Sounds good."

I go back inside to tell Lucy I'm leaving when another thought occurs to me. "Lucy, I know it's late, but would you mind coming with me? I think it would help Mia to see that there are people out there who do actually care about her. Plus, she really admires you."

Lucy stands straighter, her gaze shifting to her mother. "Do you mind?"

I take a step closer. "My friend's daughter respects Lucy, trusts her, despite not having met her in person. It would really help having Lucy there. I promise I'll make sure she gets back home safely."

Her mom looks between us before nodding. "Let me know if everything is okay."

"I will." Lucy runs over and kisses her mom's cheek. "Thanks."

We step back outside, and I'm about to call an Uber when Lucy holds up car keys. "I can get us there faster."

"Awesome. Let's go get Mia."

THIRTY-FIVE

Milo

The parking lot is bloody full. Like, all the way. I have to circle around three times before I find someone who's leaving — kind of full. And once I do get parked—of course near the back of the lot—I have to run and make my way up the pathway to the entrance pavilion to pay my entrance fee.

The young man makes sure I don't have anything on me before letting me through the gate, along with other late-night attendees.

"Thanks for coming. The park closes at midnight." The girl at the ticket booth smiles at me. "Have fun!"

I'm most definitely *not* going to have a good time.

Walking into the park is like walking into a Tim Burton film. Glowing jack-o-lanterns hang above me from black, twisted cables that resemble vines. The streetlamps are draped in orange and black fabric that somehow manage to glow. Musicians walking around in full costume—skeletons with drums that are rimmed with white glowsticks—had a crowd trailing behind them. There are suddenly so many people here watching and laughing, their phones alight as they record the mini event, that it becomes diffi-cult to breathe.

The impulse to turn and leave is so strong, I catch myself beginning to do just that. "Shit."

This is a lot. Everything that has happened with Mia, is *still* happening with Mia, along with walking away from Andie ... I'm becoming so overwhelmed, I don't know if I can see this through. I need to be strong, to get through the next hour or so. Then I can fall apart.

Quietly. At home. Probably in the shower.

Until then, I let my mind race through all the cognitive techniques I've ever learned to keep me calm and focused. I know Mia is here, but I don't have a clue specifically where. And while I can run off blindly searching, Andie will be here soon to help.

Andie.

During the drive here, my mind oscillated between worry about Mia and guilt over how I treated Andie. She didn't deserve my anger when she was only trying to help. Still, I was so consumed with my longing for something more, for a relationship that isn't centered on Mia, that I screwed up and didn't see the problem staring me in the face. Andie was right about those girls, and I ignored my gut and the creeping doubts. I could have helped Mia avoid this completely if I'd acted on those feelings sooner. If I hadn't been so distracted with the promise of a new life, of a new opportunity to live.

If I hadn't been so preoccupied with Andie.

"Milo!"

Andie emerges from the crowds and not from the entrance where I assumed she'd be. She has a glowstick necklace on, which looks strange paired with her formal dress and high heels. Shit, she didn't go home to change. She shivers but doesn't give me a moment to ask if she's okay.

"Mia's over here. Come on."

I don't know what I expected, but seeing Mia sitting on a bench smiling and talking with another person wasn't it. All the fear that has fueled me for hours evaporates. Anger swells up so fast and so hot, I nearly lose my cool. I want to yell, scream at her for scaring the shit out of me. Instead, I stride toward Mia, my hands shoved deep in my pockets to hide the fact they're balled into fists.

She doesn't see me, which gives me the chance to really look at her. Mia isn't a child. She's a young woman who's been through a shitty event, and I have to hope she'll come out stronger for the experience like I told her bullies she would. As much as I want to keep her safe from the world, to ease her anxiety and make everything easy sailing, I know I can't. There will always be things I can't predict, can't save her from having to live through. I can't always be a superhero who swoops in and protects her from the world.

The more I've tried to keep her insulated, the less resilient she's become. The easier it is for others to take advantage of her.

With my anxiety clawing at the back of my throat, I manage to say, "Baby?"

Her smile vanishes as her head snaps around to finally look at me. The next thing I know, she's on her feet, her arms wrapped around my torso and her face buried against my shoulder. "Daddy."

I hug her back hard. My little girl is safe. Hurting, but safe. "I was so worried about you."

Her fingers curl against my skin beneath my jacket.

Andie and the other girl—Lucy, her name is Lucy—begin to move away. Before they get too far, I hold out my hand, stopping them both. "Lucy, thank you for helping us. It means a lot."

"No problem." She looks around. "I'm going to check out the show. Coming Ms. M?"

I feel Andie's gaze on me, but I can't quite bring myself to look at her.

"Yup." The hurt in her voice is obvious.

The crowd is flowing around us, and the closeness is becoming a bit much for me to handle. "Can we sit down?"

I feel Mia nod before stepping away. "I'm sorry."

The bench she was sitting on with Lucy is still open, so we make our way over to sit. Mia shivers as we sit and I realize she doesn't have a jacket on. "How did you pay to get in here?"

"I have my phone with me."

I've never been so thankful for buying her the fancy case with the spot to hold her debit card. "Don't move."

Looking around, I find a gift shop that's open. I run over and grab the first large hoodie I come across and pay for it just as quickly. Pulling it over Mia's head, I trap her arms while I free her face from the aggressive hood. "That will warm you up."

She smiles, but I can tell she's embarrassed.

The urge to jump in and talk, to tell her everything is going to be okay is strong. The me from a few months ago absolutely would have. The me from tonight is too exhausted.

Mia focus flits around the park, everywhere but on me. "I'm sorry."

I still don't say anything.

She huffs. "I shouldn't have lied to you about the party. But I knew you wouldn't have let me go if you knew the truth about what was happening."

"There's a reason I would have said no." I somehow manage to stop short from completing that sentence with the *look what happened to you* part.

"I know." She brushes away the tears that escape her eyes with the heel of her palm. "I just ... I hoped that they really liked me. That ... I wasn't a freak that people made fun of." The last part is barely a whisper, the words swallowed by the cheer of a group of people passing by.

Taking her hand in mine I squeeze it. Hard. "You're not a freak."

"I feel like it. My brain is broken, and I can't ..."

When she doesn't finish, I move a bit closer. "Maybe you can't right now. That doesn't mean you won't be able to forever. That doesn't mean that once your body has stopped growing, you won't get a handle on things. It doesn't mean you won't make friends and go to university or college. It doesn't mean you won't get a boyfriend. Or a girlfriend. You know I don't care about that right?"

She rolls her eyes.

The power of my emotions make it difficult to speak. Milo Beechum can't continue, but Painbringer can. Lowering my voice, I squeeze her hand again. "I promise you this. I shall smash that mountain. Crush the rocks beneath my boot. Burn the demons to ash. I will make the path. But you must choose to walk it."

Mia looks up at me, and chuckles. "Thanks."

"I owe *you* an apology."

She frowns. "What for?"

"You're right. I probably wouldn't have let you go to that party. It's easy for me to forget sometimes that you're not a child anymore. You're a young adult who is smart and knows what she wants. Just because you have anxiety and depression doesn't mean that's who and what you are. I've held you back in a way. My intentions were to keep you safe, but I think I was actually preventing you from living your life."

"Dad, I'm a wreck. You've only done what you thought I needed from you." She leans against my side, and I get the sense that she's okay. "I turned my phone off when I left the party. I was embarrassed and didn't want to talk to anyone. I didn't want to go home, though. These last few months with Andie and filming the TikToks has made me ... braver. So I came here. I wanted to see what all the fuss was about."

An actor dressed as a bloody zombie runs through the crowd, yelling and moaning as he chases a group of screaming teens.

"It's something." I wonder where Andie's gone off to. "It's still too many people for my liking."

"Yeah. But it strangely isn't too many for me. I think ... I need to push myself a bit more. Maybe look for a part-time job. Or something."

"That's a great idea."

"It might be too much for me, but like my therapist said, if I don't try to put myself out there, nothing will change." She runs her hands through her hair and suddenly hands me her phone. "Actually, I need to do something."

"What?"

"Make a TikTok."

I'm not certain where she's going with this, but I have to trust her. Turning to get a better shot of her, I open the app and nod when I hit record.

"Hey, everyone. I know some of you may have seen the video of me circulating tonight. I wanted to let you all know that I'm okay and with my dad." Another screaming zombie races past her, bringing a smile to her face. "I'm at the Halloween Haunt at Canada's Wonderland. It's far less terrifying than other things I've seen tonight. If you're out there and someone has hurt you, I want you to know that it's okay to be upset. But reach out to people who love you for help. Nothing is so bad that you can't figure it out, can't move past it. You're bigger than the bullies. Love you all."

She nods and I stop recording. "Good for you, baby."

With a few quick button presses, the video goes live. Mia turns her phone off and sticks it in her pocket. "I'll deal with the rest of the fall out tomorrow."

I wrap my arm around her. "I'm so proud of you, baby."

The crowd parts and I can see a stage in the background. Music blares, and a man steps out, two flaming chains hanging from his arms. He spins them around to the delight of the people watching. It only takes me a moment to spot Andie toward the back, her arms wrapped around herself. She's probably freezing despite her jacket. "I should buy Andie a hoodie too."

Mia leans out to see what I'm looking at. "Are you two okay?

She didn't say very much when her and Lucy found me. I just assumed she was mad at me."

"I don't know." I don't want to make anything tonight about myself, not with Mia still struggling. "It's something we'll have to work out."

"Dad?"

"Yeah."

"I really like her." She sits back and looks me in the eyes. "I like you when you're around her. You seem happier."

Am I? "I'm not exactly unhappy without her."

"Yes, you are. In the last few months, you've seemed more like you were ... before."

Before Rachel left.

"Maybe."

"I know you haven't dated, or really done much of anything because of me and my problems. I'm sorry about that."

"It's not like you've done this on purpose."

She shrugs. "I haven't. But that doesn't mean it doesn't suck for you. You've given up a lot because of me. I don't want you to give up Andie. Not if you don't want to."

I don't.

Getting to my feet, I head toward her. Mia will either follow me or she'll be okay for a few minutes on her own. Andie didn't deserve the way I treated her tonight, even if she understands. She must sense my approach because the next thing I know, she turns and starts to come my way.

My brain instantly plays out a scene where she rushes into my arms, and I sweep her off her feet to spin her around. In the scenario, I wrap my coat around her to keep her warm and whisper an apology to the side of her throat. It's beautiful—romantic. It quickly evaporates when she stops moving and holds out her hand to stop me as well.

"Andie?"

"Is Mia okay?" She looks calm, resigned. It's not an expression I'm used to associating with her.

"For now. I'm sure we'll have more to talk about. Things she'll need to speak to her therapist about."

Andie nods. "I've been offered a job as a photojournalist for a travel company."

"Oh my God, Andie. That's amazing."

"In Texas."

Her words feel like a punch to the chest. "You're moving?" *Please don't leave.*

"Maybe." She turns her face back to the fire dancer. "I need to think."

I want to beg her not to go. I would fall on my knees right here if I thought it would make a difference. But that isn't fair to her. This is her opportunity to finally live out her childhood dream, and I'll be damned if I'm the reason she doesn't follow through.

She pulls her jacket tighter around her. "I'm going to go."

"I can drive you."

She shakes her head. "Lucy will take me back."

"I ... okay." *Please don't go.*

She steps away but smiles softly. "I'm so happy we found her. I'll leave you two to talk things out."

"Andie—"

"Bye, Milo." And before I know it, she's disappeared in the crowd.

THIRTY-SIX

Andie

It's been a week since Mia's disappearance. One week since I felt relief on a scale that I've never experienced before, knowing Mia was okay. One week since I told Milo about the job offer and saw the look of panic and upset flash across his face.

To say I've been ignoring his texts, calls, and emails out of a sense of self-preservation sounds a tad more dramatic than I'd like. Despite it partially being the truth. But I know there's no way I'd be able to work out what I need to do if I had Milo here. A part of me knows I'd default to staying because I know that's what he wants. If he never comes out and says it directly, the look on his face that night told me everything. He wanted me to turn it down.

I know he'd never make me choose between him and the job. He'd be the first one to encourage me to pack up and move to Texas. Milo has a good heart and constantly puts others before himself. Which is why I have to ignore his messages. Why I can't watch any of the videos we scheduled to post ahead of time. Or even look at the updates to our fan fics. This is a decision I need to make on my own, without the influence of others. If I make a choice and it turns out to be the wrong one, I never want to blame someone else for it, to resent them for trying to help me make the right decision.

This has to be up to me.

For the first time in my professional life, I have an opportunity to follow my dream. To get paid to travel and take photos for a magazine. To have thousands, maybe even hundreds of thousands of people see the world the way I see it and appreciate my art.

So why, sitting at my kitchen table, staring at the contract, am I not jumping for joy?

This is literally everything I've ever wanted. More so! I would be the one having my passport photo taken, the one telling others about all the fantastical trips I'm going to take. I'd be the one to see the enthusiasm and maybe a bit of jealousness in their eyes as they wished they could be me.

I probably need to talk to Holly or Cara about this but they'll no doubt ask me what's wrong, or why I'm hesitating. I don't think I could give them an answer because I honestly don't know.

Is it Milo? Have I actually truly fallen in love with him to the point that I'm willing to give up my dream? Maybe. Or maybe it's not the right offer? I'd have to pack up my life and move to another country, a place I know no one. And while yes, I have in fact done that once already, I'm not a twentysomething with her whole life in front of her. I am, in fact, a forty-five-year-old with a solid chunk of her life still in front of her. This is the perfect time to make another leap and try something new.

So, I read the contract.

There's nothing about it that screams warning. No logical reason to turn them down. It's truly everything I could want in a job. I should take it.

I'm about a third of the way through when my ring tone announces that Mom is calling me. Frowning, I pick it up as I get up for another coffee. "Hey. Whatcha up to?"

"Hello, love."

Ever get a call from someone and know immediately that

they're in trouble? Somehow the cadence of their voice is off just enough that a ripple of dread rolls through you? Just me?

"Mom? What's wrong?"

The silence stretches far past what's reasonable for anyone, let alone my direct-to-the-point mother. I want to fill the silence, to beg her to talk to me and tell me what's the matter. Instead, I bite down on my bottom lip to keep my mouth from opening.

Eventually she lets out a little sigh, that sounds nearly like a sob. "I have some news."

"Are you sick? Is Dad? Do you need me to come home, because I totally will. It's not fair to you or Cara to only have her to help if either of you are sick."

"Andie, sweetie. I need you to listen."

I bite down hard on my lip.

"I'm not sick. Neither is your father." She lets out another huff. "I have a confession."

My mind goes blank. After hearing Cara's suspicion that Mom wants to divorce Dad, I brace myself in case that's what she's about to say.

"I'd been considering leaving your father."

Considering? I get up from the table, move to the middle of my living room, and sit right on the floor. "Mom, what's going on?"

"I don't know where to start."

That makes two of us. "When did you realize you were unhappy?"

"Oh." I hear her moving around on the other end of the line. "I've been miserable for years."

"That sounds very dramatic. And unlike you."

"Perhaps. My therapist says that—"

"Wait, whoa. Since when have you been going to therapy?"

"Five years." She says it as though everyone knows and I'm being dense. "She helped me realize that I've been putting every-one's needs before my own. First you girls, then your father. When we retired, I assumed we'd be able to do some of the things I'd wanted to try. Go on cruises. Learn pickleball. Your father was content to stay home and read. Maybe garden. I thought I'd be able to adjust, but I found myself getting … annoyed."

Cara has always said the reason Mom and I butt heads as much as we do is due to how similar we are. Until this very moment, I never believed her. "I didn't know you had any interest in traveling. Why didn't you just go and leave him home? Cara would have gone on a cruise with you."

"Not you?" There's something hesitant in her voice. It's so unlike her that my heart breaks a little.

"I always thought you preferred Cara's company to mine. But you know I would have gone with you in a heartbeat. Well, as long as I'd had time to save up."

"Andie, I'm sorry. I … I never knew what you needed. You always seemed to be just fine on your own."

Knowing you're not the favorite child is a difficult place to exist in a family. That thing everyone is aware of but no one is keen to acknowledge outright. I learned early on that it was easier for me to do my own thing than to ask for help. Mom rarely fought me on things—well, not until I moved from home. "It just made sense for me to be self-sufficient."

"Is that why you moved?" God, she sounds so small, and yet there's genuine curiosity in her voice.

"I guess." I never really thought much about my reasons beyond the desire to go to school in Toronto. It was impulsive, but it always felt like the right thing. "It gave me the chance to try living a different life without getting in the way of what everyone else wanted. I know you didn't believe in me that way." When she doesn't jump in immediately to deny my statement, my heart breaks a tiny bit more.

Until she speaks again, and I can hear the quiver in her voice. She's crying.

"Oh, baby. I'm a terrible mother."

"No, you're—"

"Shut up and let me get this out." She huffs. "I've always been jealous of you."

I don't think I could have spoken if she'd wanted me to. Jealous? Why the hell would she be jealous?

"You had so much confidence in yourself at such a young age. You decided what you wanted to do, and you did it. And there I was, living a life I was okay with but wanting more. Your father is a lovely man, but the longer we were together the more I realized I was never going to be happy doing the things that he expected of me. It took me until I was seventy-two to realize that it was okay to take a chance and try something new. You learned that at eighteen."

"I ... Why are you always asking me to come home?"

"There was a horrible part of myself that was angry. If I couldn't live the life I'd dreamed of, it didn't seem fair that you got to. I'm so sorry, baby. You never did anything wrong. My therapist has said I have to expect you won't forgive me for that, and I have to accept how you feel. But I am sorry."

I swallow past the lump in my throat. "I forgive you. And I'm sorry I was never really there for you to talk to."

"You have your own life to live."

My brain finally catches up. "So, you're not divorcing Dad?"

"No, of course not."

I pinch the bridge of my nose as my shoulders relax. "What changed?"

"We had a conversation. I told him I wanted to travel, go on some adventures. He said that was fine and he'd be excited to hear all about them when I got home. I have a cruise booked next week."

I give my head a shake. "Really?"

"I'm going to the Caribbean." Something in her tone changes, and for the first time in a long while, she sounds excited. "I've joined a seniors travel group. We all go together, share meals and excursions. It will be fun."

"Mom, I'm really happy for you. I wish I could have been the one to take your passport photo."

"Maybe next time." She pauses again. "What about you?"

"What about me?"

"Cara was telling me about your situation with that man and his daughter."

"His name is Milo, and I don't know. I guess I have my own things to work out."

"I know you will. You've always been true to yourself and your needs. Don't second guess yourself now."

After we hang up, I continue to sit on the floor for a long while listening to the fridge's compressor tick away, my mind turning over everything that's happened. Mom is right that while I might lack self-confidence today, when I was younger I almost always did what felt right. That gut feeling is what led me to Toronto, what brought me to befriend Holly. It was the same thing that compelled me to apply for the teaching position at the college when I doubted they'd want someone like me.

And if I'm being honest, it's the same feeling that made me take the picture of Milo in the first place.

With my eyes closed, I try to relax and let my mind pinpoint exactly what's holding me back. If this really is my dream job, you'd think I'd be leaping at the opportunity. Is there something wrong with it that I'm in denial about?

Or is there something wrong with me?

I get to my feet and march back over to my laptop on the kitchen table, sit down on the chair, and continue reading the contract. Everything about what they're offering is perfect. Except it came twenty years too late.

Packing up my life, leaving my friends to go on a grand adventure that may or may not offer fulfillment isn't something I'm willing to do. I have Holly, my students, and I know I have Milo and Mia if they're who I want. But I don't want to go to them confused, second guessing myself. If they want me, they deserve to know I'm all in and not settling for something that might implode and wreck their lives because I was unwilling to figure out what I want from life.

I need to be an adult and figure my shit out.

"Well, balls." Gravity takes hold, pulling my chin to my chest.

If I'm not going to take the job, that leaves me in the same predicament as before; I need to find employment that gives me some measure of fulfillment. Until I sort that out, there's no way I'll be able to talk to Milo.

Fine.

I open my Gmail and sort through the influx of messages. Like before, most are companies wanting us to use their products, some even offering money. I'm about to click through to the next page when the name of one of the senders catches my attention. It's a local photography store here in Toronto who sells mostly cameras and accessories, reaching out with an offer.

Scanning the page, I cock my head and read it again. "Huh."

It's not a promise to see the world. It's not an exotic position laced with guarantees that they might not be able to keep. Before I know what I'm doing, I pick up the phone and dial the number in the email signature.

My heart pounds as I realize that while this might not be the dream job I wanted when I was twenty, it might very well be the job that gets me to my dreams in my forties.

"Hi there. This is Andie Matheson. I just saw your email, and I was hoping we could chat."

Milo

Dee's office waiting room is hot and the chairs are uncomfortable as I sit uneasy in the silence. I haven't been here in years, which only adds to my discomfort. Still, I'm determined to do this, to prove to myself that the progress I've made over the past few months with Andie isn't solely reliant on her being in my life.

Because there's a good chance she isn't anymore.

The muted thud of heels on the carpeted floor, coming closer at an impressive pace, pulls my attention from the steady stream of traffic flowing past the office's front window. Dee appears in the doorway, her hands on her hips, her brown eyes narrowed on me.

"Well." She gives her head a shake.

I get to my feet to join her. I shouldn't be surprised to see streaks of gray woven through her twists that lay heavily on her shoulders. Or the few deeper lines around her mouth. It has been literally years. We're both older, though I don't know if I've grown any wiser.

"Hi." I hold up my hand in a little wave and let it fall awkwardly to my side. "I thought it was probably time I come in person."

Her bright red lipstick highlights her smirk. "Come on."

The inner office hasn't changed much in the past several years of my absence. Some of the furniture is new—a far more comfortable-looking chair in the corner and several more plants than I remember. I move to the couch and sit down in the middle, the same spot I occupied the previous times I was here.

Dee has a stool and a computer on a little stand. The setup is portable and gives her the chance to make notes. She types something, lets out a sigh, and turns to face me. "Why are you here?"

"Was today not my scheduled appointment?" My heartbeat triples when I think I've mixed up the date. "You should have said something."

"Milo, it's fine. Today is the right day." She folds her hands on her lap, her high heels hooked on the metal footrest of her stool. "You haven't come to see me in person for years. The fact you're here in my office is equal parts exciting and curious to me. It means something significant has happened to you. You were pulled from your routine, and you came here of your own volition. So, I can't help but wonder what made you get dressed, hop in a car, and come all the way here."

It's weird seeing her as we speak. Dee has always been a good match for me as a therapist. She gives off a stern mother vibe but never talks down to me. I know where I stand with her, and that's something I only grow to appreciate more and more as I get older.

She also knows when I need time to think.

I have my phone in my hand, spinning it around and around; the constant motion is soothing. "I have a problem, and I don't understand why."

She frowns slightly but doesn't interject.

"Did I tell you I got the Painbringer role? It's my actual dream part. The game is high budget, and it looks like they're going to want me to do some motion capture for it, which is really fucking cool." I received the script from the director a few days ago, but I haven't been able to bring myself to open it up. Somehow the reality of getting the role feels hollow.

"That unspoken 'but' of yours is very loud right now." Dee shifts, putting her feet flat on the floor. "What's going on?"

Usually during our sessions I disappear into my recording booth when I have to say something difficult. The confined space, the dampened sound somehow makes it easier to get the painful words out into the open. There's so much brightness here, so much life with the green plants stretching toward the light streaming in from her window, it's nearly overwhelming.

"Milo?"

"When I got the email, the first person I wanted to tell was Andie." Why was that so hard to say aloud? It shouldn't have been. She's a good friend, and she helped me with the audition; it was only natural to want to tell her about the details of the next steps.

"Why haven't you?"

"I actually haven't been able to open the script."

It takes some effort, but I fill Dee in on everything that happened with Mia, the party, how Andie was right about the girls using Mia for her social media clout, and her subsequent running away. "Andie did everything she could to help me, to make sure Mia was safely located. And I yelled at her, cut her off, basically discounted her as being able to understand what I was going through. What kind of asshole does that make me?"

"It makes you someone who's been through a lot as a caregiver. It's easy to fall into the trap of believing you're the only one who can help when you've been the main caregiver for a teenager who has more than her fair share of mental health challenges." Dee braces her hands on her knees. "It also makes you normal."

Andie said something similar to me once; the sound of her voice echoes in my head. "I miss her so much."

"Why don't you call her?"

"I have. Texted too. She's not responding, and I don't want to turn into some psycho stalker, so I stopped. I mean, she's probably getting ready to move to Texas. She was offered her dream job as a travel photographer, and I wouldn't do anything to get in her way. I know what it's like when someone doesn't support you. The last thing she needs is some overly needy guy pining after her while she's packing."

Mia has been equally upset that Andie isn't around any longer, but she's also been embraced again by her true friends at school. I know she still has a lot of challenges to work out while she continues to learn how to manage her anxiety and depression, but the trauma of the party hasn't hit her as hard as I feared it might. That leaves me on my own more than I expected.

Alone and missing Andie.

Dee turns in her seat and makes a few notes on her computer. "That's something I've always appreciated about you."

"What's that?"

"You're self-aware." She finishes typing and faces me. "So you don't want to get in her way, but you want to let her know your feelings."

"Basically, yes."

"And what are those feelings?"

"That I love her." It took me a long time to realize that what I really feel is love. I wasn't merely obsessed with her kindness, but held genuine affection in my heart. "I love her, and I want her to stay here in Toronto with us."

Dee cocks her head. "I haven't met Andie, but I get the impression she's capable of making up her own mind about things. You need to trust that if she wants to go or stay, that's what she will choose."

My mind begins to race. Thoughts and memories of our time together make it impossible to focus on anything else. I get to my feet, the sudden rush of energy compelling me to move. "I ah, I have to go."

Dee's smirk tells me all I need to know. "Mmmhmmm. Will I see you at our next appointment?"

"Yes." I want to kiss her. "Thank you for everything you do for me."

"You're welcome. Now go."

I leave the office and pull my phone out to text Mia and order an uber.

> Baby, I need your help.

Of course! I'm done class in an hour and will be home after.

I step out of the building and am temporarily blinded by sunlight. I have to wait for my eyes to adjust before I respond.

> Don't leave. I'll pick you up.

Why?

> I'll explain when I get you.

Her pause lasts until my Uber arrives.

Is this about Andie?

> Yes.

Excellent. :)

Dee is right. I need to let Andie know how much she means to me, even if it does nothing to change her decision to move to Texas. I have a plan to let her know I care for her. Beyond that, all I can do is hope.

THIRTY-EIGHT

Andie

The meeting with Samara, the store manager for Cameron's Photos, is amazing, and more than a little unexpected. She shows me around the store—I've bought several lenses here over the years—introduces me to a few people, before taking me next door to the empty storefront.

They're looking to expand to do more to support the local art scene. Samara walks me around the space. "There's a lot of online competition for photography accessories, and high-end digital cameras aren't flying off the shelves. I want to have something that will not only support local artists but will make our store more of a destination for people to visit. Having an art gallery is the option I feel works with our mission statement. And I need someone who can help me run it."

Me.

She wants me to run it.

Not only that, I'll also be able to teach classes to beginners and have my own art on display for others to see. I won't have to pack up my life and walk away from the people and places that mean more to me than I can ever say. "The fact I've gone viral, that I'm more than a little internet famous at this stage, isn't a bit of a detractor?"

"I'm being up front here; that's one of the draws for me." Samara grins. "Social media 101 would be an easy sell with you as the instructor."

"I wouldn't mind creating some introduction courses. Maybe weekend workshops." I laugh as I shake her hand. "I have to say, this is incredibly appealing. Can I have some time to think about it?"

"Of course. But if you don't mind letting me know one way or the other, I'd appreciate it."

Leaving the store, I stand and stare up at the sign and what might be the perfect position for me. Is it the dream job of my youth? No. I've changed over the years and hadn't allowed myself to let my dreams and ambitions grow and change with me.

There was nothing wrong with wanting to travel and see the world. There was equally nothing wrong with wanting to have stability in a place where I loved to be. While I'm not about to race back in and tell Samara I want the job, I know I'm going to take it. The mild dread I've felt since the email from *Travel Now* magazine arrived is gone. The tension and low-level anxiety I've been living with has receded, leaving me with a sense of satisfaction.

Despite being more than a little lonely over the past two weeks.

My text notification dings as I take my seat on the bus. I half expect to see Milo's name on the screen, though he stopped texting a while ago, so I'm shocked when it's Mia's name and number on the display. Terrified that something's happened, I open it up only to be faced with a TikTok link.

I uninstalled the app shortly after we located Mia and I knew she was safe. Having it there, the constant reminder of my time with Milo, was more than I could handle while I was trying to figure my shit out. But that doesn't mean I can't still see the video. Popping my headphones in, I wait for them to connect before clicking the link.

I'm immediately faced with Milo walking through a thin crowd at Canada's Wonderland. He isn't looking at the camera, which Mia is holding in such a way as to get his profile. "We really doing this?"

He glares at the screen. "Yes."

"Oh boy, people. If you thought the CN Tower was a good one, just you wait."

Oh my God. What the hell is he doing?

Mia sends another link; I click it just as quickly. This time they're in line for a ride, and I lean closer to my screen, wanting to hug the panicked look off his face. "So, Dad, what ride are we going on?"

"The Leviathan."

Mia turns the phone so we can see half her face. She's having far too much fun at Milo's expense. "Are you ready?"

"I'm fuc—" He snaps his mouth shut, licks his lips, and starts again. "I'm terrified." Then he grins.

Oh dear.

I don't even bother waiting for Mia to send the next link. I go directly to the MAndM account and click it directly.

Milo has his eyes shut as he and Mia are being pulled up in the rollercoaster car to the top. I haven't been on the Leviathan in a while, but I remember that initial pull up to the first drop as long and more than a little nerve wracking. Milo is braced back hard against the seat, his face white as a ghost. Mia holds the camera on him for a moment longer, then she turns it to focus on the top of the coaster rails and the steep drop off. Milo screams before the video cuts off. It ends with one of those rollercoaster novelty photos of Milo and Mia holding a sign. Written in thick, black marker is M M with a giant sad face beside it.

The next video is them on a second roller coaster—the Yukon Striker. It cuts from the sign to Milo screaming like a fool and ends with another novelty photo of them holding another sign. This time it reads MAndM with a giant happy face beside it.

There's one final video link. I pull the bus stop bell and get to my feet as Milo's face appears on the screen. He's panting and looking as though he's going to vomit, holding the phone to the side with one hand, the other braced on his knee. "I've learned that putting yourself out there to do the scary things is hard. Life can be hard. But you can't cocoon yourself. If you do that, you can't chase your dreams. Being true to yourself means you can be strong not only for yourself, but for the people in your life. I don't think we'll be making any more videos. Not because anything is wrong, but because I think we finally figured out what is right. Thank you everyone for coming along for the final ride." He pauses, and for a moment it feels as though he's looking directly at me. "Love you."

I run down the steps of the bus as I'm checking the timestamp of the video, looking around frantically to get my bearings. They'd filmed that a few hours ago, and I assume they're back home now. I'm on the wrong end of the city from where I need to be, but that's not going to stop me. Hailing a cab, I jump in and nearly shout Milo's address at him.

The trip to his condo is a blur. My mind races through all the possible options of what I can say to him. How I can express the way I feel without assuming anything on his part.

Love you.

Does he? Was that simply a throwaway line to the online community, or is it his way of letting me know? My mind doesn't stop spinning until I get into the building. Sweat has beaded beneath my bra from an unexpected hot flash and burst of nerves. Shit, what if I read this all wrong? Is this a terrible mistake? I stare at the intercom system for several long heartbeats before giving my head a hard shake.

No. In fact, it feels as though I'm not only doing the right thing by being here, I know Milo is waiting for me. He wouldn't have said what he said if he didn't want me to come. Mia wouldn't have sent the links if she had any problems with me and her dad being together. They laid their hearts out there, showed me that they want me in their lives, and now the ball is firmly in my court.

"Big girl pantie time." I hit the button and wait for a response. "Hello?"

A shiver rolls through me at the sound of his voice. "Milo?"

The buzz up is nearly instant.

After what feels like the longest elevator ride in the world, I step out onto Milo's floor to see him standing at the end of the hallway, the door to his condo wide open. Somehow, I resist running in the hall, but I do speed walk my way into his arms.

I bury my face against his shoulder, close my eyes, and soak in the sensations of pressing against him. The lingering scent of coffee and bread clings to his shirt, and when I turn my head, I feel the pounding of his heart against my ear.

"I didn't know if you'd come," he murmured into my hair. "I wasn't sure if you'd left. But I needed you to know how much you mean to us."

There's no way in hell I'm going to start crying in the hallway. "Let's go in and talk."

He lets me step away so we can maneuver through the door, but he links our hands to lead me inside. Even after he shuts the door, he doesn't let go. I like feeling secure, cherished, so I thread my fingers through his. "You baked bread again."

"Last night. I was trying to wrap my head around some of the notes I received for the Painbringer role." He leads me to the stool by the kitchen counter and finally releases me. "One slice or two?"

"Two. Toasted."

"Andie!" Mia races out of her room. She nearly knocks me off my seat with the ferocity of her hug. "I didn't know if you'd come."

"How could I not after seeing your videos." I've never wanted to be a mother, but I've grown to care about Mia so much that if she wanted me to be a part of her life, I wouldn't think twice about it. She doesn't need another parent, but I know she could stand to have more friends in her life. "You did an amazing job with the editing."

She pulls back and runs her hands through her hair as she blushes. "Lucy helped me with some of that. She's really good at knowing where to cut things."

I have to thank Lucy again. "She's really smart."

Mia looks over at her dad and takes a step back toward her room. "I'll leave you two alone. I'll just, ah, put my noise canceling headphones on." She winks at me before bolting away and shutting her door.

Noise canceling— "What the hell does she think we're going to do?"

Milo, standing on the opposite side of the counter from me, has his hands on his hips and his gaze on the floor. "She's a teenager who might have discovered—and hated, by the way—the fact that there is a lot of fan fiction about us now."

"Nooooooo."

"Oh yes." He chuckles, but I can tell he's not really thinking about fan stories. "I have a question for you. And please understand that what I do immediately afterward will be dictated by your response."

Somehow, I know what he's going to ask me. But I keep my mouth shut and give him space. I nod, and his gaze drops again to the floor.

"I've come to realize that I care for you. A lot. I might even love you. A lot. But you have the chance to live your dreams in Texas. I want you to know if that's what you've decided to do, I'm ecstatic for you. I'll help you pack, find a place to live, whatever you need." When he finally looks up at me, he's trying to hold his emotions in check and failing.

I open my mouth to respond, but he holds his hand up.

"Let me finish."

"Okay."

"I won't—I can't be the reason for someone else's unhappiness. My marriage fell apart because Rachel tried to fit herself into a mold that wasn't right. What I feel for you is different than what I felt for her. Maybe because we were friends first, or maybe it's just because of who you are. But I love and respect you too much to put my desires in front of yours. You have a chance to live your dreams in Texas. And I need you to know I will do everything in my power to help you make them a reality."

I can't let him go on any longer. Getting to my feet, I join him on his side of the counter. I grab his hand and bring it to my lips for a kiss. "Here's the thing. I had a bit of an epiphany after I left you and Mia that night at Wonderland."

It's harder to put everything into words than I'd assumed it would be. While I know he doesn't necessarily need reassurance that my choices aren't influenced by him, it's also clearly important.

"I couldn't understand why I didn't jump at the opportunity to sign the contract with *Travel Now*. They were flexible with my start date. The pay was ... way more than I made at two jobs, and it really was what I always wanted. Except ..."

I let his hand go to cup his face. "Except, I realized that I didn't want to move. I didn't want to leave Toronto and the life and friends I've made here. I didn't want to leave you. I maybe love you a lot. I've had more fun, more excitement in the past few months than I've had in years. And I realized I could have everything I want, and no one needs to compromise."

"Wait, wait, wait, back up." His hands move around me until his palms press against the small of my back. "Say that again?"

"That we don't need to compromise?" I grin.

"You better not be fuckin' with me, missy," he says in the Painbringer's gruff voice as he smiles.

"Oh, you mean the I maybe kinda sorta love you thing?"

"Yeah, that."

I pull his face in close to mine so he knows I want this as much as he does. "I love you, Milo."

"I love you too."

The kiss starts off soft, tender. My heart pounds in my ears as a burst of unexpected nerves hits me. But this feels right, perfect.

And I realize that dreams are living, breathing parts of ourselves that grow and change to fill the holes in our lives. But the best ones are those you can share with someone else.

THIRTY-NINE

Epilogue

It took the better part of six months to get the studio the way I want it with the artists I decided to exhibit. I had to convince more than a few of those people that yes, I was serious about wanting to display their art, and yes it would be open to the public. I also spent time on the phone, calling in every favor I have to get sponsors for the evening.

Samara had to do some convincing of her own. It took her longer than it should have to convince me that my photos should also be here on display. While it felt a tiny bit egotistical to be both the coordinator and one of the featured artists, she reminded me that was one of the reasons she'd asked me to take on this job in the first place.

I turn to see Lucy standing close by, in front of the five photos she submitted to me. Lucy was one of the first people I asked to participate as an artist. She's here with her parents, dressed the way she always came to class, right down to her Raptors ball hat. I ensured she and all the other students who passed my class all had a spot in the exhibition.

But unlike the utterly confident young woman who inadvertently kickstarted my life down an unexpected path, I'm surprised to see Lucy looking more than a little nervous. "Holy shit."

"Sweetheart, this is amazing." Her mom gives her a hug. "I know I wasn't completely supportive of you taking some of these classes, but I understand now. Well done."

"Hey!" I smile at Lucy as she looks my way. "I'm so happy you were able to come. I've tried to spread everyone from the class around so you all had a good spot."

"Ms. M, you're awesome." Lucy's grin is all I need to warm my heart. "Did Mrs. Babineau make it?"

My longest tenured student finally passed my course. When I told her I wanted to display her photos, she broke down and cried. "My Stanley always told me that I had talent," she said. "He would have loved to have seen my photos shown in a place like this."

"Mrs. B is over at the refreshment table with Ronald and Fatima. I think they were waiting for you so you can stream the event or something."

Holly did all the catering for tonight—I owe her big time. It was great to see her happy after the nightmare that her work had become recently. Maybe she'd meet someone too, someone who would treat her with the love and admiration she deserved. That's a problem for another time.

"Lucy!" Mia comes tearing over, looking the most excited I've seen her in months.

She worked hard to get herself past everything that happened at the party, but setbacks still come up from time to time. Milo said the past month has been the best he's seen her in years, which makes everything better. I'm thrilled she wanted to come tonight, even if she didn't want to participate as an artist.

I made small talk with Lucy's parents for a few more minutes, before taking my leave and continuing to mingle. Samara had a tablet with a signup sheet for anyone who had an interest in taking a course with us, and there was currently a small group huddled around it, filling out the form.

I don't think I could have done anything else to have made tonight any more successful than it was.

"Excuse me?" A man in a dress shirt and pants stepped up beside me. He was tall and lanky, a full beard covered his face and his salt and pepper hair was expertly coiffed. "You're the artist of the man on the bench?"

Despite my hesitation, I'd displayed a blown-up version of the original photo I'd taken of Milo. It's off to the side toward the back of the gallery, but it's still drawing plenty of attention despite not being on the main path. "I am."

"I was wondering if it was for sale." He glances toward it. "I find I can't look away from it."

"I'm so sorry, but that's the only artwork that's not for sale tonight."

"That's what the sign said, but I had to at least try." He lets out a little sigh. "That's fine. I'll have to accept that there will be a hole in my new collection."

"I'm sorry that ... Wait, what new collection?"

"Yours. I'm purchasing all your photos. I work in a studio, and they will fit beautifully there." He smiles, and before I have a chance to register everything he said, he's gone.

Holy shit. Someone bought my art. At an exhibit. I'm not sure if I want to laugh or cry knowing my photos will be on display.

A warm arm slips around my waist as Milo comes to stand beside me. "He looked rather pleasant. Was he flirting with you? Do I need to *bring him the pain?*"

I giggle. "I think he'd be more interested in you than me, based on how badly he wanted your photo."

Milo rocks up on his toes and looks after the man. "He's attractive. I'll consider it only if you dump me. He can soothe my broken heart."

"Now I really can't sell him your photo. He was very charming, and I might find myself without a boyfriend."

"Speaking of that ..." Milo tugs me back toward the side

corridor that leads to the photo store. We're far enough away that no one can see us or any stolen kisses we might share.

"Looking to make out?" I grab his collar and pull myself up for a little kiss. "Because I can't be off the floor for long. I really need to be in there mingling."

"This won't take long." He reaches into his pocket and pulls out a small box. "I didn't know the right time to do this. Mia said I was being dumb and that I just needed to ask."

My ability to hear anything disappears, and all I can focus on is Milo opening the box and pulling out a key. "I was wondering if you might like to move in with us." He chuckles. "Move in with me. I mean, you're over almost all the time anyway. And my place is technically closer to work for you than your apartment. Plus, it would just make financial sense if you—"

I shut him up with a long, deep kiss. I want to laugh when I feel his smile against my lips. "I take it that's a yes?"

"For a moment I thought you were going to propose."

"Ah, no. I mean, not yet. I mean, I'd like to maybe get married again, but we really haven't been together that long, and I didn't want you to feel pressured—"

I kiss him again. "Yes."

"Yes, you'll move in?"

I nod. "I love you."

"I love you too." He wraps his arms around me and hugs hard. "You've made me so happy. And I'm bloody proud of you. Tonight's been amazing."

"Thanks. I wanted to make sure everyone had a chance to shine."

"You have." He brushes my hair behind my ear. "Come on. Let's go mingle. And know that I'm going to need to hibernate for a week after this much socializing."

"Okay."

Holding hands, we step out, ready for our next adventure together.

Acknowledgments

Writing this story was a journey! There were so many people along the way who helped bring And and Milo to life.

First, I want to thank you, the readers for your continued support. Over the years the types of stories I've told have changed but you continue to join me on these adventures.

This book wouldn't have made it if it wasn't for the ongoing and incredible support of Serena Bell. Oh, my friend, I don't have the words of the heartfelt love and gratitude I feel towards you. I'm constantly in awe of your talent and organizational skills. Thank you!

Misty!! Thank you so much for our calls, and your infectious positivity. I treasure our conversations, and love that you help me laugh at the chaos that's our world.

Kristina, Amy, Paula, and Kimber. I can't image a world without you there. I'll forever be grateful for our chats and the laughter we've shared.

I have the most amazing agent. Thank you Courtney for everything you've done for me, and for having my back.

Tik Tok Boom wouldn't be half as good if not for Linda's eagle eyes. I learned so much from you in such a short period and I can't thank you enough.

Kasey and Rose, you both are the lights of my life. I'm proud of you both and all you've accomplished in your lives to this point. I know you'll both continue to be amazing.

And finally, to my real-life romance hero, Mark. Your constant support, encouragement, and laughter keep me going when I feel I might stop. I love you so much!

About the Author

Christine d'Abo is a critically acclaimed author of steamy romance novels. With her quirky, funny writing style, she's won the hearts of readers around the world. Her books are filled with heart, humour, and of course, steamy plots that will leave you breathless.

You can visit Christine at her website www.christinedabo.com

Trending For You Series

Tik Tok Boom

Side Quest (coming 2024)

30 Series

30 Days

30 Nights

Sugar Series

Sugar Sweet

Sugar & Spice

Candy King

Long Shots Series

Double Shot

A Shot in the Dark

Pulled Long

Calling the Shots

Choose Your Shot